BAHAMIAN RHAPSODY

One Family's Adventure

James P. Reno III

BAHAMIAN RHAPSODY
Copyright © 2013 by James P. Reno

JEC PRESS

ISBN: 978-0-9910969-0-9

PRINTED IN THE UNITED STATES OF AMERICA

I'd like to dedicate this book to anyone bold enough to chase a dream.

* * * * *

I'd like to thank my Mother for always believing in me.

I'd like to thank my Father for giving me strength and courage.

I'd like to thank my wife for loving me for who I am.

I'd like to thank my son for being the light of our world.

* * * * *

I'd also like to thank my friend Danielle for helping me use my own voice and for showing me that it was good.

Last, but not least, I'd like to thank my publisher Jennifer. Without your guidance, patience and professionalism I probably would never have finished this project.

BAHAMIAN RHAPSODY

NOTE TO READERS:

I was not sure what to call this book. Writing an autobiography in my forties seemed premature. I have not lived enough of this life yet to think that the best parts are over and ready to be written. I'm not a novelist. I'm not that creative or organized. I can only write about what I've experienced. So, I decided to write about a transitional three year period in our lives that impacted us and was unique: our move from California to the Bahamas. It changed our lives forever.

My writing style is scattered. It floats from thought to thought, place to place, present to past, all in an attempt to describe a moment in time.

This is not an autobiography. This is a Stick Shift Biography... and yes, I made that up. It's jerky, stutters and stops, and then it clicks back into gear. It's a bumpy but (hopefully) a fun ride.

My book is one-sided. It's me-sided. It's not fair or just, right or wrong. It's just me. It tends to drift into imagination and fantasy and it constantly drifts back and forth in time. Since I'm always shifting gears, I decided to call it a Stick Shift Biography. A tale of my life, as told through a bunch loosely connected stories and thoughts.

Be warned: a Stick Shift Biography will bend the truth with artistic license. However, this story is based in fact and most of the events are true and occurred. To protect myself and the characters in this story, I'll never tell which parts are the straight truth and which parts are bent a little. The names and places have mostly all been changed to protect the innocent... but mostly to protect me from a lawsuit.

Remember, a Stick Shift is much less comfortable than an Automatic. Scenes may not transition as smoothly as you're used to, but hopefully in the end you will enjoy my style of storytelling as much as I've enjoyed writing this book.

Thank you.
James P. Reno III

BAHAMIAN RHAPSODY

INTRODUCTION

I did not see this journey as simply a vacation. I had no way of knowing just how different things would be. Like most people, we liked to visit the island because of the natural beauty of the beach and ocean, the weather, and its laid back lifestyle and attitude. The slow pace of the island is relaxing and calms the nerves of the American tourist. But that slow pace has two sides to it. I quickly learned that some things that are charming to the tourist are maddening to the expat.

In a Bahamian restaurant, you can wait ten minutes before anyone even acknowledges that you are there. It may be another ten minutes before you are asked if you would like to see a menu. As a polite person, I used to feel awkward asking for service because there appeared to be a flurry of activity going on around me. Everyone seemed to be very busy and working on something important. I hated to bother them with the fact that this *was* a restaurant and I had come to *eat*. After a while, I realized that nothing was really getting done. Most of the activity was just socializing among the staff and there really was little to no organization to the business whatsoever. After I actually got to place my order it took three times the normal amount of time I was used to waiting for a meal to arrive at the table.

I learned that there generally was no systematic way of doing things like there was at home. And I could either accept this fact, or spend my day complaining. Either way, things ran slower. My son and I once

7

waited 30 minutes for our food at Burger King in Cable Beach and there were only four people that had ordered ahead of us. It seemed that even "fast food" was defined differently.

I was surprised at the slow service in Bahamian restaurants, but I was downright shocked when I had to deal with the cable man at our rental.

"I can be there on Friday." The installer said.

"That's four days from now. I really need the Internet up sooner. Is there anyone else?" I began to plead and prepared to bargain and even bribe.

"Just me for the whole west side of the island."

"OK, what time?" I asked.

"Oh, I can't really give you a time." He said.

And I realized I'd have to wait all day for him, but I needed the Internet to run my business back in California so I had no choice. I waited all day that Friday but the installer never came. At about three o'clock I finally called the cable company.

"I'm waiting for the installer to show up. How late do they work?" I asked.

The woman on the phone asked me for the installer's name, which somehow I luckily had.

"Oh, he's here." She said.

"There? Well, may I speak with him?" There was pause and then.

"This is Robert."

"Robert, this is Jim. You said you'd be at my place in Cable Beach today." He asked for my phone number and I gave it to him.

"Ohhhhh. I see." He said.

"You see what?"

"I put you down for Friday." He said.

"Right, well today is Friday."

"I did not say which Friday." He said.

8

And I swear that is a true story. I was a bit dumbfounded. I kept waiting for him to laugh and tell me he was kidding. He wasn't. After some wrangling I was able to get them out the next week, but being new to the island at that time I really let that situation bother me. In my American mind, his comments and actions just had no place in this world. Yet, here they were.

It's easy to become quite skeptical of a move to a foreign country if you keep comparing it to your home. For example, it can take up to a year to get a local telephone installed. A year! People constantly stop their cars in the middle of a busy street to talk to friends who were walking by. And for some reason local people littered their own beautiful beaches and streets without a care. After our arrival, these were just a few of the minor things that plagued my brain daily. I did my best to put a sock into the mouth of the "little voice", but he kept at me daily.

Sometimes even I began to wonder, why live here? Why leave California? And again, I'd have a hard time explaining why we moved. It's very expensive to live in the Caribbean, so it's not like you're moving to Thailand where you can live on a thousand dollars a month with servants everywhere. Simple, everyday products can be impossible to find and the infrastructure, although older than our own in the USA, appears to be in its infancy. The roads are terrible, the power regularly goes out and the local beer costs $48.00 a case at the liquor store.

Why live here? I was reminded every time I looked out over the greenish blue ocean. The freedom of a long walk down along the shore and up across the beach that looked like a postcard can be reassuring. Each sunrise is a work of art. Every sunset is a masterpiece. The sky and the sea are imitated by

9

artists, but they never capture its beauty. Even photographs don't do it justice. The physical surroundings in the Bahamas are some of the most beautiful you will ever see.

There are many places equally as beautiful throughout the Caribbean, in the Tropics, the South Pacific, and along the Yucatan Peninsula. What made the Bahamas so alluring to me was the local people. They welcome the tourists with open arms. Partially because they know that their livelihood depends on the tourist dollar, but also because they seem to be at peace with themselves. Wherever I went, I talked to the local people, joined them at their churches or at one of their many weekend festivals. There I found the real "island love". They celebrate so often that after a while it's clear that they don't have more holidays, they are simply celebrating life.

For example, my wife and I were on a jitney (a small, privately owned bus) heading for downtown on one of our first vacations many years ago. Warm air blew in through the open windows carrying the smell of flowers as gospel music played on the speakers of the bus. We were heading for a small coin store that was reputed to carry real pieces of eight that had been reclaimed from wrecked ships that had gone down hundreds of years ago. To this day, my wife loves old coins and the thought of real pirate treasure lured her to the coin store.

We tried to figure out where the store was, looking out each side of the bus. I guess we looked confused as we peered around. A local lady spoke to us.

"Are you lost?" A nicely dressed Bahamian woman asked as she smiled at us.

"Kind of." We told her where we were headed.

"Well, I can show you. Your stop is just ahead." She said and she hollered, "bus stop", and the driver soon pulled over. The three of us hopped out and without any conversation we followed the woman (who walked very quickly) for about three blocks. After a block or so, I wondered if we were supposed to be following her this far. Then all of sudden she stopped.

"There it is." She said pointing.

"Oh thank you very much." Beth said to her. And with that the woman smiled and said "Good Morning". She then turned and began walking back the way we'd come.

I was still grinning from that international feeling I get when I'm immersed in someone else's custom of saying "Good Morning" as they leave, instead of how it's just used as a greeting at home. I suddenly had a strange feeling. "Come with me." I said to Beth. We followed the woman like two spies as she made her way back to the bus stop, ducking into alcoves, and hiding around corners making sure she did not see us. She walked the three blocks back to where we'd gotten off and stood waiting for a bus.

"She's obviously dressed for work." Beth said.

"I know. I guess she just wanted to help us."

"On her way to work?" Beth asked. "Who has time to do that?"

"Who would take the time?" I shook my head as I watched where the woman got onto the jitney.

Another time we were in a taxi headed for dinner when Beth noticed the strap on her dress was coming apart. She assured me that if it came completely undone that she'd have a tough time staying dressed.

"I'm sorry." She said. "I guess we'll have to head back to the hotel."

"It's not your fault." I caressed her sweaty, bare shoulders. And I told the driver our problem.

"You got 'em ah sewing kit back at da hotel?" He asked.

We shook our heads. He offered to take us to his house where his daughter would sew it for us.

"I don't want to put you to any trouble." I said. I was more worried that he'd take us somewhere and rob us than I was of wasting his time.

"It's no problem." He said and turned off the main road. We were told not to go with taxi drivers outside tourist areas, but Beth and I looked at each other and decided to trust this man.

As expected, the roads we were now on looked very different from the main tourist area. There were few streetlights, so it was eerily dark out. Some of the houses we passed looked like they were pieced together with scrap wood. Many people walked the streets with shopping bags. Some kids played in the street and a group of men were at a table drinking beer and playing dominoes. There were people barbecuing chicken at the edge of the road on open fires built inside with what appeared to be fifty-five gallon drums cut in half. The food smelled smoky and natural. Each corner had a large set of speakers either sitting outside or blaring from inside a car what sounded like the same music station. I enjoyed the Doppler Effect a bit as one set of speakers passed by us and the sound bent in the thick, sticky air. The place was loud and full of activity with the local people moving about in the dark like fireflies. Beth and I smiled at each other. Lord, why did I feel at home the most here in a Caribbean ghetto?

When we stopped we were a bit anxious, but went with the man inside his house. It was a modest home but it was clean and very well kept. A woman was cooking in the kitchen and she offered us a Coke. We sat on the plastic-wrapped couch and made small talk with the family, feeling like bourgeois intruders. As promised, the taxi driver's daughter sewed Beth's strap right as we sat on the couch. Soon we were on our way after thanking everyone in the house, including the house dog and an infant, for their hospitality.

We were so impressed by our driver that we invited him to dinner with us. We ate at a place that he recommended, a place Fodor's had never heard of, I'm sure. We had no idea what to order at this local place that only served real down-home, Bahamian fare, so we asked the man to order for us. He began ordering food without using the menu and his accent became as thick as brown beef stew.

We sat at the bar, drank the local beer "Kalik", and ate boiled fish soup with white bread. Our driver knew everyone in the restaurant and introduced us. For two hours we sat and talked to the owners and patrons at the restaurant. They were all as curious about us as we were about them. We had one of the best evenings of our entire trip just talking and basking in the friendliness of this man and the others at the restaurant, completely forgetting about our own dinner reservations.

I don't recommend going off with strangers in the Caribbean or anywhere for that matter. We live our lives a bit differently than most people. We're not huge risk takers, but we listen to our heart and follow our gut. By doing this we've encountered many people and places that most don't get to see.

There are many places in the world with beautiful azure waters and white, sandy beaches. Many of them are much cheaper to visit than the Bahamas. I truly believe it is the people there that make it such a popular destination. The colorful and friendly people of this island are really what make it special. The more you get to know them, the more they will fascinate, intrigue, and sometimes confuse you.

Why did we move?

The friendly people combined with the beauty of the place intersected our lives at a time when I sat on a bridge in traffic so I could afford to pay a nanny to raise my son. It was just not good enough anymore. We needed to try something different. We chose to try something that we had dreamt about for years. The timing was right, and we were bold enough to try to live our dream, for a while or for a lifetime, we had no way of knowing.

This is our story.

CHAPTER ONE
The Dream Begins

It was August of 2005. I was sitting on the San Francisco Bay Bridge in rush hour traffic heading home. I lived in the town of Walnut Creek, about twenty-two miles east of San Francisco, otherwise known as the "East Bay". Working as a real estate appraiser, I traveled all over the Bay Area inspecting homes. Usually, I was fortunate enough to schedule appointments around the predictably horrible rush hour bridge traffic, but today I was stuck right in the heart of it with fifty thousand other commuters.

The cars blanketed the asphalt like multi-colored tiles in an endless ribbon of frustration and angst, linking all of us with where we were to where we were headed. There was nothing but a roadblock of cars ahead of me, behind me, and two lanes of gridlock to either side. The behemoth Bay Bridge upper deck blocked out the sun above us so only small rays of light were visible. I thanked God that I was not claustrophobic. I had driven this bridge and tunnel crawl so many times that I was sure I'd make a good gopher or some other subterranean creature that needed little sunlight, oxygen or personal company to exist.

Situations like these were very frustrating. I had grown up somewhat poor, so waste of any kind had always bothered me. Burning time like this especially irked me. Sitting in traffic, I could actually feel the

15

minutes of my life being stripped from me like paper matches torn and used to light a bum's cigarette. When I looked out my windows at all of the people around me, I tried to add up the lifetimes of minutes burned on this bridge every day. What a waste.

I had been sitting at a dead stop long enough to actually consider turning off my engine when my cell phone rang. Whenever I was late getting home, my wife Beth asked me the same question:

"When do you think you'll get home for dinner?" She asked.

"Hard to say." I sighed. "I haven't moved in ten minutes so I suppose at this rate, *never*."

"That's too bad. I made your favorite, tacos." She said. "But now that you won't be making it home... well, I want you to know that it was wonderful knowing you. I guess we had a good run together, didn't we?"

"You were a great wife. Don't mourn me long. Perhaps once the tacos are all gone you can find someone to replace me. I really hope you and your new husband are happy." I laughed.

"At least he'll come home for dinner."

"Not if he has to drive. The traffic just gets worse every day."

"We could move to Montana. There's lots of space there." She said. "I saw on TV that there are only one million people in the whole state."

"There are more people than that on this bridge."

"Maybe the whole state of Montana is visiting San Francisco." She laughed.

I could talk to her like this all day. She could make bridge traffic fun. Traffic inched forward a foot or two and then stopped again. I looked around me at all of the frustrated faces in their shiny metal cages.

"There is a guy next to me in a Mercedes that probably cost well over $150,000.00. He looks miserable. I'll bet the Mercedes marketing crew won't use his picture in their next ad campaign." I smirked to myself as I tried not to stare at the sad man in the beautiful car next to me.

"I wonder how many times he had to cross the bridge in traffic to afford that car?" Beth asked.

"Not sure. But there are a lot of very expensive cars on this bridge. Maybe they keep all the money in bags somewhere in San Francisco and these guys just go back and forth transporting it all day."

"Did you find a bag of money today?" Beth asked. "Because, I'm tired of working. Oh, look at the clock. I still have to go pick up Jake."

"He's still there? Why didn't you pick him up earlier?" I demanded, annoyed at the fact that our four-year-old son was not home already. It was after six in the evening and he was still at his Russian nanny's house.

"You know there is a reason his first language was Russian." I grumbled.

"Well, you were stuck in the city and I had a late meeting. I had to get dinner started. Don't worry." Beth explained. We actually were thrilled that our son had learned Russian. We just wished that he'd pick up some English because now we'd have to learn Russian. "I called her and she said it was OK."

"It's *not* OK." I barked. "I don't want us to be *those* parents."

"What was I supposed to do?" She asked.

"Nothing. It's not your fault." I kicked myself for snapping at her as I watched the brake lights in front of me go off for a half second and then back on again. "Listen, I'd better hang up. Traffic looks like it may

17

actually crawl forward for a minute or two. I'll see you, *someday*."

"I'll keep dinner warm. Hurry home and be safe." She said.

"Well, which do you really want me to do?" I toyed with her a bit to get passed the little argument we'd just had.

"What?"

"Do you want me to hurry home or be safe?"

"Oh, I see you've picked up *Mr. Literal*. May I speak with him directly?" She changed her voice from "loving wife" quickly to "accusatory woman". Not good for Mr. Literal.

"Sure, I'll put him on." I changed my voice to sound uptight and anally retentive. I quickly noticed that it was not much different than my regular voice. That bugged me but Beth was waiting.

"Mr. Literal here, may I help you?" My uptight voice squeaked.

"Yes, hello *Mr. Literal*. I just wanted to let you know that sometimes when people sign off from a personal phone call that they do so with a loving wish for safety, coupled with another wish for a speedy trip simply because they cannot stand to be without their loved one longer than is absolutely necessary. You get that?"

"But given the option, which would you choose: hurry up or be safe?" I asked again.

"I'd choose *safe*. Now, which will you choose: the couch or the dog house, Mr. Ass Hat?" Mr. Literal had done it again.

"The couch. Do we still get tacos?" I eeked the words out. My own voice sounded a bit squeaky now.

"Only if you hurry home. My new husband is a very large man with a huge appetite. I'll do what I can but you know how much he can eat."

18

"You have a new husband? Already? Am I *that* late?" I asked.

"*Literally*." She laughed.

Even in that awful traffic, I was able to smile. We had the ability to poke each other, play with each other and back off before anyone really got angry or hurt. We had love for each other. We had respect and love. I kept smiling as I thought of our upcoming travel plans. In about a month, Beth and I would celebrate our tenth wedding anniversary. After being married in Las Vegas in 1995, we had agreed we would renew our vows every five years on a beach in The Bahamas.

* * * * *

We had honeymooned in Cable Beach, a small resort community on the north side of New Providence Island, just a few miles west of the capital city of Nassau. One day, as we laid upon the white sand in front of our hotel, we had a few drinks, and talked about our future as a married couple.

"Well, for me...I say that we should come back here, *a lot*." Beth said smiling.

We were on day ten of a long honeymoon and she was already in love with the island.

"How about this, we come back here every five years to renew our vows right here on this beach. I've seen lots of weddings on the beach here at the hotel. They have a wedding coordinator and everything." I explained.

"Deal, every five years." Beth said and raised her beer for a toast. "But we can't wait that long to visit!"

We caught the island bug almost immediately. Like most people, we fell in love with the laid back lifestyle, the ocean, the weather, and the smiling laughing people that wished you a "Good Morning" everywhere we went. The Bahamas seemed to be a truly blessed place and it quickly became our dream to live there. What we did not realize is that most people who visit the island had the same feeling. But for them, that feeling wore off on the plane or boat ride home. By the time their sunburn had healed, they got back to their routine, and most people simply forgot about the Bahamas.

It was not like that for us. We felt a stronger pull. We felt more at home on the island than we did back in California and it happened very quickly. I could not get back to my routine after a vacation there. All I wanted to do was plan and scheme on how I could return.

"I could come back here every month!" I said.

"How about we come back every three months?" Beth bargained with me like she usually did. It turned out neither of us was kidding or just giddy on Kalik, the local beer. We were serious.

After our honeymoon, we visited the island two or three times a year over the next ten years. Our friends and family wondered why we spent so much money on travel and why we always took every vacation in the same place. We tried to explain, but they never understood. The island felt like a second home to us and we made some lifelong friends there along the way.

"Ya'll visit here *dat* much?" A local Bahamian man asked me once.

"We do." I said smiling.

"Well, den ya'll is local." He said. "You practically Bahamian now." When he said this I felt a surge of something like pride mixed with happiness shoot through my heart.

* * * * *

20

As I sat on the San Francisco Bay Bridge, thinking of our vacations on the island, I smiled. We'd been married ten years, and as promised we would travel back to the Bahamas, back to our honeymoon hotel and renew our vows again on that same white beach in New Providence. We had already renewed our vows there once after five years of marriage. But this ten-year wedding was a little different. Some friends from the island would attend, both of our mothers would be there, and our little son would be standing there next to me, barefoot, blonde, and wonderful. At our five year renewal, Beth did not know she was pregnant with him. She only knew that the beautiful pink and coral colored dress she'd bought back in the States felt a bit tight that afternoon as she put it on.

We were really tired of the San Francisco Bay Area. We were both from there and our families were there. The place had much to offer. Job opportunities with higher pay drew most people. Moderate weather drew the rest. Can nine million people really all be wrong? It's a nice place to live, but it's a rat race just like any other major metropolitan area in the United States. It always seemed odd to me that most of our family lived within a fifteen minute drive of each other, yet we hardly ever had the time (or took the time) to see each other. I'd get in my car and drive ninety minutes to Sacramento for an appraisal job without thinking twice, but never to visit my brother who lived here. My priorities were wrong. But the freeway went both directions and he did not come to visit me either. Everyone was just too busy.

"In my opinion, if we lived in the Bahamas, we'd see my family about the same amount as we do now." I told Beth one night as we dreamed of relocating to the island and out of the San Francisco Bay Area.

21

"Sad, but true." Beth blew the words out of her mouth like a wish.

At our tenth anniversary vow renewal ceremony (otherwise known as our third wedding), our son Jake was very cranky that day. I just held him in my arms and asked him to watch for Mommy. We stood next to our minister and in front of our guests on the beach trying not to sweat through our nice shirts. As my bride stepped out of a small hotel door and onto the beach, there were some hotel guests that politely let the bride and her wedding attendant walk by. A couple of the men even clapped. She was barefoot and wearing a flowing dress the same color as the ocean behind me. She looked stunning.

I watched her walking towards where we waited, the local preacher at my side, and the small white archway decorated with tropical flowers under which we would promise again. A peace came over me that I'd never felt before. All of this seemed natural. It all felt right to be here with my family marrying this woman for a third time. It may sound odd, but we'd built a solid foundation on sand.

Jake and the grandmas stayed back at the hotel, so Beth and I could have a romantic dinner that night. We went to a small, local restaurant and sat in the open air on the rooftop terrace in an area called Arawak Caye. Arawak Caye was also called, "The Fish Fry" and it was a favorite local hangout to get conch, fish, and have a beer and a chat with friends. There were a dozen or so small restaurants that lined a small road along a public park. The ocean was a stone's throw away. Some traffic could be heard from the small two-lane road nearby called Bay Street. The air was still and sticky, but the owner had thoughtfully put a small fan near us so we would be comfortable.

"Happy anniversary and happy wedding, my dear." I toasted her with my beer..

"Happy happy to you, too." She smiled and kissed me.

We sat close to each other. "We have this whole rooftop to ourselves." Beth said as she waved her arms around like a game show hostess displaying a prize showcase.

"I'd take the credit, but I didn't do this." I laughed as I looked around and down at the slowly moving cars that drifted slowly by. The usual large groups of people walked by on the sidewalk and laughed the loud Bahamian laugh. It was infectious and we laughed for no reason other than it felt good.

This place had been popular for many years. It was vastly improved since the early days when Beth and I first visited the place.

"I remember riding that broken down scooter that we'd rented on our honeymoon. I heard the loud music and began to turn in to Arawak Caye from the main road to check out the party and you tried to stop me." I laughed.

"The place was barely lit with a muddy road. It was crowded with people and the music was deafeningly loud. I was sure that our scooter would just slide out and we'd end up in a puddle. If we actually made it in to the party, I was afraid we'd get mugged...

"And take us for what? The obviously rented scooter or the twenty bucks I had in my pocket? Maybe my Casio G-Shock watch?" I asked.

"Maybe. I didn't know." She said. "I was not as comfortable in situations like that as you were."

"It was just local people having a good time." I teased her. I understood her trepidation but wanted her to relax and trust a bit more. "Funny how back then they called the fish stands 'conch shacks' and that they still do. Compared to back then, everything is so clean and updated. I actually prefer the way it was over the new restaurants and all the pavement. It's nicer now, but it was more Bahamian then."

"Things don't have to be third world and filthy to be local, honey. There were rats everywhere and no bathroom. That was fine for you men who could just pee behind a palm tree." Beth said. "There were nights when I thought I would pee my pants!"

"Well, you're the one who drank 13 Kaliks in one night. What did you expect?" I laughed.

"I suppose I expected to get sick and throw up." Beth laughed and poked my chest.

"Mission accomplished." I laughed with her. We had laughed about her 13 Kaliks night many times.

That same night a shark had shown its fin in the small bay where the conch divers dropped their catch for the conch shacks to prep and sell. A man in a Cadillac opened his trunk and pulled out a 12-gauge shotgun and aimed at the shark. We all just waited, while our hearts beat together. The man aimed but never took a shot.

"Da shark got his way tonight." He grumbled sternly and then laughed loudly.

I figured the fish was too far for his scatter gun to do any damage. That or he was just showing off. Either way, he had all of our attention for a minute.

That same evening, we got a ride home to the hotel from a man who described himself as "The Minister of Partytime." I imagined there were many such "ministers" but we'd been hanging out with him and some other new friends that first night at Arawak Caye, and I could tell he was well known and liked by all. I would not have taken a ride from Shotgun Man, but the the Minister of Partytime...why not?

The hotel was only a few miles away and he said he'd give us a ride in his big Lincoln.

"Should I get one more round of beers?" I asked him as he pulled his car up to the conch shack.

"Ya mon. Get tree." He said.

I'd noticed that most people drove around the island with a drink in their hand. It seemed to be the norm and I was here on vacation so I was willing to go with the flow. Beth got in the back seat and I sat down in front. I reached for my seat belt when the Minister spoke up.

"We voted against dat, mon."

I noticed he was not wearing a seat belt. I nodded.

"What about the beer?" I asked.

"Oh we voted fer dat." He smiled as he turned on his stereo and pulled away from the conch shack and on to the main road. He played some unrecognizable local music on the stereo, but we loved it. He also pulled out a spliff and lit it. He took a long pull from the cigarette and handed it to me. I held it and looked at him.

"Any vote on this stuff?" I asked and the Minister just laughed loudly. I had never been a fan of marijuana so I did a "Clinton" just to be polite and took some smoke in my mouth but did not inhale. I handed it back to Beth who may or may not have tried it before handing it back to me.

Suddenly, very suddenly, my thoughts began to get complex. I began to think in patterns that reminded me of those scenes in The Matrix where the world was depicted electronically. I wondered if Clinton had felt this way and looked over at the Minister.

"Just weed, right?" I coughed.

25

"Ya mon. Jus da weet. But it da Jamaican chronic."

"Oh. Is that bad?" I asked him and he just grinned and looked forward as he drove.

"Why you aks?" He asked.

"They must have sprinkled this chronic with polio." I said. "Because, I can't move."

He laughed and I struggled to turn my head to see Beth in the back seat.

"You OK?" She asked.

"Oh yeah. Just rewriting Bob Marley's 'Legend' album in my mind. I'm thinking of just doing it all acoustic. I was also thinking of my childhood. That time in school when we were told not to kick the red rubber ball and I did it anyway and that ball flew soooooooooooooo, far. Hey, you want to get a snack later? Oh, wow look, there's that truck I like. It's a Jeep. Funny thing about Jeeps. Jeeps aren't really cars or trucks, but you know what I mean. Their like a mixture. Like a 'cruck' or a 'trar'."

"You tink a lot of tings, mon." The Minister said laughing.

"I guess I'm multi-tasking." I said.

Beth laughed. She knew I was inexperienced when it came to marijuana. She was not a user, but she hung out with the rock and roll kids in high school during the 1980's which meant smoking weed was pretty much a rite of passage.

The Minister dropped us off in front of our hotel. We thanked him and he sped off. I looked upwards and thanked God for watching over trusting souls like us.

* * * * *

"That was a heck of a night." I giggled as I remembered how stupid I must have sounded.

"I've seen that guy so many times since then. We could not have been safer." Beth rubbed my neck as I shook my head laughing.

"I know. I've seen him too. He's a very nice man." I was talking to my wife and paying attention, but my mind kept wandering. I forced myself to be "in the moment". The air here just felt so right at that moment. All the sounds and smells were so comfortable. It was all so very intoxicating and it made me feel like I felt earlier on the beach with Beth. It all just felt calming and normal like I was doing the right thing.

"We need to own something here." I said.

"An investment?" Beth looked at me. We were doing better financially now ten years into our union. Long gone were the Top Ramen and Kool-Aide days and we could comfortably invest in things for our future.

"Sure, I guess. But mostly because I just want us to have some connection with this place, something real."

"Well there is nothing 'realer' than real estate." Beth said. "I'm with you. We've talked about it for years. Can we afford it?"

"We can. We can't go crazy but we can afford a condo or a small house." I said. And before we knew it, we were making plans to buy a place.

Beth smiled and looked out at the small bay water near us.

"Oh, I'm going to hate leaving."

"Who says we have to leave?" I asked.

"Don't tease me."

"I'm not." I said and we looked at each other.

We thought the same thing, again. It was just like when we got first got together and decided to get

27

married less than a year and a half later. Everyone asked us if she was pregnant. She wasn't. In fact, we had agreed not to have children. We just wanted to work, be successful, and to be married. And then, almost seven years later, we decided to have our son. We had changed our minds. We decided to do so at the same moment, the same day, together. What might have been a "deal breaker" for some became something that bonded us even closer.

We agreed that night that we'd try living in the Bahamas. Jake could attend one of the private schools for expats. He was only going to pre-school and we both agreed that (regardless of what the uptight parent groups at home said) he could attend pre-school or kindergarten anywhere as long as they taught him social manners and how to count and read. As I remembered it, Kindergarten was little more than socializing with other kids and not pooping your pants at school. It would only be for one year and then we'd head back to California. The way we looked at it, we'd just be on an extended vacation.

Once we had decided to make our move, I contacted a Bahamian real estate agent I had found on the Internet to assist us in finding a home to rent and then ultimately one to buy. I'll state here and will probably do so again and again: I have conflicting feelings about real estate agents. I have worked with them for many years at my appraisal company in California. Many of them are professionals, but a lot of them are just people who were not successful at anything else. Some worked very hard but many used the job as a hobby. I hoped that we could find a good one.

I'd spent years scanning Bahamian real estate web sites, dreaming of one day living on the island. One of my favorite sites that I visited often was easy to navigate and had many attractive properties. We chose to visit this office because we had no local connection and the site looked professional.

We drove to the real estate office to see about getting a rental. Having no referral, we simply walked into the real estate office on the east side of New Providence and asked for an agent. The man who came out to assist us (we'll call him "Spencer" for the purposes of this story) was a tall, well-groomed black Bahamian man who spoke with a voice affected by either education, pretension, or maybe a little of both. I had explained to him that we wanted to rent a place, while we looked for a home to buy.

"It just does not seem likely that we can find a place and close on it in three months, but if we can, then we won't need the rental." I said.

"What is your planned return date?" Spencer asked.

"We can leave right after New Year's. We plan to watch the Rose Bowl with some friends and then fly out that night." I made up this plan as I spoke. Beth smiled and nodded.

"I can help you with both the rental and the purchase. Which island are you interested in?" He asked.

"We'd like to stay here on New Providence in the Cable Beach area." I explained. "We've visited here for many years and always used Cable Beach as our home base."

"And how much would you like to spend?" He said as he took notes on a small clipboard. He looked up at me now. I thought this was a very unprofessional question, but chalked it up to cultural differences. It felt like going into a casino and being asked how much you would be losing that evening so they knew how well to treat you. I decided to answer cryptically.

"We'll spend what it takes to fulfill our needs." I said without trying to sound like some soulless, ivy-league trust baby with money to burn. This seemed to sit well with him. Perhaps he thought we were the good kind of trust babies or maybe even lottery winners with money to burn.

Spencer smiled at the prospect of two commissions and said he'd happily work with us. Shortly thereafter, Spencer found a small beach rental condo for us and we signed a three-month lease. He agreed to meet us at the airport when we arrived and get us settled at the condo.

* * * * *

It was September of 2005 and once we got back home from our vow renewal trip, we immediately made plans to return. I could keep in touch with my staff via the Internet and a VOIP phone, and Beth could do the same with her job in sales. The unbelievable thing was that her boss actually allowed her to do this. As long as her numbers did not suffer and she made regular trips home to see clients, he was fine with the idea.

Once we'd made up our minds, we shifted to high gear. Our plan was to leave right after the holidays. After a lot of planning and re-planning, we'd decided to move to the Bahamas for at least a year. My mother was single and retired so she volunteered to stay in our home and watch our dogs. My staff was trained and ready to watch over my company in my absence, and truthfully, I was only a phone call or email away.

Our bags were packed and sitting by the door. Our driver waited impatiently in the street. It was January

4th, 2006, the night that USC played Texas in the Rose Bowl. Jake's godparents were over watching the game with us, saying their goodbyes.

"I have no idea what you're doing. But I wish you nothing but luck." My friend Bill said to me.

"I don't know what we're doing either. But that's part of the fun, isn't it?" I said.

"I can't believe this day is here." Bill said. "You are really doing this?

"You guys have to come and visit." I pleaded. I heard Beth and Bill's wife Brenda in the other room laughing loudly as they said their good-byes. Jake was busily going from room to room saying good-bye to his dogs and the house.

"We will." He said. "But can I ask you something?"

"Sure, anything."

"How can you leave your house, your business, family and friends? I could never leave my home." He looked puzzled as he asked me this. He'd lived here his entire life and did not have the vagabond spirit I had. He did not suffer from wanderlust. He did not feel trapped.

"I guess I'm still trying to figure out where 'home' is. It may not just be where I've been the longest. A house is not a home to me. You guys are my home." I grinned but strained to hold back. I did not want this to be a tearful good-bye but suddenly the weight of our actual departure was upon me.

"Well, we'll be here when you get back. And I'll help your mom take care of the house." He said and he hugged me. I hugged him tightly. He was a good friend and I'd miss him a lot.

The doorbell rang.

"There's our driver again. It must be time to go." I said. We went to let the driver in.

31

"Good thing you brought the big car." I said to the driver. We had nine bags for him to shoe-horn into his limo.

"Are you visiting or moving?" The driver asked.

"Good question." I said. "We're not sure yet."

The Rose Bowl was a tight game and we chanced being late to our flight to see the end. Our driver was getting nervous in the driveway. In the end, Texas won 41-38.

"I guess California lost, daddy." Jake said.

"Yeah, California lost. We'd better go." I said. We all hugged each other at the same time in a huddle as we began to cry just a bit in the foyer. We hugged and kissed our friends again and got into the limo. They followed us for a mile or so to the stoplight where we turned left, and they turned right, honking the horn in their Chevy truck as we waved.

We settled in for the forty-five minute ride to San Francisco International Airport. The limo sped through the darkness a bit like a rocket to the moon. We'd prepared as much as we could for this trip and now the candle was lit.

No turning back.

I thought about what my friend had said to me just before we left. He really had no clue why we were leaving a perfectly good life in California to go live in a third world country. And I had no clue why he wanted to stay in the congested, expensive, and crime-ridden San Francisco Bay Area. I had tried unsuccessfully to explain it to him and everyone else I told of our plans. They thought we were just going on a really long vacation. But I knew better.

CHAPTER TWO
Sean Connery Is A Local But Not Our Neighbor

Cable Beach is so named because in 1907 it became the landing point for the Trans-Atlantic cable, which connected the Bahamian islands with Jupiter, Florida. It is also known as "The Bahamian Riviera" with many upscale hotels, resorts, and a large casino. Beth and I originally honeymooned at the (now renamed) Radisson Hotel, which was built on over a thousand feet of beautiful white sandy beach. Over the years we returned to the Radisson many times and used it as our "base of operations" from which we would visit many other islands in the Bahamas. Our familiarity with the area and the fact that a bazillion-dollar resort was scheduled to be built in the area made us want to own something there.

"Cable Beach is a wonderful area to purchase a home. Are you interested in a house or condo?" Our real estate agent Spencer asked.

And here is where the long line of choices that brought us to the home we ultimately bought began.

* * * * *

But first, let me backtrack a bit to our rental. Spencer had arranged a rental for us in Cable Beach at a small development called Harbour Place. The condo was advertised as "ocean view"; however, our unit did not have an ocean view unless you leaned out the window of the third floor and looked across the neighbor's property. The third floor was called the "Horse" room, I was told. Horses? Not with those windy, wooden stairs!

We rented a dark three-story end unit that backed to the parking area. With all the bright colors I saw on the other units, our color was a bit disappointing. But right near our unit I saw a solid black condo and wondered what kind of person would paint their house black in a Caribbean nation where the national color was pink? Who would have a black house anywhere? Especially here where the sun shone about 20 hours a day?

The townhouse was plain, anonymous and sparsely furnished, a true rental. My wife said the kitchen had very few dishes and such, but that it had recently been updated. This was a good thing as she loved to cook and the rest of the place appeared to be original, probably built about fifty years ago. There was a hellishly dangerous, slippery, wooden, spiral staircase that led to the upper floors. The middle floor had two small bedrooms surrounding two small bathrooms and as said before, and again, the third floor was the "Horse" room with a vaulted ceiling and a glimpse of the sea out one of the windows- if you were a giraffe and could stretch your neck that far.

I still did not get the "horse" thing. If the horse room was on the third floor there was no way any horse could get up those narrow stairs and the horse urine and manure would have ruined the wooden floors.

It was not much for the $4,000 per month we were paying. It really was a shabby little place. Short term rentals were more expensive than long term ones and we had only contracted for three months. I was sure our real estate agent had used his limp-wristed

34

negotiating skills that insured him a fat commission and me an overpriced rental. But, I was still in my "who cares" mode when spending money those days. If we wanted something, we just got it. I did not want being cheap to affect the happiness of our move. I'd figure it all out later.

The more I learned about the local real estate game, the more suspicious I became of Spencer's ability to put a deal together. I was not sure how tough he would be in negotiations. He seemed more like someone who could make introductions and reservations at a restaurant. Maybe he could make a sandwich and an afternoon cocktail but he was no hard negotiator. The deal he got us at Harbour Place was not good, but it would have to do. He seemed affable enough, but lacked the gregarious "get it done" nature of some of the better agents I knew in California. Perhaps I just needed to get to know him better and see what he could do.

As we settled in to Harbour Place, I realized we needed a few other things besides a place to live. We needed school for our son Jake and a car. Jake was four years old and would be ready for kindergarten or pre-K, whatever they called it here. Back in California, I searched online and had found a private school in Cable Beach. The owner had extended an invitation for our son to join their school when we arrived. This school was started in the eighties by a woman from the USA. She was a petite woman who had somehow maintained her southern drawl over three decades of living in the Bahamas and had a reputation for being rather tough. I can say that from personal experience that she was a wonderful, caring woman who had done her level best to insure that our son got a top-notch education. She adored every kid in her care and we adored her.

We also needed to purchase a vehicle, so I began searching online and in the local papers. With the tiny roads and the crazy drivers, I did not plan on walking Jake to school even though it was just a few blocks away. We had rented a Suzuki Grand Vitara but the cost of renting was far too high to keep doing so for long. I needed to buy a car.

Don't get me wrong as I lay out the minute details of our move. It was not all business, believe me. Our first few months were filled with meeting new friends, house parties, beach parties, festivals, birthdays and a lot of rum. I was not working, so my days were wide open. We spent many hours at our little beach with our newfound friends hereafter known as "The Texans".

The Texans were young twenty-somethings; a married couple from a small town in the hill country of Texas. He was a tall, happy-go-lucky computer whiz with an accent that blended both Texas and surfer-speak. She was an attractive yet tough Texas blonde. If a Texas whiskey company began manufacturing firecrackers, she could be on the label. She was generally the loudest and the life of the party wherever we went. We fell in love with them immediately and they rapidly became our best friends on the island. They too lived in Harbour Place and so we spent almost all of our free time together. Mr. Texas worked in the fire alarm business for a local contractor. They did work for all of the large resorts and hotels on the island. Mrs. Texas, a former rodeo and beauty queen in Texas was a beach bum here in the Bahamas. She probably should have just walked around with the Mrs. Texas banner draped over her shoulder but it could have caused some odd tan lines.

It was about noon and Mr. Texas was due to come home for a beer. Mrs. Texas wore her tiny bikini and lay next to Beth and me on our little beach, while Jake played with two thousand Star Wars army men, lining them up for yet another epic battle. It was one of the many lazy days we had spent the first few months there in the Bahamas decompressing from decades in the San Francisco Bay Area.

"I have to go make his sandwiches for lunch." Mrs. Texas suddenly announced.

"How sweet." I said. "I did not know you did that for him."

"Well, to be honest, I never do. As a matter of fact, today is the first day." She said and laughed. Mrs. Texas was so honest. It was easy being around her. She hopped up and wiped some sand from her arm.

"Jake, when is our next battle?" She asked our son. At our first meeting, she was immediately enamored with him and he with her. She and Mr. Texas wanted kids in the worst way, meaning they were struggling getting pregnant. For now, they could practice with Jake.

"Ummm, how about in two minutes?" Jake asked as he held up two sandy little fingers. He was just four years old and still spoke with that voice midway between baby and little boy. I cherished every day with him. He was the center of my universe. All I wanted was more of him. Again, I was glad we'd moved to this tiny island.

"You got it, little man." She held up two fingers as she walked away smiling at him.

Jake did not yet know the difference between two minutes and two hours so she could take her time. I was suddenly reminded of the fact that we could not have any more kids. Beth's body would not do it. Her second pregnancy nearly killed her. We decided to be happy with the healthy son God had given us. But not a day passed that I wondered what it would be like having another two or three kids. Children remind us of why we're alive and if you chose not to have one, I'm sorry. You missed out on something wonderful. If you can't have one, I'm also sorry. I know how you feel because I would have had ten.

Mr. Texas showed up at the beach a few minutes after his missus had left.

"She at da house?" He said in his adopted Bahamian accent. He worked with locals all day and it had rubbed off on his dialect.

"Ya mon." I said, playing with my own words. I grabbed an ice cold Kalik from our small cooler and opened it with the bottom of my flip flop, which was ingeniously equipped with a bottle opener. What a great time to be alive. I handed him the beer, which he drank half of in the first sip. It was hot and he was fully-dressed in work pants, shirt and boots. He was acclimated but still sweated in the midday sun.

"Ya know, man. I's a thinkin'." He said as he looked out over the sea and lit a Parliament cigarette. "You probably stepped in a lot of potcake shit in dem flip flops and now you open my beer like dat. I thought we was friends." He said this and grinned widely. A "potcake" is a term for a stray dog in the Bahamas.

"That's a possibility, brother. But I'm sure that I must have walked that potcake shit off on the beach and in the sea by now. Besides, I thought Texans didn't take shit off of anybody." I said.

"Well, now that is true." He grinned and flicked his cigarette ash.

"Then I suppose you're clear." I loved talking to him. He was one of three men in the world I know that

38

don't always have to be right, the center of attention or always one up on you. He was comfortable in his own skin. His kind demeanor and non-threatening attitude made others want to be around him.

Mrs. Texas walked back towards us from where our condos were, her hands full with a big bag and another cooler. She looked hot, sweaty and completely frazzled. I went to get up to help, but Mr. Texas held me back as he chuckled. He was enjoying this.

"Here comes trouble." I laughed quietly.

Mr. Texas looked back over his shoulder at her and smiled. He adored his wife. They had been friends since early childhood.

"Hey baby." He said. She walked up to him with her little dog on a leash, handed him a big brown bag and the small cooler.

"Whew! That was heavy!" She said. "And little Missy here kept winding her leash around my feet and legs."

"What's in the bag?" He asked her.

"Sandwiches, spaghetti, a pork chop, chips, pretzels, an apple, and some chicken." She listed the items like a diner waitress. She had packed what I considered a Texas-sized lunch.

"I'm afraid to ask what's in the cooler." Beth said.

"He deaded him, Daddy!" Jake held up a handful of storm troopers covered in sand and I took one and played with him.

"It's ten sodas on top with six beers underneath, smothered in ice." She said.

"Texas pirate booty." He laughed.

"Buried treasure." I said.

"Well, those local boys never eat right. Just a plate of fried fish with peas and rice every damn day. If it wasn't for us, they'd never get to try anything." She said as she tied her little dog to her beach chair. The small dog immediately took her place under the chair in the shade and laid down.

She was right. The locals had a very limited diet and most of the food was fried fish, fried chicken, fried plantains, and fried something all of the time. Want to become rich in the Bahamas? It's simple: buy a Kentucky Fried Chicken franchise that sells rum.

"And the beer, that is for the ride home." Mr. Texas said.

"Oh yeah, that brutal ten mile drive. How can you stand it?" Beth asked.

"Ten miles in bumper to bumper traffic on a two lane road that crawls along at about a mile an hour." He complained.

"So it takes ten hours to get home?" Beth asked.

"Sometimes fifteen, Mrs. Reno." He laughed.

He always called my wife Mrs. Reno. We weren't that much older. I figured it was just one of the many Texas niceties that made their state the greatest of the whole union. I had always said that I love California, but California's problem was that it's full of people from other places. California was full of individuals. Texas was full of Texans.

"OK, so the six pack of beer sounds a little light for that ride. But what's the soda for?" I inquired with real interest. Soda?

He leaned over to me and almost whispered. "Far as I'm concerned, it's to break up the rum so I don't feel like a total alcoholic." He laughed.

We did share a lot of rum and cola and went through ice like an NFL locker room after a tough game.

As far as friends went, they brought out the best in us. However, with all the beach time we did together,

I'm sure we took a few years off of their lives. Oh well, they were young.

* * * * *

So that I did not spend all of my time either shopping for a house and car online, or relaxing on the beach, I decided to get some exercise. I saw an ad at the local super market community board for a sea kayak, and even though I'd only been in a kayak once before, I knew this kayak would be mine. What a great way to exercise! Out on the sea, in the sun-it sounded perfect.

I drove the cheap little car we had rented at the airport. The rental price was not cheap at $100 per day, but the quality of the little SUV was questionable. It was a Suzuki Grand Vitara. We called it the "Viagra" because when you stepped on the gas, the engine still remained limp for about 30 minutes. I headed west to Love Beach, just a couple of miles along the shoreline to meet with the owner of the kayak.

"I'm asking $800 for it and if you're not interested I've got another guy coming by in a minute or so." He said curtly.

OK, non-local white dude from Canada I guessed from the accent. I supposed we could dispel with the pleasantries. For some reason, North Americans and Bahamians are very polite to each other, but not so much to their own kind.

Kayak Boy was a tall, beefy white expat guy with a nerdy slant to his appearance. He was overweight, poorly dressed, and unshaven. Just inside his first floor condo, there were video game cases and computers everywhere. There was every geek's dream date, a 60" flat screen TV and a couch that appeared to double as

41

his bed. This apartment simply stated, "I HAVE NO GIRLFRIEND AND MY MOTHER GAVE UP ON ME YEARS AGO."

"I wouldn't have come by if I wasn't interested, sport." I said looking at the kayak. "But eight hundred is a lot of money for a used kayak."

"Well, then I should go back inside." He said.

He had the best negotiation technique available: not caring. He was willing to walk away. He had me. He knew it. I wondered if he could help our real estate agent learn how to close a deal.

He kept the kayak outside his front door, fixed to a post by a small, rusty chain with a tiny lock almost rusted through. A five-year-old girl could kick the chain and break the kayak free.

"Well, if you'll throw in that high-tech security device, we have a deal." I said.

He thought for a moment and then said, "Well, OK I guess." I could tell he really wanted to keep that chain. I rapidly learned that sarcasm had no meaning in my adopted home.

I knew that my "who gives a toss" attitude with money would only last so long. I gave myself three months before I would have to get serious again. For now, fat, geeky Kayak Boy could have his money. I took the boat at his price. I wanted to go for a paddle.

* * * * *

"Great boat, Daddy!" Jake said as I untied the kayak from the roof of the Suzuki.

"Yep. And look at the pirate treasure Daddy found. Here, you keep it." I handed him the chain and lock.

42

"WOW! Thanks, Daddy." He said and just stared. "REAL pirate treasure!" MOM!" He ran off to show the chain to his mother.

I grinned as he ran into the condo. That was worth $800 right there.

* * * * *

I took the kayak out for her maiden voyage. The water was flat and the sun was warm, so I threw on a swimsuit, some shades, and a little sunscreen before paddling out. Once I had gotten a couple hundred yards offshore, I leaned back and looked up at the sky. With no mountains or large buildings, the sky and ocean seemed to go on forever. Some small birds flew overhead as I looked up at the clouds. Then I sat up and looked down into the water. I had to catch my breath for a moment as I felt like I was going to fall. The water was so clear that I felt like I was floating in air.

The buildings back on Cable Beach all stood guard on the water's edge as some seagulls flew by talking to each other. I splashed water on my body to keep cool in the midday sun and took the whole scene into my memory. Another one, locked in my memory vault that was bursting at the seams. Moments like that stack up in your mind in the Bahamas and after a while you may want to leave the island, but your memory won't let you go. You'll want to stay and won't even know why. The memory lock will hold onto you.

* * * * *

In January of 2006, we soon found out that if you want to live on the ocean and are not fantastically wealthy a detached house in Cable Beach was out of the question. They could cost many millions of dollars and the upkeep maintenance could break your budget. Just off the beach, there were many houses available ranging in price from about $200,000 on up. Condominiums on the beach could be found for under $200,000 if you only needed one bedroom and one bathroom, but for two or three bedrooms the average price would be closer to $500,000 on up.

Our first problem was price. Beth only wanted to live right on the beach, but all the houses there were out of our budget. We did not want to live in a condominium, so I convinced Beth to look for homes not directly on, but near the beach. She drug her feet a bit, but went along with me.

Our agent showed us a few homes, but nothing really inspired us. He kept trying to get us to move to the east side of the island where he lived. I got the feeling "Viagra" that he was more comfortable with that area and that he might not be an area expert in Cable Beach, so I kept searching for homes on my own. Truthfully, I wished I could just find a home without his help. But if a home is listed in the Bahamas, you are going to have to pay the agent whether he does anything or not. That was the rule there so you might as well get whatever help they could offer.

One day, Spencer phoned and offered to take us to lunch in neighboring Lyford Caye, a private country club sub-division on the far western side of the island, and one of the most prestigious and expensive areas in the nation.

"I have a golf membership there so we may dine at the beach restaurant." Spencer said, rather proud of himself.

I'm not that bright, but I could tell he was feeling us out by taking us there. It would be so much easier if he'd just ask. But on we go with another tiresome game of charades. He wanted to see if we would spend the millions it would cost to live in Lyford Caye that would garner him a hefty commission. I knew we would not spend that much, but thought it might be fun to be toured around Lyford anyway. It's always fun to see how the pampered folks lived.

As we passed through the guard house and entered lifestyles of the rich and obnoxious, Spencer began pointing out certain homes.

"That one is Sean Connery's place. He's owned it for many years. I believe he became enamored with the Bahamas during the filming of the movie, "Thunderball" back in 1965." Spencer explained.

I must say that Sir Sean's home did not have a lot of what we call "curb appeal" for what I expected of an international movie star and a knight. I read somewhere that Sir Sean had stated that he would not live in Scotland again until it became independent of the UK. I respected that but realized that he'd probably live out his days here in the Bahamas. Perhaps I should make some kind of similar statement that would force me to remain here.

"I'll never return to the US until they adopt the flat tax system." I said.

"What was that?" Spencer asked?

I realized I'd said it out loud. So much for my inner monologue. I just shook my head and looked out the window.

"This big white place was owned by a rich *woman*." He said.

I looked at him to finish the sentence, but he didn't. He just kept driving and looking about. "Well, of course it was owned by a *rich* woman." I thought. Who else could afford to live here? I was glad we did not pay for this tour. Then I wondered if the fact that a "woman" could own a house like that was the interesting part to him. From what I could gather, women's rights in the Bahamas were not on par with men's. We kept driving, looking at the huge homes.

"You know, this home is listed for three million. I could get you a tour." Spencer said. Now, either he had forgotten who he was taking to lunch or he was making a bad joke. Spencer's sense of humor was dry and he always had his "I'm your agent" persona on. I could not really read him yet.

"A little out of our price range I'm afraid." I said. But I took note of Lyford Caye. "Someday", I thought to myself. These people knew how to live.

"These homes are nice, but none of them are on the water." Beth said. "For that money you should at least have a view."

"Beach front homes here get really expensive." Spencer explained this in his usual second-grade teacher drone.

"I saw one online for around twenty million." I said. But homes in that range were just poker chips for millionaires, a way to keep score. Affordability was really not a factor.

"Ten to twenty million sounds about right." Spencer said and grinned.

I just knew he thought we were secretive millionaires and he was licking his chops. He was in for a big letdown.

"Here we are." He said.

He parked the car and we walked across a large, manicured lawn toward the shoreline where the clubhouse was located. Sarcastically, I thought *how convenient that they put the golf club right next to the yacht club*" but I felt out of place and a bit envious.

46

A waiter took us to a small table located in an outdoor café that backed to some sand dunes. The gentle waves could be heard from just beyond the dunes, but the ocean was not in view. Around us, WASP's from around the globe noshed on snacks and talked about how they would continue ruling the world. To say I felt out of place would be a massive understatement. Not that I am broke or don't know which fork to use, but I never really felt comfortable where all the people sitting and eating were white and the people serving and cleaning were black. I imagine this observation was not lost on the staff. I figured the patrons were oblivious.

Spencer bought us a surprisingly awful lunch and talked about real estate options. He had a habit of speaking so low that it seemed he attempted to keep anyone around us from hearing our conversation. I was sure no one around us cared about or what we said. And my annoyance meter was straining almost as hard as my ears as I struggled to hear him, trying to read his lips.

He spoke of his family, his grandchildren and his wife. And now, I began to see a human being behind the agent. We spoke of getting our son together with his grandkids for a play date, knowing we would never actually do it but it felt good pretending we might. I'm sure that was the idea. After a bit of talking, we made it clear that Lyford Caye was beyond what we wanted to spend on a vacation home.

"There's a new development of town houses near Cable Beach I'd like to show you. The units are brand new and very well done. As a matter of fact, many of the American embassy people live there because it's so safe. There are lots of children there and safe places for Jake to play…"

47

"Sounds great." I said. Beth remained stoic.

I noticed that Spencer used the word "safe" in back to back sentences. I should point out that while the Bahamas was a great place to visit, when you live there it was obvious that it was a third world nation. And in such nations, there is a large rift between the haves and the have-nots. This distance creates friction and tension, which causes the have-nots to steal from the haves. For this, the haves built gated communities with high walls and razor-wire fences. Almost all shopkeepers in the Bahamas have installed buzzers at their doors so the door remains locked until they see and scrutinize you before opening their door. If you pass their "profiling", you get buzzed in. Man, would the pamphlet-passing hippies back in Berkeley have a field day with that practice. They could lawyer up and retire!

An expat who had lived on the island for thirty years recently told me a story. She was working at a department store on the island when two gunmen came in and fired a shotgun at the ceiling telling all to hit the floor. They then robbed the place and made off with all they could carry.

When the ordeal was over, she said to another woman, "Well, it appears that the rightful owners have reclaimed their property."

This was a stunning concept to Americans who believe in personal property rights to the very core. It's not something that happens every day but it is interesting to hear how some people view what you may consider *your* property. Something to keep in mind when you're a tiny minority in a foreign country full of people less fortunate than you.

* * * * *

The new townhouses Spencer spoke of were in a brand new development called "Nautica". Spencer had not lied. It was gated, the attached units all had two stories, and the one we were looking at had a deck looking out over a small, man-made pond, including a one car garage, a common pool and was right across the lane from a little playground for the kids. It was brand new and the smell of new carpet and fresh paint tickled my nose as I inspected the place and imagined living there.

"I like it, babe." I told Beth as we walked around the unit.

"Yeah, it's nice." She said. I could tell she was less than impressed.

"What's the matter?" I asked. "You've been kind of quiet."

"No, this place is nice. And the others were okay too."

"So, what's the problem?" I asked.

She motioned for me to follow up upstairs and we stopped in the master bedroom.

"The problem is that these houses could be *anywhere*. Did we really move three thousand miles away, to the *Caribbean*, to live in a *suburb*? I thought we moved here to live in the *Bahamas*. This place looks like *Walnut frigging Creek*." She said.

And she was right. But for the abundance of palm trees and the constant sweating from the balmy heat, this place felt a bit like any other nice, new suburb in Florida or parts of California. Nice, but not on the water. Did we come this far just to cling to what felt comfortable, I wondered.

"I want to live on the water, Jimi." She said. "I want to see and hear the ocean. I want to feel the breeze and walk on the sand."

49

"Even if we have to live in a condo?" I asked.

"Yes, even in a condo." She said.

"OK." I said. I'd do anything to make her happy, even live in a condo... something I detested. Having people above me, below me, and to each side of me felt like I was back on the San Francisco Bay Bridge again. And the lack of privacy in a condo did not attract me, either.

Imagine a real estate agent listing like this:

SUPER SMALL MICRO-CONDO. NO SECURITY. FLOOR-TO-CEILING WINDOWS CONTRIBUTE TO A FISH-BOWL, AQUARIUM-LIKE QUALITY. THESE SAME FLOOR TO CEILING WINDOWS MAKE IT EASY FOR ALL TO SEE INTO YOUR HOME LIKE YOU'RE LIVING A CARIBBEAN REALITY SHOW.

WIND AND WAVES WILL PROBABLY DESTROY THE WHOLE PLACE WITHIN A DECADE DUE TO GLOBAL WARMING. DIFFICULT NEIGHBORS FROM AROUND THE WORLD ARE SURE TO MAKE MAINTAINING THE PLACE IMPOSSIBLE. GOOD LUCK!!!

How odd, that we would ultimately buy that very place?

That's how we made the decision to buy a condominium on the beach. For us, the whole reason to live in the Bahamas was tied to the beauty of the water. The beautiful blue and green colors cannot be described with words, they must be painted and even then the beauty is not properly conveyed. The clarity and the warmth is unlike anything I've ever seen or felt back in California.

Beth was right. For expats like us, what other reason was there to move to the land of sun and fun?

Begging forgiveness from the local people, but if the Bahamian waters were dark and about thirty degrees colder the island would have few residents and certainly would not be the tourist attraction it is today. We decided to try to live on the number one attraction: the beach.

The problem was we were certainly not the only people who felt this way. Global warming or not, good beachfront properties proved to be both scarce and expensive. We would have to increase our budget, get lucky, or both if we were to find the right place. Or we could simply buy across the street from the beach and wait ten years for the ocean to rise like Al Gore had promised.

TV Announcer on popular talk show at home in San Francisco:

"HE'S THE MAKER OF THE WORLD WIDE WEB... LADIES AND GENTLEMEN, PLEASE WELCOME ... MR. AL GORE AND HIS BAND, GLOBAL WARMING!
(APPLAUSE!)
WITH YOUR HOST AND DEBATE MODERATOR, MR. AL GORE!
(APPLAUSE!)
TONIGHT'S TOPIC (SPONSORED BY THE GOP):
'IS THIS ALL JUST A BUNCH OF CRAP OR WHAT?'
(CANNED LAUGHTER.)
WITH OUR RETURNING GUEST, MR. BLAME THE SUV!
(HUGE APPLAUSE!)
AND HIS OPPONENT, MR. BLAME NATURE, *NOT MY EFFING SUV.*

(SMALLER GROUP OF APPLAUSE.)

From the prices of beachfront in that area, no one was listening to old Al. The debate would rage on and we would have to side (at least for the short term) with Mr. Blame Nature and hope for the best.

CHAPTER THREE
Fake Estate

Back home, I owned a real estate appraisal company. In order to do an appraisal you must deal with real estate agents. Again, let me be perfectly clear: I have never had much love for real estate agents and still don't to this day. The problem was that there were so few really good agents. A good agent could save your financial life while finding a dream home. And then there were many that really should have just been assistants to the really good ones. If you're reading this and you are a real estate agent, either you're one of the few good ones or you're part of the problem. If you are part of the problem, try law school, another one of those last bastions for those with no direction. I've done both and sucked at each so I can say this with a straight face and self-defacing honesty.

I had been searching online for a condo for months with no luck. They were either too expensive, too old, not on the beach, or had monthly maintenance dues that were ridiculous. When I found one called "Bonita", I was very surprised. I found it right on my favorite real estate site. How had I missed this before? Or was it a new listing? It had two bedrooms, two bathrooms, and it was listed as being right on the beach.

All of this sounded great, but $500,000 was a lot more than we wanted to spend. I was finding out that our original budget of $300,000 would only get us a shabby house with barbed wire on the fence about two blocks from the beach. In the Bahamas, most of the beaches are private. The rule is that none of the beaches are "private" and that the beach is public up to the high-water mark left by the tide. However, these "public" beaches are all blocked from the road by private condominiums and houses. You could walk to one of these beaches from a true public beach with a public entrance, but it would be a long walk and most people did not bother. This was just another of the little nuances of the nation we now called home that sneaked up on us. However, it would serve me as I wanted to be a homeowner on the beach.

One such listing our agent had given us to view was right behind a huge supermarket. The agent said this was a benefit. Of course! Who doesn't want smelly trash dumpsters full of rats and flies right by your property line? Why is it that those dumpsters are always emptied at 4:30 AM by huge garbage trucks? I guess it's to avoid the traffic. Perhaps the real benefit was that you would not need an alarm clock or even a rooster. The garbage trucks would wake us up every morning.

When we went to view the place I thought the agent was on the lawn talking to another agent, but it turned out it was just winos pissing in the yard. There was high-intensity security lighting that stayed on all night long to make sure we did not fall asleep waiting for the garbage truck at 4:30 AM. I did some research and found out that the local crime rate in the neighborhood was so high that the windows were actually made of concrete.

"So…do you want to make an offer?" The real agent had finally shown up and walked us through the shabby place.

"No, but I could make a few suggestions." I said. Beth shushed me and we thanked the agent and left. She was good at being a social muffler for my sarcastic soul.

My mother stayed with us for a month at Harbour Place, and she, like I, was completely enamored with island life. She loved the beach, the warm water, and could stay in it all day. As she enjoyed the beach and all that sun, she wondered why I was wasting such beautiful sunshine indoors as I scoured the Internet for a house and a car.

The picture of the building at Bonita looked very familiar, so I walked to West Bay Street just outside Harbour Place and headed west , passing a couple of condo buildings and there she was: a boxy looking five-story orange building with a green awning. It was kind of like one of those juice boxes Jake took to school. It looked like a huge square orange that had rolled on its side with the stem and leaf still intact. "Bonita" the sign on the wall said. The 1980's letter font style on the sign gave a clue of the building's age. It reminded me of Crocket and Tubbs speeding through Miami in a white Ferrari Testarossa. Ahhh, the 80's. My decade.

The parking lot was gated and locked, so I headed back to Harbour Place admiring their security. From the Internet photos, I could not tell if the building had an actual beach or just a sea-wall with a view. I decided to put on some shorts and head for the beach at Place. I walked west along the waterline and only got a little wet as the low-tide waves splashed my shins a bit. I made it to Bonita and looked upwards toward the building. There was a sea wall that formed a little protected square of a beach about thirty by thirty feet surrounded by sea walls to the rear with some stairs leading up to the patio and pool. It looked good so far.

As I walked back to Place, what bothered me was the fact that Spencer had not found this place first. It's a condo on the beach in the right neighborhood and it was listed on his company's site. The place was literally two doors down from where we were staying. What was I missing here? My confidence in Spencer took another step down the ladder, but I called him anyway.

"Spencer, the place looks perfect. When can I see it?" I asked.

"Let me contact the owner or agent and call you back. Do you have the phone number?" He asked.

Was he for real? Why was I paying this guy?

"Yes here's the number." I sighed and read it off my laptop.

"I hope it's really for sale." He said. I did too. Another thing I'd found out while searching for a home is that Bahamian real estate agents aren't very quick to clean up old listings on the web. More than once, I would find a place and call Spencer only to find out that it had sold three years ago.

Another problem was that many owners put their place up for sale just to test the market with no real intention of selling. It could get very frustrating. I learned to not get too excited about a place listed online until the details were clear.

We had been interested in a few places at Harbour Place. One beach front condo I had found online was particularly unique. The owner had taken two units that were side by side and turned them into one large unit. From what we could see through the windows as we walked through the garden, it looked like he had done a great job of remodeling and decorating the place.

When we contacted the listing agent he said that the owner currently had the place rented out to some

56

French people and that the lease absolutely had to be honored.

"Well, when is their lease up?" I asked.

"Three more years." He said. I wondered who rented a place for three years. This was very different from home. Still, I thought, for the right price it could make a nice investment and provide some rental income, so I was still interested. Perhaps we could buy this place and use the rental income to rent another place until it was vacant. The possibilities in my head always spun and never needed oil. It still made me dizzy sometimes.

"Well, may we see the place?" I asked.

"No. The tenants are kind of skittish about people coming into the property."

I imagined a bunch of skinny people all dressed in black wearing berets and smoking cartons of cigarettes, eating stinky cheese and complaining about American foreign policy.

"Well, we're not going to bother anyone. Photos are just not enough. I need to get a feel for the place." I explained. "Can't the owner give them proper notice?"

"They're not going to let anyone in." The agent said.

"How about an appraiser or home inspector?

"Nope."

"Handyman?"

"Uh-uh?"

"A pizza guy? I could get a uniform…"

"What?"

"Never mind. So, you want me to buy a place that I can't even get a look at for three years?" I asked.

"Yes." The man said.

I won't repeat here what I told him.

There was another unit we wanted to see in Harbour Place. I had also found it online. I guess my agent did not like using computers because he was not finding any of these listings right in my back yard.

I was suddenly struck by the strange world in which we lived. I was using the Internet, sending electronic signals racing through thousands of miles of wiring, and many more thousands of miles wirelessly out into space and back to discuss a home for sale that is actually two frigging doors down from where I was sitting. I then used a VOIP phone that bounced off more satellites to talk to the agent who was just across town. I was doing all of this instead of actually walking two doors down, knocking on the door, and asking the owner if his place is for sale. I did all of this in a place where falling coconuts killed more people than bicycle accidents. I was doing all of this with a big grin on my face as I thought this over. What a world!

I finally got ahold of the listing agent and he gave me the owner's phone number and told me to talk to the owner directly.

"You can't tell me anything about the place?" I inquired doing my best to get more information.

"That place? You'd really be better off talking to the owner." He said.

And for some reason I did not believe him. That was very odd, even for here, but he gave me the owner's phone number.

I phoned the owner.

"Yeah." A gruff voice barked.

"Hi, I'm calling about the townhouse you have for sale in Harbour Place." I said politely.

"Call the agent." He said.

"Well, I did that and the agent gave me this number."

"Hey, how'd you get this number anyway?" He asked.

"The agent gave it to me." I said.

"What agent?"

"The one that has your place listed for sale. You may have met him and spoken sometime when you were signing the listing agreement?" I said getting annoyed.

"Well, the place is being renovated." He grumbled defensively.

"I understand. I'd just like to take a look."

"It's under construction. We're doing some repairs." He explained.

"I was in the construction field for many years and can probably look beyond any work being done. I'd just like to see the place and check out your view. I'm literally just a few doors from the place. If you look outside your front window, I can wave to you. May I come over?" I asked.

"Uhhhh, well, you see, my dog was kidnapped by my ex-wife and she took her to Africa. I've got the whole back patio wrapped in plastic and yellow police tape. It's a crime scene, ongoing investigation." He said officially as if he was reading from some legal documents. "I have to leave everything as it was until the police are done with their work."

"Sorry to hear that." I said. "How long has this been going on?"

"Three years."

"You've had your patio wrapped in plastic for three years?"

"These things take time."

At this point I knew I was only moving forward with this out of morbid curiosity or some sense of masochism.

"Well, I really could just take a look at the inside of the unit. I mean that's where we'll be doing most of our *living*." I pushed him as I pried hoping to just gain entry to the unit.

"Not a good time."

"So is it safe to say that the townhouse is not for sale?" I asked.

"Oh no, it's for sale."

"Well how much do you want?" I asked.

"Just a fair price." He said. "I'm not asking for any more than it's worth."

"Do you think we could nail that down an actual figure? Or should I just estimate?" I began to slip into my American sarcasm. It fit like a well-worn glove, but it was useless here. Bahamians don't get sarcasm.

"Ohhhh, the agent has all that information. Look, I really have to get back to work." He said.

"Oh sorry, what is it that you do?"

"I retired from the local police here and now I dabble in construction and real estate." He said.

"Really? Well, as it turns out I know some people who could use your services." I toyed with him.

"Sounds great." He said and hung up.

I grabbed my laptop, walked out of our townhome and looked over at the place I had just been discussing with the man on the phone. I looked down at the laptop screen. That was the place. I just had to assure myself that the place really existed and that our conversation had actually happened. I needed a quick reality check. I walked over to the friendly, but useless manager's office and asked her about the unit.

"Oh he hasn't paid his monthly dues for years." Hattie, the manager said. She kept a small office on the grounds of Harbour Place. Hattie did not do anything but sit in her office with the door open. She was good for a conversation or some gossip, but at Harbour Place she couldn't get a light bulb replaced or keep the night watchman from sleeping on the job. He snored so loudly that I complained that he was keeping me up at night. Hattie said she'd talk to him and get him to sleep quieter, but he just changed locations and slept in the laundry room.

"That man has not paid his monthly condo dues for *years*? I asked.

"That's why we cut off his water, sewer, and power about a year ago. But he don' move."

"That man has lived in there for over a year with no power, water….and no working toilets?" I asked.

"That's right." She said as she nodded and then switched to shaking her head in disbelief.

The man was right. That place probably was a crime scene at this point. I gave up on Harbour Place.

Spencer called back a few minutes later to tell me that the owner of the Bonita unit was also a local real estate agent and that he could show the place to us now. Now? Right now? Things did not usually run that fast. Beth was still back home on a business trip to California and Jake was in school until three. I guess I could go check it out alone. I grabbed my little Sony digital camera, put on my flip-flops and headed out.

"Mom, I'm heading a couple of doors down to look at a possible condo for us." I said to her from the patio window. She was reading on a lounge chair and waved to me.

"Good luck!" She said.

I was so glad she was here. She had raised us as a single mother and struggled so that her three kids could have more. It didn't really work out the way she'd planned but we learned to work hard and appreciate what we had.

61

She deserved this life. It was my plan to make sure she had it any time she wanted. My mother was my anchor, my security. As a boy, I had always promised her a house with a pool. If I could get her a house with a pool in the Caribbean on the beach, I would feel like I had delivered on my promise. I looked at my mother as she lay in the sun, so happy, so content. I had to make this work.

Spencer said he would meet me there in two minutes. I translated that to his normal timing and figured he'd show up in an hour or so. Since the owner was there, I'd just go on my own.

When I showed up and dialed the door code Spencer had given me, the gate opened and I walked into the parking lot towards the building. A small, thin man approached me from the main entrance door.

"Are you Jim?" He said with an accent I could not place.

"Yes. Do you have a condo for sale?" I asked.

"I do. Please, come in." He reached out and shook my hand. "My name is Geraldo."

I could go on and on describing him, but just imagine a man, advanced in years, and balding. Geraldo appeared to be a frail, insomniac mortician who looked like he had been on a diet of nothing but coffee and cigarettes for many years. Believe me, not everyone in the Bahamas looks like Lenny Kravitz or some tanned white expat like Jimmy Buffet.

We walked together into the building. Of course, Spencer was late but I was not going to wait for him. There was an atrium entrance area, a long hallway with one unit on the right and a party room with a wall of floor to ceiling windows on the left. At the end of the hallway were some double doors. Geraldo opened the doorway and motioned for me to enter. Something about the man gave me a creepy feeling, but his age doubled mine, and he appeared about as threatening as a skeleton made of cigarette ash. As long as he did not cup my mouth and nose with a chloroform-soaked rag, I figured I would be fine.

"So, you're looking to buy a home?" He said in a low monotone.

"Right." I said. I realized that no matter how much this guy creeped me out that he owns the condo I may want to buy, so I'd better check my attitude and be friendly and polite. "I've been looking for a little while now."

"Are you married?" He asked. For some reason even his voice made my skin crawl. Where had I seen him before? Oh yes, he was the Crypt Keeper!

"Yes", was all I could muster.

"Family?" He asked.

"One child. A boy."

"How fortunate." He said as if we were going to put my son into his stew pot. "Would you like coffee?"

"Coffee?" I wondered. It's ninety-five degrees outside with 90 percent humidity. There was no breeze and not a cloud in the sky. There were people downtown renting space under shade trees to tourists by the hour. Earlier today, three seagulls flew by and two burst into flames. Coffee? Sure, why not? And how about a parka and a nice rousing camp fire song? Gimme that guitar!

"No thank you. I've had mine already." I lied.

"Where is your family?" He asked.

"My wife is out of town on business. Son is in school. I'll want her to see the place in a few days if that is alright." I said.

"Of course." He nodded.

63

The accent. Was it Cuban, Puerto Rican, or Addams Family? I did my best to separate the condo from its owner and began looking around.

"May I take photos? I'd like to email them to my wife."

"Be my guest." He said.

Upon entering the condo, I was first struck by the décor. Apparently, the owners were front row fans of the colors gold, black and pink. Almost everything in the entire place was either one color or the other. There were Roman columns made of plastic (or some kind of ceramic) painted gold with busts of stately looking, long-dead Greek men on top of them. Pink leather couches jumped out at me from the living area. There was a lot of black lacquer furniture, which someone had apparently thought would be more attractive if it were faux-painted with speckled gold flake. But the piece de resistance had to be the rectangular glass dining table supported by clear acrylic flames. Don Johnson would have loved it here.

"Nice place, pal!" Crockett said to the drug dealer. "I guess crime DOES pay!"

Don may have loved it, but Beth would have thrown up.

I forced myself to look beyond the furnishings and tried to assess the place. My professional training as a real estate appraiser kicked in. I had to look beyond the owner's vision of décor to see the real value of property. While this place would be a challenge, I began to envision it as it not as it was but as it could be. Would this work for us? A third bedroom would be nice, but the master bedroom was big enough for a desk next to the bed. If people came to visit, Jake could sleep with us and there were two twin beds in the second room so we could accommodate guests. The grounds appeared well maintained. There was a pool with a large patio area and the small beach. The biggest selling point of this unit was the view.

The unit was on the ground floor, which was good for us as we liked being able to see Jake playing outside and my Mom had bad knees. There was an unobstructed view of the ocean and a neighboring island that was breathtaking. That water was mesmerizing and the view here was unbelievable.

"So, how long have you lived on the island?" The thin man asked. Or maybe he said something else. I'm not sure as I was not paying attention anyway. My mind was spinning as I tried to take it all in and do mental calculations.

Manners, I thought.

"I'm sorry. What did you say?" I asked, smiling.

"Have you lived here long?" He asked.

"No, not long. But we've visited regularly for thirteen years." I said.

"Working?" He asked.

"No. Not yet." I said and he smiled and nodded like we had a dirty secret. I thought he even winked at me. Had I just given the password for some kind of dark, secret society? I imagined him slowly motioning toward the hallway where he pulled a long, gold rope which opened a secret passageway of stairs behind velvet drapes that lead down, down, down... I was really wishing Spencer would show up.

"Excuse me a minute. I need to make a call." I said and the man just nodded slowly.

I went outside and called my wife on my cell.

"I think I found it, baby." I felt so right telling her this.

"Are you sure?" She asked.

"I believe so. Do you trust me to make the deal without you?"

"I do." She said. "If you think it's the one for us, get it. I trust your judgment."

One good thing about my marriage: we have the same taste in just about everything and we were definitely on the same page when it came to our life plans. I knew she'd love the place. I just had to get her to imagine it redecorated. That would be the tough part.

"Do you mind if I take some more pictures?" I asked as Spencer finally walked up the side of the building through the garden area. I gave Spencer a quick glance and half smile, trying to communicate my disgust with his constant tardiness.

"Be my guest." Geraldo said.

He and Geraldo shook hands and probably knew each other. Maybe they were brothers in a local secret society. Skull and Cigarettes. At this point, I did not care. I found the place and I'd make the deal. I'd done enough research to know that it was priced right. I also knew that under Bahamian rules, if a place is listed by an agent, he gets paid no matter who makes the deal. Spencer told me that the deal was $500,000 triple net, which means I had to pay all fees. I took photos of everything and planned on emailing them to Beth later that night. I could grind on the guy, but I wanted to make a statement and get it done. I did not want this one to slip through my fingers.

"Geraldo, I'll take your place at asking price if you promise me you will not show it to anyone else. If you do show it and get a better offer, take it. I'm not getting into a bidding war." I said to him.

Both agents were a bit stunned. I guess it's not often that someone makes up their mind this quickly.

The truth was, I already knew it was priced fairly well, I had the money and I wanted the place. There was no reason to play games. Although, again I probably could have negotiated better and saved a little money, but I was not in the mood. I'd made up my mind and wanted to be bold and brash in hopes of just securing the deal. Club Caribe Fever was a real disease locally and I had to make sure the crypt keeper did not suddenly come down with a case of it.

"Okay." He said. We shook hands. And I'm sure I aged at least ten years during the three seconds I held his bony hand. I let go quickly but maybe not quickly enough. I was sure I'd find some ashes in my palm but I did not look. What have I done? Yikes!

I learned later that he showed it to at least one more person that day after I had left. He probably showed it to many other people in the following days until they finally accepted our offer. And to be honest, if I would have known that earlier, I would have walked away from the deal. An old boss of mine once told me, "You can't make a good deal with a bad man." But the deal was accepted with no quibbling about price so we both got what we wanted.

Spencer and I walked out to the parking lot.

"Need a ride home?" He asked.

Was he joking? I could never tell. Our rental was practically next door, but in the other direction of a one-way street. To bring me home, we'd have to circle about a half mile of one-way roads. I knew he may have been trying to be funny but I still did not really get him. He did seem very happy, and why not? He just made 3% of $500,000 for doing nothing. He did not find the place, nor did he save me any money in negotiations. When I offered full price he just drooled a little and kept quiet. Fifteen grand for him. No high-five, no nothing? I was sure he saved his celebration for later.

I wished there was a way to get around this, but the only way would be to wait until the listing expired and then make another offer. Chances were that it could be sold by that time. The owner was an agent so he'd just renew the listing. The thing that really irked me was that since the owner was also the listing agent, I had to pay him fifteen thousand dollars for the privilege of buying his home. What a racket. Lawyers, bankers and real estate agents... pretty much the same everywhere.

"No. I'll walk." I said. I wanted to say something sarcastic to him about how much I appreciated all of his hard work, and to thank him for helping me find this place. I also wanted to point out just how useless his total silence had been in the whole thirty second negotiating process, but then I realized that there really wasn't a negotiating process. I was just angry at him and the seller for reasons I could not even put into words at that time. They just appeared to be money-hungry speed bumps on the road to my dream. Soon, they would be just fading memories and I'd still own this beautiful condo on the beach. They'd spend their commissions and I'd still own the place. Geraldo would dry up somewhere and turn back into sand and ash while I'd still own Bonita. Hateful bastard, aren't I?

I had gone in without a game plan. I winged it and offered asking price. It does not take much to do that. I had never been impressed by people who drove expensive cars because any idiot with the money can buy one. I figured I was the idiot with the money this time but I did not care. I had looked for years for a place like this and when I found it I just bought it. I suppose all of this explanation is my way of disguising the fact that I now feel like an idiot for not negotiating harder and for buying on emotion. But, live and learn. I could not kick myself too hard for allowing myself to realize a dream, even if it cost me a few extra bucks. Heck, I knew I was going to marry my wife on our 4th date and that was almost 20 years ago. Sometimes, you don't look long before you jump. I had read that it's best not letting yesterday take up too much of today. Maybe someday I'll get that and start living it too.

I decided to hold off on saying anything sarcastic to Spencer. Part of living in paradise means letting go of who you were and becoming who you will be. And for me that would mean learning to be a more gentle person. Living in the San Francisco Bay Area of California, one gets a bit jaded and callous. I wanted to change that. I knew that I had a very defensive and sometimes hostile attitude. A lifetime of freeways, middle fingers, construction sites, Army barracks, and fighting people I grew up with just for a wave to surf on had changed me. I wanted to change all of that again. Perhaps I could work on that here.

"Thanks, Spencer." I said as I walked away. "I'll call you tomorrow. You take care." And I walked the two minute walk back to Harbour Place floating on air. I had found our new home and I was not an asshole to our agent. Win/win.

Back at Place, my mom was anxious to hear all about the condo. She was excited for us and was eager to get redecorating, but I knew we had just passed step one of a long journey. Closing a real estate deal at home was not easy. I knew it would be especially difficult in the Bahamas.

* * * * *

"Any word from Beth in your email?" Mom asked.

"Not yet, Mom. It's three hours earlier there. I'm sure she's sleeping right now." We were floating up to our waists at the beach at Harbour Place on our mid-morning swim. It was the day after I'd seen the condo and sent photos to Beth. I was anxiously waiting for her reply.

"Oh yeah, I always forget the time difference part." She said as she paddled around in the tiny waves. The sun was out and the sea was dead flat. Mom was in her element: water. I loved to see her floating on her back, eyes closed, not thinking of anything else. She was warm, happy and drifting around in the Caribbean Sea which makes all of us weightless and warm. I decided to copy her and we floated together holding hands. I would hold this moment in my heart forever. How long had it been since I had held my mother's hand?

"I'll call her later. I sent her the pictures of the condo. I can't wait to see what she thinks. I just hope she can look past the interior." I said.

"There is so much you can do to that place to make it nice. Don't get hung up on furniture, paint and bad art. It's the location that makes it special. Well, that and this view!" Mom reassured me like she always did. She had an artistic eye and I was glad she understood.

"A little paint here... some new furniture there." She said. "Before you know it, you've turned it into your own. A home." Mom had always fostered the dreamer in me. She had spent hours looking online with me when we were back in California. For a long time, before even Beth was convinced, she was the only one who believed in my dream. She made it easy to dream because she believed just like I did. We saw things like children and we did this together often. Perhaps we got

70

so good at this together because we had practiced since I was born. She taught me to dream. Without her guidance and belief in me, I would not have amounted to much.

Mom was right. A condo was basically four walls with a big air pocket inside. We could redecorate the place any way we wanted. I could donate the pink furniture to the Pepto Bismol Foundation, the black lacquer-faux-gold painted stuff could go to the retro-eighties store, and all the gold-headed busts and columns…well, we could only hope they took those with them when they moved.

I poured over the photos I'd taken of the condo. I wrote down notes of everything I could remember so I could explain it to Beth when she got up. It was ten-thirty here so seven-thirty there… I could not wait. She should be up by now. I phoned her in California.

"Hello…" Her morning voice answered, a bit raspy and child-like. I knew I'd have to ease in and not barrage her with a bunch of info and questions like a kid at Christmas.

"Good morning, hon. Sleep well?" I asked.

"Mmmmmm hmmmmmmmm." She said. "Did you really like the condo?" So much for easing in, it looked like her head was right there with mine.

"I did. The view is amazing. It has white porcelain floors that look like marble. The guy said porcelain does not chip as easily as marble."

"Is that true?" She asked.

"I don't know. I thought porcelain was for toilets and little statuettes. But I've never broken a toilet." I tried to remember.

"Well, there was that one time."

"Thanks. I still say that was faulty plumbing." I grumbled. Only a husband and wife could have

71

conversations like that and consider it normal. Only a good wife still thought it was funny to talk about your bathroom adventures. And only a great wife thought that your bathroom adventures were somehow endearing. I had married well.

"Hey, when you get up check the pictures I sent you, OK? Let me know what you think. I even labeled them for you." I must have sounded like a child about now. I was pretty excited.

"How many did you send?"

"Oh just a few. Not too many. Sixty? No more than seventy." I explained.

"You took seventy pictures of a two bedroom condo?" She was wide awake now. "The owner must have thought you were insane. Jeez, Jimi. Seventy?"

"No. I said I *sent* you seventy pictures. Those were the best of the *bunch*."

"I don't even want to know how many pictures you actually took. Jimi, you're detailed. I'll give you that my sweet husband. I can always rely on you to be thorough." She said laughing a bit. "Does anyone know what a geek you are?"

"Just you." I laughed. "Right?"

CHAPTER FOUR
Taking Out The Trash

We had an appointment to go see what just might be our new home in the afternoon and Beth and Jake were excited. We all were. They had only seen the interior from the photos I had taken. I had done my best to describe what I had seen. We had stared at it from the street and from the beach. We had already allowed ourselves to think we owned the place. This was a dangerous thing to do but we gleefully set ourselves up for disappointment.

The owners were not very receptive to my calls for us to set up an appointment, until I mentioned in my last voicemail that we would be looking for another place if we did not hear from them soon. Right after that we were able to make an appointment for later the same afternoon. I guessed it was the right amount of prodding. We had to at least appear ready to walk from the deal.

When we showed up at Bonita, Geraldo the mortician answered the door.

"Hello, hello, hello." He said to each of us, one at a time, moving his head downwards with a bouncing motion like a basketball, losing energy as he noted our shrinking individual stature with a cartoonish glee.

"Hello." We all said in unison. Jake looked up at me without moving his head. I knew how he felt. We were all very stiff at this meeting.

"This is my wife, Beth and my son, Jake." I said and suddenly I had a vision of all of us being drained of our fluids in some scary movie. I looked down at Jake and he appeared normal. Perhaps they were only needing adult blood and wanted to fatten him up a bit for the soup pot. What was happening here? This man truly scared me.

"Hello." Beth said. "Nice to meet you."

"Yes, it is." He grinned. Beth just smiled politely but I could tell she immediately disliked the man.

Jake was trying to look into my eyes, but I just shook my head and squeezed his little hand.

"Dad." Jake whispered. I did not lower my gaze just yet. I just kept looking forward with a frozen grin on my face.

Beth entered the condo commenting slightly on the decor.

"Mmmm, so unique." She commented quietly, trying not to reveal her real thoughts. I was so proud of her and at the same time kicked myself. What was I doing?

Jake kept trying to get my attention but I was afraid to look at him and speak. We should have brought our agent. We should have brought a cross and some holy water, some garlic, silver bullets or maybe a priest. We entered further inside the condo, slowly. Beth looked like she was Indiana Jones entering the Temple of Doom.

"Oh," was all she could say.

"Beth?" I answered in a low whisper. But she did not answer me.

"Daddy, is this man a friend of yours?" Jake whispered.

"No." I said. "No, he is not." I whispered back through my perma-grin and rubbed the top of his head.

"Please, do come in." Geraldo said and Jake and I followed our fearless female leader.

Beth's eyes were like little cameras recording all she saw. If she was annoyed by the décor, it did not show. I was pretty sure she was already redecorating in her mind. Jake stuck to his mother's side and looked around like a small furry animal trapped inside a snake hole.

I was struck by how calm and demure this man was. He seemed just too mellow. He moved like he took a nap in between each step, sloth-like, no, he was slower than a sloth. He was like a large old tome slowly turning pages as he moved. It was then that I noticed he wore a sundial for a watch. I was sure not to accept anything he offered us to drink. The last thing I wanted was a Valium and Robitussin cocktail and to wake up in a dungeon below the building with my family chained next to me.

"My wife." Geraldo motioned towards the bedroom door as she made her entrance.

The décor all suddenly made perfect sense. We were inside a genie bottle and she was the genie. Her hair was pulled back very tightly into a high ponytail of long blonde hair that went past her shoulders. The sides of her wrinkled face appeared to be held up by the tautness of the ponytail and I wondered what would happen if the rubber band broke. I remembered that time at Jake's third birthday when the bouncy castle air compressor came unplugged and the castle just listed to the side as it slowly fell in on itself. The children all trapped inside screaming. I remembered that it was hot that day and his little birthday cake had melted a bit, too. Yeah. That's about it. Daddy's nightmare.

Genie wore a lot of jewelry and make-up. She dressed very provocatively for a woman of her age, which I guessed to be close to seventy-five. It's hard not to look when there is a car accident three feet from you and it's harder not to look when an older woman shows twelve inches of sun-damaged cleavage through billowy drapes of fabric, but there we were. She floated towards us, her light garments flowing as she moved.

"So nice to meet you. What a nice little family. Just one child? No more?" She asked and stared at me.

I guess in Cuba, or wherever she was from, a man's virility was measured by how many children he could father. With only one child, I must have looked just this side of cross-dresser to her.

"No, this is our only child."

"Too bad." She made a very animated sad face.

Mom warned me, make faces like that and it might stay that way. I guess Genie did not listen to her mom.

My comfort level was at zero and my patience was tapped. But somehow I had to remain polite to these two elderly Latin folks as we perused their genie bottle. Like most people, I have no tolerance for strangers commenting on my family. I knew she probably meant nothing about the "small family" comment, but then again, she was not there the night my wife miscarried our second child and almost bled to death. The comment brought up this memory to me and for a moment I hated her for it. We were content with the beautiful, healthy child God gave us... thank you very much, *you bitch*.

I told myself to relax. She was just an old woman, oblivious of her words. Most people had no clue how to talk to each other. The adult in me just smiled a bit and politely nodded, but the evil child in me wanted to splash water on her and watch her face melt all over the floor leaving nothing but a pointy witch hat and a big pile of white hair. I really needed to grow up. Adults should not even have thoughts like that, should they? After we closed on this place, I thought I would seek therapy. At that moment, I had no idea how much I'd really need it.

As Beth and Genie strolled the condo, I talked to Geraldo.

"I received a notice from our attorney that you're going to need more time before you move out." I said.

"Yes." He smiled.

I guessed he was going to make me pull it out of him so I got my verbal pliers ready.

"But we agreed on a closing date. I've already given notice at our rental and the owner has planned a trip to the island. There's no way I could extend." I explained.

His face did not change.

"It's in the contract." He said. "We have the right to extend if necessary."

"Well, actually the contract stipulates that in the event that our loan does not go through that we have up to thirty days to procure other financing. There is nothing in the agreement that extends the sellers stay under any circumstances." As I said this, I'm sure I sounded like a wanna-be attorney but I had gone to just enough law school to be dangerous. And I'd read our contract back to front about thirty times. It's my nature.

"Actually, it's understood that any concession goes both ways. That's how it works *here*." He said and grinned.

He was always smirking underneath his narrow moustache. It was becoming annoying. I wondered what his Etcha-Sketch face would look like if I just shook the shit out him for 10 seconds. I was sure his moustache would look very different. Again, I reminded myself to remain calm and adult. I did have my son with me.

"Daddy, why did you shake the old man?" Jake would ask and I would not have a good answer. I would just sport a grin and an evil laugh that I would hate myself for the rest of my life. Be calm and maintain.

"Well, why do you need to stay anyway? You see, my son is in school and has activities and teams. We'd have to go back to California and take him out of school. It would cost us considerable trouble and expense." I explained.

"Well, he is young." Genie said as she patted Jake on the head. I guess she had been listening. Jake squinted his eyes under her hand and tried to shrink lower. I felt the same way he did.

"His age has nothing to do with it. His education is important to us. We had an agreement that we have acted in good faith upon. What is the reason for your needing to extend?" I asked.

"Well, I just need more time to pack. We've been here ten years." She said and waved her arms at the dining and living areas.

This condo was a two bedroom, two bathroom unit and only about 1,500 square feet. They had no children and per the contract would have over a month to pack. Steven Hawking and Helen Keller could pack this place in a month!

"If you need help packing, I can help." Beth said.

The genie just smiled and slowly shook her head. Beth was grabbing at straws. I did not like seeing her this way.

"We could hire professional movers to help you pack and move." Beth said.

But the genie still shook her head. At this point, I realized that these were pretty unreasonable people. I'd have to talk to our attorney to see if they in fact could do this. I took Beth's hand and squeezed it.

"Well, I guess we're done then." I said, the evil child in me reaching for a bucket of water to throw on this witch was sounding more and more convincing with each moment. I headed for the front door with my small family and made sure that I was far enough away to avoid shaking any hands as we said our good-byes. The last time I shook his hand had surely taken years off of my life.

We made our exit. Despite the news that we would be delayed, we were happy that we all liked the place and we formally agreed as a family that this place was our choice. We were a bit stunned knowing that we had to find a place to live for three weeks or go back to California and wait for the closing and immediately began discussing how we would handle this latest costly twist.

No one we could find would rent us anything for just one month and the hotels were too expensive for a stay that long. As much as we fought it, our attorney was a limp mess and could do nothing. We had no choice. We'd have to leave for California for the three weeks to wait out the closing of the condo.

* * * * *

Since we closed escrow on Bonita while we were back in California, we had instructed our real estate agent Spencer to give a set of keys to the Texans so they could do our final walk-through inspection. The Texans had also been kind enough to store a lot of our boxed up personal stuff at their place while we were gone.

Per our agreement, most of the major pieces of furniture in the condo were to remain and the home was to be left in clean and working order. We did not want

79

their furniture, but it would have to do until we bought new stuff.

Once the old owners finally moved out, Mr. Texan called me.

"I've moved a lot of people, bro." Mr. Texan said to me on the phone. "But I've never moved anyone while they were still out of the country."

"You *moved our stuff* into the condo? You didn't have to do that." I said. "I'm in your debt, man. Thank you."

They had moved about twenty boxes of stuff for us and even signed for our new bed when it was delivered. They saw to it that our phone was installed before we even got back to the island. I still do not know how they got that done. Apparently, Mr. Texas had friends at the phone company. Good friends like these are hard to come by.

When we finally landed back on the island, it felt odd the first time we walked into the condo and looked around. It felt so different without the presence of the previous owners. All the cluttered belongings of their decade-plus stay had been removed. All the little ceramic figurines, the phony Chanel perfume bottles filled with pink and green water, and the ridiculously huge faux Asian artifacts and vases were all gone giving the place a very relaxed and open appearance. The heavy assault on the olfactory senses by the presence of perfume, powder, make-up, cigars, cologne, and many years of colon-wrenching spicy cooking was all fading away now. The thick-accented voices no longer pelted the walls with the machine-gun staccato of that Latino-Whatever-Spanglish they spoke. The air felt lighter, the windows appeared larger, the floor spanned farther and the walls no longer flexed and cramped from the tonnage of useless warehouse, bargain-store art.

Now that they were gone, the home felt *relieved*.

What was left was some white wicker furniture in Jake's room, some large, cheaply-made, particle-board curio cabinets painted black and then faux-splattered with gold flecks.

Looks like somebody had been watching the craft channel about twenty years ago!

Also left behind was a glass dining table with six Lucite and felt chairs. The table supported by what appeared to be Lucite flames, the chairs resembling flaming forks made of the same material. Plastic hell.

Looks like somebody had been shopping at Z Gallerie back in the 80's... probably around the time when a Nagel print cost $500.00... and everything in the store was black, white or red... and they gave out a free cass-single of Boy George singing, "Do you really want to hurt me?"

It was as if the owners pressed play in 1980 and then hit pause in 1985.

In the living area, the previous owners left some couches that they swore were made of fine Italian leather. A leather couch in the Bahamas was not a good idea unless you wanted to slither around in your own sweat as you lounged. But the pink color of these couches was what really made them candidates for the sidewalk. Luckily, they were not pink like a Valentine's Day card, but more like the pale pink found on the inside of a conch shell, so we could live with them until we got something else.

You learn a lot about people when you remove their belongings and see where and how they lived. When we attempted to move the black and gold faux-painted curio cabinets outside to the dumpster, we found out

81

why the previous owners had left them. They were stuck to the floor. They were not adhered or fastened, but stuck. It seemed that someone liked to mop the floor right up to the bottom edge of cabinet and let the water and soap just soak right into the fibers of the particleboard. This caused some of the glue that held the furniture together to fuse with the tile floor. The furniture just fell apart when we attempted to move it out. And the metaphor was not lost on me for a moment. It was cheap furniture, faux-painted to resemble a long, lost era that had rotted to the ground and eventually just fell apart. The old owners were finally gone and it was time to get the rest of their belongings out as soon as possible.

I sat and sweated on the pink leather couch as I looked out over the garden and the beautiful ocean. The bruise of the entire purchase ordeal was already beginning to fade away. I was reminded of how women could endure childbirth, fall in love with the child immediately and then shortly thereafter create another. We had been left with something beautiful that would quickly erase the trauma of acquiring it.

It was going to take some work but we could turn this place into a home.

CHAPTER FIVE
The Color Wheel Is An Instrument Of Torture

Downtown Nassau was described in an American tourist book I read recently as, *"...a bustling Caribbean city, full of noisy activity and some old-English charm...a jewel that has lost a bit of its luster...."*

True enough, the downtown area of Nassau was a bit aged and run down. It's pretty far from "quaint". It was where the cruise ships disembarked their huge, overfed, and sun-burned American and Canadian passengers like a horde of chubby red ants. During the daylight hours, downtown was a very busy area with trucks, buses and a non-stop flow of traffic heading east on Bay Street. The truck drivers constantly felt the need to blow their loud horns, mostly just at each other, a needless greeting in an inappropriate place. The constant flow of traffic and trucks ruined any sort of quaint, cobblestone "oh honey, look at that!" experience. It was more like, "Shit! Hold on to the kids...here comes another truck...now RUN!"

Once the tourists headed back to the ship for their fifth feeding of the day and another soak in the ship's petri dish-sized pool, the purpose-built Bahamian downtown went dormant for the night right around six or seven in the evening. It was like Main Street USA at Disneyland except it was dirty and a little dangerous. There was a drive-by shooting when I lived there, the Straw Market was burned down by an arsonist, and I almost got my ass kicked by a drug dealer when I told him I was not interested in his wares. The only thing that kept the tourists safe in downtown Nassau (in my opinion) was the fact that there is strength in numbers and the tourists outnumbered the locals about ten to one. The little pretend-police that patrolled the downtown area were similar to the Guardian Angels in the USA. They had little to no power, no weapons and merely called the real police if something happened.

Throughout any Caribbean tourist area, the sidewalks were lined with jewelry stores, perfume shops, and all sorts of tourist traps selling cheap gifts. There were stores selling three logo t-shirts for $10.00 everywhere. How did they retail three shirts for $10.00?

"Wash and tear," my local friend told me.

"They don't last long? Well, that makes sense." I asked.

"Long?" He asked. "Dey last one day! Den you wash it, put it on and it tear. *Wash and tear*. But by 'den the tourist already home." He chuckled to himself.

"Perfect timing." I thought. I suddenly felt like Steve Martin's character Navin R. Johnson in the movie "The Jerk." He was working at a carnival guessing people's weight and failing terribly. His boss told him it did not matter because the prizes were almost worthless so they made money no matter what.

"So….it's a *profit deal!*" Navin exclaimed suddenly relieved.

When we were visitors here, we would go downtown a few times during each visit to get gifts for everyone back home. As much as I disliked it, we would head for the Straw Market (which was really just a huge concrete structure at the water's edge downtown) where hundreds of Bahamian vendors sold tourist gifts. Most were just the same cheap "made-in-China" knick-knack items that you saw at any cruise

84

ship port. Every now and then you'd see a swarm of women surrounding someone bold enough to sell knock-off copies of Chanel, Coach, other famous designer bags. The government had been cracking down on the sale of these fake items. Some vendors still risked it as they sold quickly. It's all really just more Chinese junk, but everyone wanted to pretend they're rich, I guess.

Once inside the Straw Market, it could be a bit confusing as you wound through the maze of vendors all vying for your attention. The heat outside was compressed and there was little to no ventilation inside the big concrete structure. Instantly, you sweated right through your shirt and began bumping into people. The whole area was not designed well and each aisle was single file wide. Add to that the average girth of your typical American cruise ship traveler and the place clogged up quickly.

"Hey pretty lady! Hey big guy! Want your hair braided? Be my first sale today! I got dem discounts!"

The vendors all tugged at our ears and eyes with their voices and expressions as we politely pretended not to hear, or be otherwise distracted. It's just not a part of our culture to have people barking at us to buy things. It was always uncomfortable telling each one no, so you just pretended to be interested in an item just beyond them. If you talked to each you'd never get out of there. If you bought from each vendor you'd go broke.

Tourists shuffled through, elbows rubbing, wiping each other's sweat onto their arms. The stickiness of the air mixed the natural scents of each vendor and tourist in a cacophonic stew of sweat, body odor, bad breath, suntan lotion, cologne, tobacco smoke and dust.

After five minutes, I usually got dizzy. After ten minutes, I was looking for the exit.

I longed to exit the place when I was struck by the most vulgar t-shirt I've ever seen. It was worn by a tourist, about fifty years old. American or Canadian, I could not tell, but he wore this shirt with zero expression. It read:

"I'm no gynecologist, but I'll have a look."

Have you ever laughed and vomited at the same time? It must have been the heat. But his t-shirt was typical of the garb worn by my American cousins when on a cruise ship in Nassau and suddenly I was sad that I was related to them.

"How much for the straw coin purses?" My wife asked a huge Bahamian lady. She was apparently sitting down on a chair, but it had been completely enveloped by her mass. You could not see the chair so it looked like she was crouching in mid-air trying to sew something into a straw beach bag and fan herself at the same time. Strong legs! She looked up over her reading glasses at Beth for a moment, then back down at her work.

"Dem five dollars each. I give to you for 'tree'". She said with the usual auto-discount that is prevalent in third world countries. Everything here has five or six different prices:

1. The price initially offered.
2. The discounted price that immediately followed the initial offer.
3. The price that followed as you wrinkled your brow and shook your head.
4. The price that came as you began to walk away.
5. The price you got if you bought more than one.

6.   The laughable price they actually paid for the damn thing, which still netted them a profit even after all of the above occurred. *It's a profit deal!*

FYI: *90% of the stuff at the Straw Market may be purchased in bulk right on the island if you knew where to go (ask any taxi driver). Of course, you would need to buy a dozen of everything, but if you have a lot of people to shop for, it can come in handy.

Beth was a shrewd buyer. She was not afraid to walk away and rarely was attached to anything, especially at the Straw Market. Your average American was not used to haggling over price and was not generally comfortable with the custom.   Bahamians knew this and capitalized on it every day. American tourists were on a time clock and would rather pay the higher price, just to get the vendor to shut up and let them go. Pay full retail and both sides were happy.

My wife was charming enough and shrewd enough to get bargains at the Straw Market. And as long as I could stomach it and not pass out from the heat and the constant human exchange of basic humanity, I loved to watch her work.

"How much if I buy ten?" She asked.

"Ten fa two-fiddy each, twenny-fife." The lady said, not batting an eye.

"How much if I buy twenty?" Beth asked. Now the woman took her glasses off and focused on Beth to make sure she was not kidding around.

"You wan twenny?" She asked as she cocked her head.

"Depends on how much." Beth said.

Uh-oh, it's a retail showdown!

"Twenny-fife is a dolla each." She said.

"How about thirty for twenty-five?" Beth asked.

"No problem." The woman said and began packing them into a plastic grocery bag. "What else you need?"

"Oh that's it for now." Beth said.

"For the girls in the office?" I asked.

"Yep." Beth said to me, but her eyes were already off somewhere else. She was already planning her next hit.

When we lived there, the newspaper warned that the average cruise ship tourist only spent about $50.00, while in Nassau, a statistic that had the local businesses scratching their heads wondering how they could wring more money out of each tourist. Polls have shown that like me, many visitors found Nassau to be dirty, noisy, and just a bit dangerous. They got off the ship and wandered around downtown a bit looking for a watering hole, some pictures and perhaps a cheap memento to prove they were there. In a city where a gallon of gas was over five dollars, a gallon of milk was over eight, and reading your dinner check could (and often did) cause a stroke, fifty dollars was nothing. Fifty dollars was lunch in an average restaurant. Fifty dollars was half a tank of gas in a small car. Fifty dollars was just over a case of local beer. Twenty-five dollars was half-way to fifty and this was why the big lady was glad to get it from Beth.

I felt myself getting a little overheated. I wanted some ice cold water but the only thing near me was a daiquiri shack. Jake was still at school for a few more hours so it was OK to get a quick cocktail to ease the Straw Market pain. Beth agreed, so we stopped at one of the many daiquiri shops for some bottled water and one strong drink. I ordered a Bahama Mama and Beth had a Goombay Smash. Both of these beverages were very tropical, icy and smooth. Tip the man right and you could get him to convert your touristy rum-sprinkled daiquiri into a high-octane rum rocket that would make Hunter S. Thompson stand up and salute. Beth usually got hers pretty stout for a lady, but I ordered mine like I was Ted Kennedy with an iron-clad alibi.

After our stop at the daiquiri shack, I felt much better. The sharp corners of my obsidian personality were being worn down to smooth, round little river rock edges. The noisy, rude people suddenly became my brothers and sisters. The annoying cries from the vendors now sounded like an old friend calling me for a chat. The man selling barbequed chicken could have been selling dog or pigeon on that filthy grill and yet it was now calling me to dinner. And it smelled good! *And I had three…whatever it was!*

All that "junk" that was for sale before was suddenly gone and now there seemed to be bargains everywhere I looked. Rum was really just a retail lubricant. They knew that too. We all loved to shop when we had a glass of it in hand.

"Babe, we'll have to remember this store." I said to Beth as I slurped from my boozy cup of friendly.

"Yeah." She said. "It just seems like the stuff here is better quality."

"And there is quite a selection. Did you see the man carving wooden parrots over there? We gotta get one of those." I said.

"Cool!" She said. "And what about one of those woven hammocks? They can weave our names in to it! Wouldn't that be great in the back yard?"

"And we'd better get something for our moms." I said. "Perhaps one of those electric conch shell lamps."

From there, we fell into one of our customary shopping binges where we bought tons of things we didn't really need, but the rum was flowing and our moods were high. Each bag we carried around with us was like a memory of a good relationship. We became quite friendly and conversational with the vendors now. A friend was made at the wood carving shop, the jewelry store, the t-shirt emporium, and many more at the Straw Market. After a while, the buzz faded, the sun began to go down and we headed for the car.

"That was fun!" Beth said as she put on her seatbelt.

"Good times, good times." I said as I put the radio on full blast. We usually played the local music when we were really feeling the island vibe, so now was a good time.

On the way home we noticed a shop that advertised that they did catering, weddings and remodeling. Kind of like the store near our condo where I could buy bathroom caulk, life insurance and firecrackers. There were places like that are all over the island. People had to be multi-faceted to make it here.

Beth got the number from the window of the shop and called the number. The woman who answered the phone at the catering/weddings/remodeling shop seemed to be more than helpful. I'm almost twice Beth's size. But for some reason she usually went one for one when drinking with me. Since I'd eaten the three barbequed pigeon-on-a-stick things, I felt fine. She had not eaten anything so she was a bit chatty.

"So can you like come out and take a look at our place and stuff? It's like, really *sad!*" She spoke into the phone. Beth slipped into her California-speak pretty quickly. I have been told that I do it too, but I don't sound like a Valley Girl. At least I hope I don't.

Beth babbled on for a while with the lady on the phone and I tuned her out to pay attention to the road ahead. Driving in the Bahamas was actually easier if you relaxed because you tended to flow with the idiots better. And most people there drove like idiots. As an American tourist, you had to do something really stupid to get into trouble in the Bahamas. Lord help you if you were to actually cause an accident. (That would be bad.) I listened to the music and tried to sing along to the songs, but did not know the words.

"Ohh girl your love is like....a...mmm-hmmm, ummm...yeah baby." Due to the thick traffic on Bay Street, we were crawling along at five to ten miles per hour. I bobbed my head as I drove and stared at the beautiful shoreline. Yep, traffic or no traffic, that's a good reason to live there.

"Oh that would be *awesome*! I'll meet you there then, thanks!" Beth clicked her phone off and turned to me.

"I just got us a decorator." She said.

"Just like that? Were we looking for a decorator?" I was stunned.

"Well...." She began but I cut her off.

"Did you bother to ask how much she charges or look at any samples of her work?"

"Huh?"

"Did you call any of her references? Oh yeah, that's right, you couldn't have because you're in the car with me!" I chastised her.

"I didn't write her a check or sign a contract, *honey*." She snapped back at me. "I just talked to her and she sounded so cool. I think she'll be great."

"Of course we'll get other bids on the remodel?" I said poking for info.

"Yeah, of course." She grinned.

"And we'll talk to some of her past clients for reference." I stated firmly for us both to hear.

"Sure." She agreed. "Gotta do this right."

But we didn't. We didn't do any of that.

91

* * * * *

We met the decorator at our condo late one afternoon. Francine was a large, white Bahamian lady with a smiling face and a strong handshake. I decided right then that I'd rather be on her good side. She was really huge and seemed powerful. Her teeth were so strong when she smiled she looked like she could bite through cable.

"Pleased to meet you both." She said as she entered our place. We all introduced ourselves properly and then we walked into the main living area, whereupon she sat down and asked us to give her a "minute". We glanced at each other and were quiet while she half-closed her eyes and tilted her head back a bit.

"I just need a minute." She then stood up in the middle of the room and then fully closed her eyes. "I need to *feel* the space."

She looked around for a few minutes, breathing in and out deeply as if to inhale the condo. Beth and I just stood there quietly as I thought, *"Uh-ohhhhhh, artist on board. Duck or be hit by low-flying bullshit."*

I grew up in Santa Cruz, California and then moved on to live in San Francisco, so I'm pretty accustomed to dealing with artsy types, stoners, space-cadets and whack-jobs of many different flavors. I once went to the Santa Cruz Psychic Fair with my father when I was a teen-ager and watched my dad pay twenty dollars to have his "aura" massaged. After my father sat down on the bean bag chair, the *carnie*...I mean, *masseur* walked around my father with a perplexed face for a moment.

"Something wrong?" Dad asked.

"Well, your aura is very strong. I'm going to have to start from a few feet away and work my way in." The hippy said as he stroked the air in circles from a few feet away, slowly working his way toward where my father sat. Oh, man did this reel in my father. A man who's ego actually cast a shadow. He was in love with this treatment. In later years, my father told this story with the hippy starting from twenty feet away... but the tales of my father's BS'ing ability were for another book. It's legendary.

Suffice to say here that Dad's aura may have been massaged but it was the stroking his ego received that made him gladly pay another $20.00 to the sheister for a second rub-down. Apparently, there was just too much energy in his aura for one round. I just stood there eating my falafel, alfalfa sprout and hummus pita, watching and silently laughing my ass off inside my own head. The psychic fair must have felt my negative vibes because the falafel and hummus sandwich staged a revolt in my gut that had me racing for the nearest redwood tree for relief. There were no bathrooms at the psychic fair. I guess any good psychic would have known when they have had to go and would have planned accordingly.

"OK, I've got it." Francine said as she stood up straight. "You want ocean colors, earthy woods, and an open, clean space that has a lot of natural light."

"Wow, you nailed it. That's exactly our style." Beth said.

She was hooked. I was not so sure. Our condo was right by the ocean and we had almost floor to ceiling windows everywhere. Lots of light would be simple. Would we get a discount on the light?

"Not too ostentatious but with subtle tones of tradition." Francine walked through the condo

93

spreading her wings as if she was going to fly and Beth followed her nodding.

"Just the right blend of old and new." She said and the two of them looked at me for approval.

"Oh yeah." I said. "Old and new."

"We'll have to balance the lights and the darks." She said and again they looked at me.

"Right, lots of *this*, with just enough of *that*." I said smiling, but neither laughed with me. They were in sync. I'd heard women could do that...but this quickly?

"I'd say we'll need to balance the overstated with the understated, you know? Merge the lights and darks, but not using too many extremes." Again, they looked at me.

"Light and heavy at the same time, but without being overly one-sided or too balanced either." I said and shook my head. What was happening to my wife? I was playing with them, but they seemed to think I was on board. Kind of like how frat boys thought the Beastie Boys were fighting for *their* right to party instead of making fun of them. They were not getting the joke here.

"Exactly. Are you a decorator?" Francine asked me.

"Hang on. Let me feel the space." I said. "I'm feeling this now. I'm ready to take some wild chances here while remaining completely conservative. I mean I'm totally open to having two pillows on one side of the couch and none on the other. I am totally open to that. As long as we can add two more pillows if balance is needed." Again, crickets. Beth was buying this crap. Neither of them was laughing.

Beth and Francine nodded to me and ignored me at the same time. Had they completely agreed with my sarcastic rant? Apparently they did. Or, they did not. I could not be sure if Beth was just putting up with me or flatly did not get me. And Francine, being Bahamian and not getting sarcasm, she probably just thought I was simple-minded.

They rambled on to each other about balancing light with dark.

"Soft with hard." Francine said.

"And rough with smooth." Beth chimed in.

"Scotch and soda?" I asked them but they again ignored me as if I were a toddler pulling on their leg for attention.

As I listened to Francine babble on and on, I cringed and was reminded of all the newspaper horoscopes I'd read in the past. This experience felt strangely similar to a horoscope or a palm reading. Vague, tag-line laden phrases fitted every random average anyone; yet the words were seemingly pointed directly at you, making you feel cosmically connected to the random arrangement of stars that suddenly aligned when you picked up the newspaper, opened the fortune cookie, read the tea leaves or paid the palm reader. Somehow the cosmos gave you divine premonitions and advice to live by. It could be entertaining, but it was a load of crap.

This was not a man's job. I was just there as decoration or as an accessory for my wife like a purse or a five-pound dog. When women connect like these two were, men were really not needed, yet it was demanded that I be present. Perhaps I was there for support, or more likely, I was there as a possible co-defendant to help take the heat when the Blame Police came to arrest us for completely screwing up our condo and blowing through our budget.

At that moment, I could have said that I wanted black lacquer cabinets, pink leather couches, and Lucite flames holding up our dining room table and they would not have batted an eyelash. These two women would decide on how our home would look. It was my job to nod and smile, pretend I could help make a decision between thirty different sofas, chairs and tables, (as if I even cared) and to try my best to stifle my cynicism. Then I'd be forced to offer loving support and understanding when my wife waffled back and forth between different shades of green on that male torture device: the color wheel.

Hmmmm, which one? Pea Green, Car Sick Green or *Shouldn't Have Fed The Baby Peas and Then Taken Him For A Ride In The Car Green?*

They all look the same to me. It was my job to feign enthusiasm, but the check I'd have to write would be very real. This whole process would be painful. Perhaps I needed to get my aura massaged.

* * * * *

Some things were just expensive. Regardless of what you may read, you cannot do Paris on twenty dollars a day. It may sell books, but I've lived in Paris and twenty dollars doesn't even buy ten dollars there. The proposed expense of redecorating a small condo began to really add up. I'll bet that if we let her go wild, Francine could have spent $250,000 on this project. Just like my wife, Francine was very good at finding creative ways to spend my money.

Beth had been out shopping on her own for a few hours one day, which made me feel like a dead man walking, on my way to the gas chamber, and just waiting for my last breath. The inevitable was on its way and it was best to just accept it. Beth was a curious personality type. She was in sales so she was at the same time very shrewd and a total sucker. For some reason, sales people are susceptible to their own schemes.

She had decided (or had been helped to this decision by the friendly salesman) that to insure our back health, we needed a Tempurpedic bed. She'd been to our local bed store and apparently had fallen in love.

"Jimi, this bed is amazing. It's the most comfortable thing I've ever laid on. You've got to see it." She said.

Well, at least she was asking me to come and see the thing. It wasn't like the time she called me out of my office in California to show me a new convertible BMW.

"Do you like it?" She asked. The top was down, it was sunny. Who doesn't like a convertible?

"It's nice. Where'd you get it?" I asked.

"The dealership. I borrowed it for a bit." She said.

"Can I go borrow one too?" I asked.

"No, silly. I'm *demo'ing* it."

"Can I go demo one too?"

"I guess." She said.

"Where's *your* car?" I asked.

"It's at the dealership."

"When do you pick it up?"

"Well, actually...." She began to stammer just a bit, but smiled instead. She had the most beautiful smile.

"I like your new car, honey. I just hope you made a good deal on your trade. See you after work." She smiled again and sped off in her new car.

What could I say? It was her car. But it would be our payment.

We went to the bed store and I lay down on the bed. It felt very different than any mattress I'd ever tried. It felt like it exhaled and held you in a soft sponge that kept compressing until you were totally suspended. When you moved it took the mattress a few moments to reform, inhaling where you left, and exhaling where you now lay. It was different, but it was wonderful.

"Wow." I said.

Beth looked over at the salesman who grinned. Cha-ching!

"I'll even throw in the pillows and our large teddy bear made of the same material for free." She smiled. "That bear is normally $100, sir."

Wow, a $100 teddy bear! I'd seen one of those at FAO Schwartz in New York City. How many of those could there really be? Hey, maybe this bear was HIM!

Of course we bought the bed. I was stunned to find out it was $7,000.00 and protested to Beth, but she was prepared. She had a very strong trump card. She pandered to the absolute techy geek in me and showed me that the bed was independently fully adjustable via two wireless remotes. We could each have our side of the bed in any configuration we wanted. And it vibrated, too.

"*Wireless remotes*?" I asked, feeling one of my eyebrows raise as the other lowered. My knees felt weak. I salivated wildly as I practiced with the remotes, doing yoga poses without effort as the bed folded and bent my body like a pretzel-eating yogi. Beth laughed at me as she filled out the paperwork.

I felt my usual buyer's remorse that I get whenever I spend too much money, but the salesman had left me with some words of encouragement:

"What price your back?" She asked with a caring look. "Can you put a price on your health?"

I can now. I suppose it was around seven grand.

* * * * *

Those home makeover/craftsman shows on TV incorporate a lot of staples and hot glue guns along with miraculous garage sale finds that make the final outcome so easy on the wallet. I've been to garage sales and all I found was stuff that looked like what we weren't able to sell in our last garage sale. I once fired up a glue gun and stapler to recover a chair. I ended up with something not even on par with my son's first grade science fair project that a kid would not put in a tree fort.

What these shows don't show you is the years of professional expertise that these people have that they use to transform a fixer into a stunner. Time-lapse photography and commercial breaks divide the job into easy to swallow segments and help to make the process look easy and FUN. Watching those shows make the whole thing look so simple. And they never show the charge for the decorating team's time, just the cheap materials, and antiques they find at unbelievable prices.

Back in the real world, I tried to corral my wife's hopes and dreams, while at the same time attempting to balance our decorator's hypnotic charm wheel with my wallet. There were moments when I tried to enjoy myself along the way, but it was futile. I'm too much of a realist to get caught up in projects like that. It's a fault of mine. I'm sometimes not able to see the beauty of something because I got so bogged down in micro-managing. I could get downright anxious and nasty during big jobs. I don't mean it. I guess I just get nervous and don't know how to soothe myself. Beth helped to keep me in check. She had to press the horns on my head down really hard sometimes to keep them from surfacing. I'm lucky the world does not know me as well as she does.

We needed a budget. Having never redecorated a condo from top to bottom here in the land of sun and fun, I was at a loss. Any sort of budget we'd have would be a blend of what we wanted balanced with not only what we could afford, but what was available.

"A lot of what you might want won't be available here on the island. The choices are sometimes very slim. Of course, we'll probably have to get a lot of things from the States." Francine said. "No worries though. I travel to Florida often and can have my shipper send what I buy. We'll just have to add shipping, his fee, my fee, and the duty to whatever we get there." My brain was literally buzzing from that last statement.

Here is a breakdown of what the little calculator in my mind just heard:

"A lot of what you might want won't be available here on the island."
-Add twenty percent
"The choices are sometimes very slim."
-Lower your expectations.
"I travel to Florida often…"
-One round trip ticket to Miami.
"We'll have to add shipping…"
-Another 5%
"His fee…"
-Looks like another 5%
"My fee…"
-Probably 15-20%
"Shipping costs…"
-rent a ship

"And the duty…"

Why do they call it "duty" when it's just *tax*? They should call it a "fee" or maybe a "charge". "Duty" sounds like it lives next door to "honor" and "courage". But it's really just the word before "free" in the airport when you need to buy some cigarettes, booze, a new watch, a Mont Blanc pen or some perfume. Now, those are items I always wait to buy when I'm rushing through a crowded airport, don't you?

I suppose that the choosing of colors and such actually *was* the fun part. The hard part was figuring how much this would all cost. I was perplexed at how Francine's fee would be calculated. Would it be a percentage of what we bought? I still was not sure and she never really made anything clear. I was swimming in a dark ocean, blindfolded. In a symphony of costs that included her fees, duties, shipping, contractor costs, and materials she would weave together a contract for us. She promised to line item everything, so I shined up my microscope. I couldn't wait. A written contract felt like a breath of air for this drowning man.

We began the process of looking through design magazines and web sites, picking colors and major pieces of furniture. Francine dragged us around the island to different stores showing us pieces of furniture: a decision at this store, a haggle here, a compromise there. The things we needed in the States were mostly wall art, finishing touches like lamps, vases, a little water sculpture that made me feel like I needed to pee all the time, and a couple flat screen TV's I had picked out. We left the actual colors and finishing touches to her. We gave her a theme and an idea of what we wanted, but left her with the minutia. There was no way I wanted to go blind looking at color wheels trying to determine which shade of pale yellow I wanted: the *Sienna Sage*, the *Mountain Morning Sun* or the *Dog Peed in The Snow*. Aren't they all really just pale yellow? The torture! Leaving the actual details up the Francine was not just part of the fun, it evaporated some of the decision conversations.

In the end, I was actually pretty pleased with her ability to read what we wanted. She picked furniture I would have picked. She chose colors I liked. Hmmmm, maybe she could mend my broken aura with her artistic hands.

It was our plan to head back to California for July and August during Jake's school break, giving the condo to Francine and her crew for two months to create her masterpiece. With everything, it looked like we'd spend about $40,000.00. I guess that's not bad for a lot of new furniture, electronics, paint, fixtures and some finishing touches and artwork. But what did I know?

We would be leaving the job to Francine. We trusted her. And we'd gone over the major things together, so there would be no big surprises. We also regularly met with her husband, a large black Bahamian man with an easy laugh and a friendly disposition. He handled the actual rough construction for Francine. After so many meetings and conversations with them, we felt like we'd made some new friends. We all made plans to throw a welcome back party when we returned.

Cynicism, cosmic feelings, and auras aside I felt pretty good about the whole situation.

CHAPTER SIX
Christmas In August

We had turned Francine loose on our condo with ideas on how we wanted our place to look when we returned to the island at the end of the summer. But, we had left some of the design details up to her. Jake's Bahamian school was closed in July and August. It was a nice break to go back to California during the miserable Bahamian summer to see family, work some, and do a bit of traveling. Those late summer months in the Bahamas were dreadfully hot and muggy. I could do without the $1,000 power bill from running the AC all day and night. It was nice to go back to our home and just have the dry heat.

I normally would never have done anything like this, but it was exciting having a professional decorator, and it was twice as exciting leaving the details in her hands to see what she could do. The idea that we'd come back to the condo, not really knowing what to expect, was like giving ourselves a big present to welcome us back at the end of summer.

When we returned, the Texans picked us up at the airport with cold Kalik beers, sunglasses pushed up on their heads to hold back their long hair, and tans that belonged in a Hawaiian Tropic ad. They appeared to be the perfect expat couple. They had completely adjusted to the island. They were always so damn relaxed. I wished I could get to that place soon. I hoped that now that our condo was bought and upgraded, so that we could move in and let my blood pressure finally settle.

The early evening air was sticky and I felt that that familiar balmy, sweaty feeling that you either love or hate. It hits you as soon as you exit the airplane and wraps itself around you like a blanket. To me, it felt like home.

"Man, did we miss ya'll!" Mr. Texan said. He was standing in the airport parking lot as he surveyed our mountain of luggage. "How many bags did ya'll bring anyway?" He asked as he handed me a beer.

"The max, nine altogether." I said as I hugged his wife spilling beer on her back. She yelped and then just laughed at me. Jake ran back and forth between both of them like a dog when you came home from work, hugging their legs. "Oh yeah, and we all brought two carry-on bags as well!" I laughed.

"We're gonna need a bigger boat!" He said. "How you doin', little man?" Mr. Texan asked Jake. He was particularly fond of our son and his face always softened a bit when he spoke to him.

"Good." Jake answered. "We got to watch cartoons and wrestling all the way from California to here!"

"Man, I bet Dad loved that!" Mr. Texan grinned and lit a smoke.

"I watched football and an old Led Zeppelin concert. We all had our own TV's and about forty different channels. Beth watched cooking and The Nanny. We all wore separate earphones and watched TV. Not exactly quality family time but it is a long ride." I told him.

"No kidding." He chuckled as he and I loaded the suitcases into the hatch of our car and the trunk of theirs. They were smart enough to know we'd need both vehicles. The Reno's travel heavy. We always brought the hard to find things we'd need here from home. Besides the furniture and TV's, we'd pretty much stocked our home completely via suitcase from California. One time, Beth returned from a business trip and the Bahamian lady checking her through noticed that she had a bag of oranges in her carry on.

"You can't take these with you. This is not allowed." She said.

"Have you ever had a California orange?" Beth asked. The lady shook her head and Beth handed her one. The lady smelled it, smiled and just passed her through.

On the way home, the two ladies rode together in one car babbling to each other so much that they barely came up for air. They had missed each other.

Mr. Texan and I rode in our car sipping our beers and flicking our ashes out the windows. Jake was in the other car so we could talk guy talk, smoke, and curse freely. Heck we could even scratch ourselves if we wanted. It was man time.

I watched the headlights of the cars coming at us and immediately had to remind myself that we were back in the Bahamas where we drove on the other side of the road. A good shot of adrenalin subsided as I recognized that fact again.

"How's it feel to be back home?" Mr. Texan asked me.

"It feels great. We really missed you guys. It's always good to go home to visit everyone because you're a minor celebrity for a while. But after two weeks it's pretty much the same old stuff. Who's mad at who? Who lost their job? Who's getting a divorce? It gets really real, really quick." I said. "Now we're back in Shangri-La and I'm Peter Pan. I'll never grow up." Mr.

105

Texan was a bit younger than I was so I always wondered if he got my dated references. "Shangri-La?" Did I really say that? I guess I did.

"Well, things here are pretty much the same. Summer was hotter than hell. We started a few new projects at work and most of them had AC already so it wasn't too bad. Not much to tell, really. Everything here is pretty much the same as you left it." He said.

"Well, not everything." I grinned at him.

"We decided not to even look at ya'll's place for the last couple weeks. Seems like that was when they were most active doing last-minute stuff, I suppose. We want to be surprised too, ya know?" Mr. said. "Hell, they didn't do much for the first month or so. I kept checking like you told me to but that Francine started getting annoyed so I left them alone. I think it was a mad scramble at the end to get it done."

"I kept in touch via email, reminded them of when we would be back and they assured me it would be complete and ready, bro." I told him. "I really don't know what to expect. I sure hope they got the job done."

"Well, either way I'm sure it turned out great." He laughed. "Man, it sure is good to have ya'll home!" He said as he hit my shoulder.

I smiled. It *was* good to be *home*.

We unloaded the bags by the parking area lights at Bonita and headed into the entryway of our building. The anticipation had all of us grinning and giggling. All four adults were almost equally excited, and Jake was literally spinning circles as I put the key into the door lock. It felt like I was opening a Christmas present we'd sent to ourselves. I counted 1-2-3, and opened the door.

The smell of fresh paint hit my nose first. I turned on the light in the foyer and saw a beautiful new painting of an Adirondack chair on a beach with some flip flops nearby. Now that's my kind of art! Down the hallway there were glass sconces holding candles and more paintings of beach scenes. As we entered, we saw different colors of blue on the walls, all seemingly pulled from God's paint set for ocean jobs. She had picked good colors.

Where there was once gaudy pink leather couches there were now tasteful sea-green couches and chairs. Where there was once a hideous glass table with Lucite flames was now a hand-carved, hardwood bar complete with marble top and inlaid design on the curved front. Where there was once a cheesy chaise lounge in the master bedroom there was now a man's desk with a comfy leather chair. And our $7,000 Tempurpedic bed had been delivered and put together complete with two wireless remotes that twisted and changed the bed like origami. I had earlier guessed it was for when you want to do yoga in bed. Pretty worthless option to me, but at the time we just had to have it. I'd never have spent this much on a bed at home, but it was a way of tattooing ourselves here in this country, proving to us that we were serious about staying here long term.

Jake's room had white wicker furniture, a bare wood desk, cubby boxes, and his name in big wooden letters over the double-closets: JAKE

"Daddy, this is MY room!" He exclaimed as he jumped around. Even the huge Tempurpedic bear was resting on one of the twin beds in his room. The bear seemed to be smiling too.

"How 'bout a drink?" Mr. Texan said.

"Yo, yo." Mrs. Texan said. "I'm in."

"Deal me in, too." I said as I looked at the new breakfast table and chairs in the nook area.

"Me too." Beth almost sang as she looked at all the candles, the shadow box of family pictures and shells and the center table in the living room, with its glass top showing off the shells and sand below. Francine had added some personal touches that helped make it feel like a home.

"How 'bout Annie-Joe and coke?" Mr. Texan asked and we all nodded in agreement, wandering from room to room calling out what we found to each other. "Annie-Joe" was actually "Bacardi Anejo" which we bought locally on the cheap. "Anejo" is just Spanish for "aged." How long it was aged? Probably about fifteen minutes longer than the other stuff.

We were giddy from traveling and even a little of the rum was going to push us right over to the happy, teary-eyed drunk that I generally don't visit too much. I was truly happy and pleased with the job. And it was absolutely wonderful to have the Texans with us to share these moments. They were rapidly transcending the friend level to the extended family level.

It was only about 9 PM, so I called Francine and thanked her for her work. I told her that I did not expect it to come out this good, which should have been music to her ears but she responded rather coolly. I did not think much of the exchange and went back to our reveling, which went very late into the evening.

Life slipped back into a comfortable groove. Jake was back in school, Beth and I were working remotely again, and our new life in our new home felt good. We had removed almost all traces of the creepy people who lived here before. Our realtor and lawyer were busily spending the tens of thousands we'd given them, like hyenas tearing the flesh off the bone in a nature show on TV. The Texans were regular visitors, the sun was bright, the sea was calm and warm, and we had many "come and see our new place" get-togethers with friends.

Francine had a few things to button up to complete the job. She made a few visits with her workers to install curtains in Jake's room, fix a light they'd broken, replace a picture that had broken glass, etc. Little things that probably itched under her saddle as I'm sure she wanted the job to be done. We did too. She had two whole months to paint, decorate and furnish a small condo, but I was not going to make a big deal about it even if the guys on the reality channel can do it in sixty minutes less commercials.

I looked for my tool set just long enough to determine that it was not here. One good thing about having a small home is that it is hard to lose things. It was not a very expensive set, just one I'd brought from the States for household chores, but I needed it regularly to fill my "honey-do" list that Beth handed me each week.

"I can't find the good alarm clock, babe. And there are a couple other things I can't find either." Beth said.

I began to feel a bit paranoid. The more we looked, the more we noticed that random things were missing. Some tools, some small electronics, and a flashlight. Nothing big, but I felt sure that someone had helped themselves to our things while we were gone. The odd thing was the utter randomness of the missing items. It was if a blind man had wrapped himself in double-stick tape and bounced around the place for a while.

"Just make me a list and I'll deduct the cost from your total bill." Francine said. She apologized for her workers actions, but it really was not good enough for me. I felt violated and was not sure just how long it

109

would take us to figure out everything that was missing, since the items were all so random and you did not know they were gone until you needed the item.

A little weed began to grow in our Garden of Eden. I tried to convince myself it was no big deal, but what kind of contractors steal from a person's home? This thing really made me feel negative in a deep way. I begged myself to just let it go and not get too hung up on this situation. I'd deduct the amount we lost from the thieving contractors from what we paid Francine, but that hardly made things even in my mind.

The other thing that was bothering me was that after we paid Francine her final bill, we never heard back from her again. Ever. There were some other little things she'd left undone and they just remained that way. We had remote-control fans put in each room, but they had not installed the remote control electronics in all of them so they did not work properly. We had a picture that was supposed to hang over our bed but they had broken the glass, so she had it repaired. When I picked it up, the picture itself had been scarred and was warped. Not exactly the best workmanship, but I figured I was stuck with it. She had removed our vertical blinds because they were ugly, but neglected to install any privacy curtains in any of the rooms and instead left us with decorative sheers. They were nice enough, but left us wide open to the outside world. Living on the first floor is fish bowl enough and now we had no way to hide from the outside world. Where were the bamboo roll-downs like the other units had? I imagined we would be living a reality show like "Big Brother" now, our neighbors looking into everything we did as they walked to the pool or the beach.

I made a laundry list of things that needed doing, or redoing, and kept emailing and calling Francine but she never responded. Beth finally got hold of her on the phone once and she promised to come by to take care of everything, but never showed up to their appointment. What had happened?

As I thought of my remedies, I really did not see any. This lady was a local and her husband's Bahamian family roots went back a hundred years or more. We were expats living here on the edges of what was legal. I'd heard stories of local people getting angry at expats and turning them in to the police for immediate removal. The last thing I wanted was to make an enemy here and have them retaliate in a way that would really screw up our lives. As Americans, you may have some rights, but it's really better to just fly under the radar.

We decided to exact our revenge in more subtle ways. Anyone who asked us about our decorator was told the whole story and I can't tell you how much business she lost that way. There is an old saying: Do something right, a customer tells someone. Do something wrong and they tell EVERYONE.

I remembered a time when a friend in California built a huge deck for us. He was a good carpenter, but a bad businessman and really underbid the job. As a friend, and without his asking, I gave him an extra five thousand dollars to make the deal right. That's the kind of world I want to live in, one that is fair.

When I combed through our contract I noticed that Francine had really underpaid herself for her work. I think she bit off a bit more than she could chew and perhaps this is why she disappeared once she got her final payment. Funny thing was, I was going to give her a nice completion bonus to make the deal right in my mind. Considering how she left things and the unprofessional disappearing act she pulled in the end, I decided to keep the money. Even though she left some

111

things undone, in the end, we got her services very cheap. She only cheated herself.

CHAPTER SEVEN
Can't Pass The Bar

The auditorium was filled to the windows with proud parents all waiting for the show to begin. At Jake's school, the kids' productions were called "pageants" and they were very popular with the parents. The entire school only had about two hundred kids in all of the classes from pre-kindergarten through eighth grade. Jake's class only had sixteen kids, a teacher and an assistant teacher. Back in the States, the same class would have thirty-five kids and one cop. The small private school was about half expat kids and half privileged local kids. It was not cheap, but it was worth the cost.

It was very warm and muggy on that evening. The small school grounds area outside the auditorium was packed with parents, students, staff and friends. There were tables set up with snack food and soft drinks. And low and behold, there was a full bar right there outside the second graders' classroom.

The Bahamas have a very different view of alcohol than we do in America. People drink socially more and drinking in public was not done only by bums and derelicts. I read somewhere that the Bahamas had more churches and bars per capita than any place on Earth. I'm not sure if that was true, but our church had a bar too.

Our church was built mainly as a church, but also did duty as a community center and hurricane shelter.

113

It was a fairly new structure so it was strong against the wicked storms that seasonally plagued the area. It also had food and water for hundreds of people for up to a week in case normal services and stores were closed for a while after a hurricane. In the back of the church on the patio, there was a place to get food and drinks. And if you wanted it, the drinks could be alcoholic.

When we first went to inquire about the church, we were invited to sit down for a meal with the head pastor. We all met on the back patio and had a light lunch and a few beers. It was odd at first and then it felt completely normal. We weren't getting hammered. We were being adults and having adult beverages. I never ordered one, but you could even get a powerful rum cocktail called a "Hurricane" if you wanted one. Needless to say, we joined that church immediately. But for some reason, being able to do this took a bit of the naughtiness away and we honestly never drank at the church again for almost three years. Still, I told everyone that we could drink at our church because it was a cool story.

The production that evening was an abbreviated version of "Joseph and The Technicolor Dreamcoat". For a small school, the shows the kids performed were always very entertaining. The music was good and the teachers really went all out to set the stage and provided good costumes. I have to admit, having a few cocktails before the show gave all the parents a very friendly glow. We clinked our bottles together during the show when one of the kids did something particularly cute. We took hundreds of photos and then shared them with each other later. Parents at events like this tended to bond a bit more than usual. Add to that the alcohol, and we were like old friends.

The hot evening combined with the radiant heat of hundreds of parent bodies defeated the weak AC's attempts to cool the large room. Add to that the fact that alcohol raises your body temperature and the auditorium felt a bit like a sauna.

Thankfully, Bahamians were very clean people and they wore gallons of cologne. And the productions were never longer than an hour. At the end, we all stood up and clapped and then hustled outside for more refreshments. The air in the Bahamas stayed thick and warm late into the evening, but it was cooler outside than it was in the auditorium. There were four productions per school year. Somehow we packed hundreds of people into a small building and the fire marshal didn't close the school down. Somehow all the cars were parked in and around a parking lot that held about fifteen cars. And somehow, a large group of adults drank and sweated together without any issues or confrontations.

The Bahamas made people adapt to survive. Dealing with the lack of conveniences en masse tended to align people with a common experience. And the small size of the nation tended to make people friendlier. It's easy to be nasty to others on the American freeway as we speed past each other, knowing you would never see each other again. Island life was more like two travelers walking by each other on a dirt road in the country. As you pass, you would certainly reach out and at least say, "Hello."

CHAPTER EIGHT
The Bahamian Blank Stare

Being a Californian, I was used to very good food and I did not realize how spoiled I was with regard to produce and meat. As compared to local supermarkets in the Bahamas, we Californians entered the local store, removed our shoes, donned flowers for our hair, wrapped ourselves in silk tunics and played the lyre as we floated through our bountiful produce sections listening to New Age tunes and sipping purified water. In the Bahamas, the avocadoes were six dollars each. They were so small and so hard that the local kids used them for practice at the driving range. The tomatoes were so hard and green that they resembled limes, and the best salad lettuce available came in a plastic bag from Mexico. The produce department left much to be desired for a Californian.

The meat department was not much better. There was no friendly, helpful butcher to answer questions about the special of the day or how best to cook a particular cut of meat. There were just open freezers lined with meat that was slowly thawing out because the freezer was not set low enough. The meat packages all had little pools of blood and other meat juices formed as the meat thawed.

The older I get, the more looking at meat makes me queasy. I'm dangerously close to becoming a vegetarian. I have a very hard time eating steak anymore. I had gotten to the point that if I do eat meat

I needed it cooked *with* something or *in* something like a burrito. To me, if meat had to be on the plate, it should to be in friendly shapes. Triangles have worked well. My son's dinosaur-shaped chicken nuggets were fine. As long as it does not resemble an animal's body part or something you see in a car wreck or horror movie. Call me hypocritical, or weak but I need to separate what I'm eating from what was recently prancing around the meadow. I still don't understand why the "meat is murder" protestors back home were all wearing leather coats, belts and shoes, but I'm getting the "don't" eat meat part. I don't have politics about hamburger. I just don't want to have to grind up my own cow carcass to have a Sunday barbeque. I'm a spoiled, modern man just like you.

* * * * *

In our first home back in California, Beth and I once grew a small vegetable garden. After weeks of work and waiting we had some lettuce, strawberries and cucumbers growing in our back yard. For a guy who had bought all of his food at the market, seeing this garden was nothing short of magical.

"Go into the yard and get me a head of lettuce." Beth said to me one day as she was preparing dinner. Being the new, self-sufficient gardener I now was, I happily complied.

It was a great feeling walking outside to collect nature's bounty. I selected one of the heads of lettuce and cut it from the plant with a small knife. I remembered seeing a deer hunting show where the Indian hunter smeared some of the deer blood on his face to show respect for the sacrifice of the deer. I took a small piece of the lettuce leaf and put it over my ear.

117

"Thank you for your sacrifice, brother." I said solemnly. I shook some pieces of dirt off the little head of lettuce and then flicked a small ladybug from the leaves. Then I saw another bug on another leaf. Suddenly, something about this did not feel right.

I took the lettuce in the house and gave it to my wife. She washed it and prepared the salad and when we sat down to eat I commented,

"I'm not sure I can eat this salad."

"Why not?" She frowned.

"Well, the lettuce was just in the *earth*." I said. "Like, laying there, *on the ground*."

"Where do you think lettuce comes from?" She asked.

"I know where it comes from. It's not something I think about. I just buy it at Safeway." I said.

"But you did realize the lettuce grew in the ground." She probed.

"Yes. I did. And I also know that steaks are really sliced up cow and that ham is a pig's butt."

"Go on." She grinned.

"I know that pepperoni and sausage are made of whatever is left on the floor of the meat packing plant."

"Gross." She laughed.

"And I also know that Slim Jim's are made from whatever is left over at the pepperoni and sausage plant. I just don't like to think about it." I said.

"Double gross. So how are things in the little town of Denial?" She laughed.

"We're doing well. We usually do." I said.

* * * * *

My mother was visiting us for a while and she wanted to cook something for dinner that night so I took

118

her to the super market. We had two markets in our neighborhood. At the time Mom was here, one of them was a real dump. It smelled bad inside and to think that you would actually buy something to eat there was more than most Americans could stomach. (They rebuilt it later and it became the nicest store in the area.)

We decided to shop at the other store which at the time was nicer, but its name was a contradiction of terms. Without going into a whole list of price differences, suffice to say that food was expensive in the Bahamas. Take your grocery bill in the USA and multiply it by at least 150% to 300% depending on the items.

When shopping for food in the Bahamas, get ready to use brands of products direct from exotic and wonderful places like Mexico and China. I think the lead count in our milk alone would give everyone in my family gout for the next three generations. I thought the fancy English coat of arms on the label meant "quality". But upon closer inspection, I learned not to buy dairy products from a company called, "*The Madness of King George*" made in China.

When comparing prices and the quality of products available at the markets, it is no surprise that the American fast food joints are taking hold in the Bahamas. It does take a bit of the shine off your Bahamian vacation when you're staying on the beach at the Royal Bahamian and across the street lie Burger King, Domino's Pizza and Dairy Queen, all right next to each other. When you see what's available on the menu at the Royal Bahamian and the prices they charged, you'll find yourself in line with the rest of the tourists at Burger King. Just don't expect to get your fast food *fast*!

119

"I'll have a cheeseburger, fries and a coke." You would say.

"We all out of coke." The local at the register would reply.

"Hmm, OK, just the burger and fries."

"No burgers today." She will say.

"Fries?"

"No."

"Well, what do you have?"

"Try Domino." And she would say all of this while texting on her cell phone and never looking up at you once. For the most part, you don't go to the Bahamas for the food or the service.

But, *gee that water sure is beautiful!*

Mom seemed perfectly happy walking up and down every aisle in the market. Being a devout Christian, she enjoyed the loud gospel music they always played there, and the AC worked very well that day. Bahamians are musical people and they loved their music loud and constant. They played it in the buses, gas stations, stores…everywhere. It was not uncommon to see two Bahamian ladies sitting on the bus singing along to the same song and not even notice the other singing. If you ever wondered about the "soul" decedents of Africa always referred to, you can find a lot of it in the Bahamas.

"Do they play this music every day?" She asked.

"Pretty much, yes. Some days they play a local radio talk show where people call in and they debate local issues. Most of the time I can't understand what they're saying and when I do understand I still am clueless about the issues they are debating. I'm still just a glorified tourist here." I grumbled.

"You should read the local papers and watch the news channel." She lectured. Mom was an avid

120

political watchdog. She read volumes of historical data and studied ancient languages and nations. It was the kind of stuff I used to struggle through, get graded on and then frown. Mom was retired and single. She had time to pay attention to the different dialects of ancient Arabic and Greek. When I studied those things in college, I was more interested in the girl next to me and if she'd go out with me. There were distractions. These days I'm too wound up in family, work, and travel for intellectual pursuits. I guess the distractions remained. But I did get the girl.

When we got to the checkout counter, I noticed that the young lady there was leaning over on top of the register apparently asleep on her feet. It seemed that much like government workers in the USA, Bahamians were very good at relaxing at work.

"No worries, Mon! Don't worry! Be happy!"

I looked over at my mother and we decided not to wake her. We went to another line where there was one only person ahead of us, and we hoped that the new checker might even be conscious. Conscious or not, she must had been invisible because we did not see anyone at the register. We figured she was on a break and would be right back. There were two girls that appeared to work at the store, busily chatting and laughing loudly at a nearby register where the sign read "CLOSED".

The checker in our line had still not come back. After our line had not moved for ten minutes, I said to Mom, "I guess we're waiting on a price check." We both smiled smugly. We waited a few minutes longer and then the woman in front of us grumbled something and left the line so we moved up.

"Hey, now we're first!" I said to Mom, a bit embarrassed about the service in my adopted nation. But still, being first in a line that did not move for fifteen minutes was not much better. We were just standing in a large building listening to gospel music. It could have been church but for the foul smells from the meat department.

There was still no one there to check our groceries. I spoke up to the two girls at the next till.

"Excuse me, do you work here?" I asked.

"Yeah." One girl said without looking at me. The other just looked down at her cell phone.

"Do you know where the checker is for our line?"

"She right here." She motioned to the girl next to her on the phone. The other girl never looked up from her phone.

"She's the one working this line? I clarified.

"Yes." The checker said annoyed.

"Is she on a break or something?"

"What?" The girl with a voice said. The mute one remained silent and still looked at her cell phone.

"Sorry, let me rephrase, is she visually impaired or can she actually see us waiting here in her line to check out?" I asked.

"What?" Now both girls looked up at me.

"We've been waiting here for almost fifteen minutes. There was a lady in front of us that gave up and left. I'm beginning to understand why. There are more people working here than shopping here and we still can't get anyone to help." I explained.

And then I received what I call the BBS, or the Bahamian Blank Stare. The BBS appeared to be a natural defense mechanism that kicked in when some rude American (like me) was sarcastic with a local. Ask a stupid or sarcastic question and the Bahamian will just look at you blankly, stunned. The BBS was a very powerful defense. The BBS also can come into play when a Bahamian simply does not have an answer for you.

For example:

At a conch shack I once said, "I'll have a conch salad, please."

The conch salad man said, "We all outta conch."

"Is that all you serve?" I asked.

"Just that and the salad." He said.

"OK, I'll have a salad then."

BBS.

We looked at each other for a minute and then I said, "No salad today either?"

"Da salad is da conch, mon."

More BBS.

"Right." I said and then walked away.

Back at the market, the checker and I looked at each other for a few moments after my question regarding the other checker's vision. Neither of us were willing to back down and then I finally said, "Do you think one of you could please check our groceries?"

"She can. I'm going on break." The talking girl finally said. The quiet one angrily checked our groceries.

"You were on your cell phone a long time." I said. "And now you look angry. Did you get bad news today? A lot of bad news? Was it serious?" I smiled as she BBS'd me with a precision glare.

As I pushed our cart to the car outside, Mom commented on the earlier exchange.

"That was odd." She said.

"Not here." I replied.

"Really?" She asked.

"Really. Let me tell you a story. When Beth and I used to vacation at the Radisson there was one lifeguard tower on the beach that held one older lifeguard who would take his post for about five minutes and then fall into a deep sleep. No one would wake him. This went on for years. Nice man when he was awake, just very sleepy. Beth and I just figured he had a night job and took this gig for extra money. We felt a bit sorry for him and we made sure we waited thirty minutes after eating before we swam, just to be safe."

"You know that's a myth." Mom said.

"It's a myth you told me."

"Oh, I told you lots of things. But here you are, so it must have worked." Mom said smiling at me. "But about the sleepy lifeguard, what if someone was actually drowning?"

"Oh Mom, the water here is so salty. You would need a weight belt to sink."

"So why do they have lifeguards?" Mom asked.

"Same reason they have street sweepers, I guess."

"But the streets here have a lot of trash on them." She said.

"Now you're getting it." I said and smiled.

I then told her the story of the time Beth and I shopped for some outdoor carpet at House Junction back home.

* * * * *

At House Junction, the employees wore orange clothing. I figured because most of the workers there were probably already used to wearing orange at their former position in the state pen.

Along with the orange, the workers also wore huge buttons on their shirts that read:

124

I CAN HELP IN ANY DEPARTMENT!

The problem was, catching a House Junction employee was a bit like catching a greased pig. They were quick, nimble and always seemed to be on their way to a very important job elsewhere in the store. They literally whizzed by you, eyes averted, and they wouldn't stop if you were bleeding or actually on fire.

"Excuse me, would you mind...?" I tried to stop the first employee that came near us. I grabbed his hind leg and had a good hold on his hoof, but he squealed and wriggled free before I could grab him tightly and headed for an employee break room. Damn! He was safe. I almost had him.

"You're going to have to try harder." Beth said.

"What do you suggest?" I asked. "They're so fast today." More orange clad workers sped by just out of my grasp, eyes elsewhere, or talking on little microphones attached to their walkie-talkies.

"I'd use bait." She said. "Put a twenty on the floor."

"What? Are we fishing now? I asked.

"Forget it." She said. "Watch and learn."

A male employee was headed in our direction. We nodded at each other. He looked ripe for the picking. Beth stood about ten feet from me. I took my position and pretended to be examining a small bag of grout.

She got ready to cast her net, adjusting her blouse a little. She put on her best poor-little-kitten eyes and purred.

"Um, Hi. Do you think you could help me?" She almost whispered. She must have looked like a tabby with a broken leg because this hot dog stopped dead in his tracks.

"Of course, *I can help in any department?*" *He* said pointing to the plate-sized button on his orange bibs. "How may I assist you?" He said this, smiled and leaned just slightly against some large boxes of terra cotta tile as he sucked in his gut a bit. He'd taken the bait, now to set the hook. Just then, like when a game show contestant picked door number two only to reveal a lifetime supply of manure, I made my entrance.

"What my WIFE and I need is some outdoor carpet." I said.

Beth gave a pride of ownership slide of her finger gently down my arm. Orange Man's smile went flat. He knew he had the hook in his mouth. He chewed hard but even the bait was just a plastic worm. He was caught. We spoke to each other like spaghetti cowboys waiting for high noon in our lowest Clint Eastwood growl.

"What do you need?" He asked.

"Outdoor carpet." I replied.

Our eyes squinted at each other. The midday sun was always making cowboys like us squint just before we shot each other when the town clock struck noon. *Imagine both of us with a guttural, high-noon growl here.

"Oh, is *that* all?" He said.

"Yeah. *That's* it."

"Aisle five." He said and tried to leave.

"I'm afraid you're gonna have to show me." I said, blocking his move.

"I'm actually on break." He played his trump card.

"I've seen the break room. It's on your way." I trumped his trump.

"Fine." He said with an angry grin. He folded. I won.

We headed for the outdoor carpet area in the next aisle.

"This is the stuff we need. Let's just measure off fifteen feet and use this cutter here." I said reaching for a hacksaw blade that had been tied to a post with some twine, obviously put there by the store for this purpose.

"I'm afraid I can't cut the carpet for you." He said and I saw an embryonic grin forming on his face. What was he up to now?

"Why not? Your button says you can help in any department."

"Well, yeah. I can *help*." He said. "I'm not trained to use the cutter."

"It's a hacksaw blade tied to a piece of twine." I said. "*Anyone* can use it."

"Sorry *sir*, it's against our union rules." He said. "I'll send someone qualified to operate that tool." And he walked away.

I stood there dumbfounded. Beth frowned at me. He'd won.

In the Bahamas, they have the BBS. In the States, we just have the usual BS, but in both nations service was similarly dismal.

CHAPTER NINE
Fly Talking

Beth and I were watching some old concert heroes on VH-1. JetBlue played this channel and when you flew the red-eye from SFO to JFK. You could catch some good old concert footage on the headrest TV that was sent straight from Heaven. How bored we used to be on cross-country flights before this simple addition.

Led Zeppelin was one of those rare bands that our parents loved, but were still very cool when we were in high school. They were one of my favorite old rock bands and would surely always be in that category.

"Wow, look at Jimmy Page and Robert Plant!" Beth said as she spilled a little vodka and ginger ale on her lap.

"Yeah, Jimmy looks like he has a serious case of Ted Kennedy head." I said as I munched on a bag of blue potato chips. They were awful, but I always ate them because they were free.

"And is that Robert Plant or is it his mother?" Beth asked, straining her eyes a bit.

"I'm not sure, but she sure can sing." I said. "Man, they have not held up well."

"You know who has? Steven Tyler of Aerosmith." Beth explained.

"Yeah but he started out already looking funny." I laughed.

"He still does today. But at least he still looks like he did when he was younger." Beth said with authority.

128

"I guess heroin really is a good preservative." I poked her and she laughed aloud.

CHAPTER TEN
Enter Bali Hai

It was our anniversary. I decided to take Beth to Atlantis to a newer upscale beach restaurant there called, "Dune". Dune sounded like the perfect place to take Mrs. Reno for an evening out. The Texans offered to watch Jake for us, so I began ironing my pure white linen two-piece suit.

"Mon, all da bruddas wear dat. Dat is *tight!*" My Bahamian friend Kelly told me one day when he took me shopping. I knew what he meant by "tight" but I was still not so sure I had gotten the right size.

Recently, I had complained that I could not find any clothes that were reasonably priced on the island, so he took me to what he called "the ghetto."

The ghetto was really just the inner island and compared to ghettos in America, this one looked very nice. I did not grow up with money so places like this did not faze me. Most poor people were just that, poor. The violent ones were the gang members and drug dealers. Stay away from them and you are fine.

While in the ghetto, we got two-dollar haircuts (mine was completely crooked but I tipped the guy anyway), had some beers and did a lot of shopping. But all I found that I liked was a linen suit. I'd seen Kelly wear these before and he looked great. It was just pants and a long-sleeved shirt with a v-neck, but it looked elegant on him. I bought a dark blue one and a white one thinking of how island smooth I'd look.

I brought out my white linen suit to press it, turned on the music and opened a beer. Beth was in the bathroom getting ready, so I took the ironing out to the living area. I turned the music up. I was in a great mood. I loved being married to Beth. She was the perfect woman for me. She was beautiful, loving and fun, but my favorite part of her was that she was pure. I'd never met anyone so honest and absent of pretense in my life. What you saw was what you got. There was no game playing or mental/emotional BS of any kind with her. She was easy to figure out, trust and love. And everyone loved her. It was our 12th anniversary and I wanted to treat her right. She deserved it. She was open-minded enough to come on this journey with me and I needed to tell her how much I appreciated her.

I began ironing the linen suit, which took a lot longer than I thought it would, and even though I was underneath a rapidly-spinning ceiling fan I was sweating like I'd been in a sauna. I looked out the windows to see if my neighbors were anywhere outside, but there was no one. One of the nice things about living at Bonita was that we hardly ever saw the few neighbors we had. Most times it felt like we had the place to ourselves. The view from our condo was stunning and I took it in for a moment. It was why we lived here. The ocean was flat as a lake and the sky had its usual fluffy little clouds that floated by, like scattered cotton balls on a blue floor. In all my days in the Bahamas, I had never seen a perfectly cloudless blue sky like we had in California. There were always at least a few little clouds and I wondered about this as I sipped my beer.

"Can you please turn that down?" Beth yelled. I snapped out of my daydream and turned the volume lower. Ahh, marriage. Accountability and compromise.

"What's wrong?" I asked.

131

"Nothing. I was just trying to talk to you and you seemed deaf." She said.

"Oh, I was just enjoying the view."

"Are you trying to iron?"

"Trying? No, I'm getting it done. I know how to iron." I said. "I learned it in the Army."

"Well you must have learned how to keep it a secret in the Army because I've never seen you iron before. Do you mind if I just sit and watch for a bit?" She sat down and grinned.

"Suit yourself. Watch the master." I said. I focused on the ironing now and tried to appear cool and at ease, but the linen suit was fighting me. It was pure white and the linen was a bit sheer so I had to be careful.

"That's what you're wearing?" She asked.

Here we go.

"What's wrong with this?" I asked.

"It's practically see-through." She pointed at me and then to the mirror.

Uh-oh. I'd better investigate this accusation.

"Have you even tried it on?" She asked. "Of course you haven't. What was I thinking? Why not go try it on now?"

I went into the bedroom to try the white linen suit on so I could come back out to surprise her with how great I looked. We had large mirrors on one wall and I looked at myself. The ironing had made the suit appear like a huge piece of paper that hung on me like I was a news bulletin. I looked like a guy from the 1920's walking in New York with a sandwich board ad on my body. There were two other problems, too. The suit was almost see-through and I could see the dark boxer underwear I wore. The insult to the injury was the fact that the suit was way too big for me and made me look like a giant, fat marshmallow with a tan face. There was no way I could wear this, but I walked out into the living room to model for Beth. I posed like a GQ model and made kissy Zoolander faces.

Beth roared with laughter.

"You look like you're in the KKK! That may not fly well here, honey!" She laughed loudly and held her stomach, while I spun and turned, still posing and making provocative faces and sticking out my rear end.

"No good, huh?" I asked. "How about it I just wear the top part?" I took the pants off and the top hung down to my knees like a nightshirt the Three Stooges might have worn.

Beth continued to laugh but then sat up and tried to be serious.

"Take that off so you don't sweat it up too much. We have to return that thing!" She laughed.

I obeyed and stripped the shirt off, standing there in the living area in my boxer briefs just as one of our older neighbors walked passed our window with some friends. Of course they all looked in and saw me so I grabbed my beer and toasted their direction and smiled. They just looked the other way and kept walking.

* * * * *

We arrived at Dune and found the exterior bar area to be absolutely exquisite. In the warm night air the setting was perfect. As we waited at the bar for our table we met a nice young Canadian couple. He sported a totally shaved head and could have lost the same twenty or so pounds I was trying to lose. His wife was thin, blonde and a delightful combination of a good listener and funny story-teller. Both of them were clicking with us so well that I would have thought we'd known them from somewhere. It turned out that our kids went to the same school and we'd spoken briefly at one of their little soccer games. They lived in Sandyport just down the beach from us and had apparently recently purchased a boat named, "Bali-Hai." They invited us to go out with them sometime and we gratefully accepted. The waiter came and took us to our table almost on cue. The evening had been perfect so far if you didn't count my linen suit fiasco.

We saw the Canadians quite a bit over the coming weeks. We bumped into them at school, soccer practice and we'd joined them for dinner at a few of the nicer restaurants in town. They were a great couple and we loved being with them. Their having kids in the same school Jake attended helped too. The boys all got along very well and entertained themselves while we laughed and talked by the pool or at the beach.

Then one day, Mr. Canada called me to remind me that he'd purchased a boat and he wanted to take me for a ride. We met at a local beach restaurant near Sandyport and had a beer at the bar before heading into Sandyport where he lived and had the boat docked.

"I made a deal with my boss. Rather than take payroll while my work permit is being sorted, I took the boat as payment." Mr. Canada explained.

"But, technically…you're still working, right?" I asked.

"Of course." He smiled. "But no one knows and my work permit paperwork has already been submitted so I'm all good."

He seemed so calm and cool about all of this. I was not so sure. Was I just being overly cautious? It seemed to me that most people here just tended to write their own laws.

134

Sandyport is a nice, gated development on the west side of the island, not far from our place, that was pre-conceived as a boating community complete with brightly-colored houses along small roads and winding canals. Almost all of the homes there appeared to have access to the canals and many had nice boats tied up to the docks in their back yards. There was a central parking lot that adjoined a group of small businesses to include a bank, a gas station (for cars and boats) that had sundries and other boating supplies, a church, a gym, a great fish restaurant, a yogurt store and some other small businesses that all seemed to suffer just a little from the fact that Sandyport was only about 2/3 complete. There was a lot of construction going on everywhere that was a noisy eyesore. Hopefully, it would all be done soon but things like this take time in the Bahamas. A lot of time.

We parked his little SUV near his house, walked around the side of the building to the rear where the canal was and there she was, Bali Hai. A beautiful white Mako 280 with teal trim and a new teal Bimini top. She was fully rigged with huge deep-sea fishing outriggers and two Mercury 225 horsepower outboard engines. I was in love the first time I saw her. We boarded her and sat at the central captain's station under the Bimini top while Mr. Canada flipped switches and turned on the batteries. I was overwhelmed. I'd always loved boats, but this one was beautiful. I could not imagine how much she had cost him. I figured the better part of a year's salary to be sure but then again I had no clue what he did or made. I knew very little about Mr. Canada's work from our little chats and dinners. He had one of those job titles that tells you absolutely nothing; something like a Firmware Station

Engineer or a Seismic Hydraulic Geo-Technical Analyst. I just smiled and nodded. I really did not care anyway.

"We'll just take her out and blow the dust off, eh?" Mr. Canada asked.

"You're the captain." I said.

"Know much about boats?" He asked as he fired up engine one.

"Lots." I said. I'd grown up on boats all of my life and was a licensed sailboat skipper back in San Francisco. I untied the lines and waited for him to signal.

"Good." He said. "This is my first boat and I don't know shit!" He gunned the engines backwards hard making me lose my balance. I grabbed one of the thick aluminum support posts that framed the Bimini cover and tossed the bowline to the dock. He then jammed the engines forward and headed quickly for the gate where there was a guard shack and a long chain that crossed the canal.

"Starfish number 336!" He shouted to the sleepy guard in the shack who reluctantly lifted the chain on his end and lowered it into the water with a long rope so we could pass safely over the chain and then under a roadway bridge overhead. The water ahead began to get choppier as we got within 50 yards of the open sea. The water got a lot lighter in color here which meant shallower to any captain and I waited for Mr. Canada to notice but he did not.

"You'd better trim up a bit here." I said. "It's getting really shallow."

"Trim?" He asked.

"Lift the engines so they don't scrape the bottom and ruin your props." I said and pushed two buttons on the dashboard.

"I'm on it." He said nervously with a cigarette in his teeth.

I could tell he was not sure of what he was doing. I decided to watch him very closely. We finally cruised outside the small channel and now the fully-trimmed engines were slapping in and out of the water giving us no forward thrust.

"Trim down now." I said and he did. The engines dug deeply into the blue-green water now and Bali-Hai chugged forward, the bow now slapping up and down on the waves. I waited for him to power up and plane the boat out. There was no way he could see very well with the front of his boat aimed up at about a 30 degree angle. This guy did not have a clue. I headed back for the captain's cockpit bench and sat next to him.

"I checked, you're all clear to run 'er up." I said.

"OK, running up." He said as he gunned the engines and Bali-Hai almost jumped out of the water. Soon enough she began to plane out and without asking I adjusted the engine trim for less drag and evened her out on the water. He looked at me and grinned.

"She's going now, eh?" He grinned behind his aviator shades. And indeed, she was. We were doing about thirty-five miles per hour and she felt like she could do twice that with ease. As we headed east towards the touristy hotel beaches I watched for wayward Jet-ski's and Hobi-Cat sailboats. I was not sure he'd realize that Bali Hai did not have brakes. Another boating newbie (who swore she knew what she was doing) had shown me that mistake once before and almost rammed a bridge piling as her feet scrambled for a brake pedal.

We passed by my building and I watched as it drifted by to our right. It looked so small from here. It

137

was hard to believe that we had so much of our lives and livelihood wrapped up in that little concrete box. All that work and all that money tied up in that tiny piece of the world. I began to feel very insignificant.

I guided him out deeper into the ocean now so we could avoid the shoreline activities of the tourists and he responded with more speed. We cruised quickly now at about forty-five miles per hour as I dialed in the trim plates with the angle of the engines for maximum speed. Mr. Canada just kept grinning and finally, so did I. He was no captain, but I was here to watch over him. Just now Bali-Hai reminded me of how much I loved boats. I was so happy as we cruised passed the hotels where Beth and I had honeymooned and revisited so many times over that last decade or so. The water was calm and flat as we sped over different colors of blue and green, Cable Beach to our right, Sandals tiny island and equally small Chicken Island to our left. I looked over at tiny Saunders Beach where good friends had swam with us years ago and the locals still swam and cooled off daily.

"Where are we headed?" I asked loudly over the whipping wind.

"There is a channel over here that connects our little bay with the main cruise ship entrance." He shouted.

Well, this was probably not a good idea. I was sure Mr. Canada was unfamiliar with the "big boat/little boat rule." In a nutshell, the big boat has the right-away because it can't turn or stop quickly. Cruise ships were like floating death. If you got near them in a small boat even the water near the props was deadly. Mindlessly, soullessly and without remorse a cruise ship would devour your boat into its propellers and splinter you to shreds without even feeling that it had hit anything.

138

Nassau Harbor held up to five of these monsters at a time and they came and went every day and night. Add to this the constant freight and delivery ships along with the sailors, fishermen and pleasure craft and Nassau Harbor was a very busy place.

As we got closer to the channel he spoke about, I saw the derelict Coral World tower to the left. That place was fun once with its underwater viewing room where you could walk downstairs about twenty feet and look out at the ocean floor through little windows. There was an outdoor aquarium with sharks and the like. A strong hurricane wiped the place out and almost all that remained was the spaceship looking tower we passed now.

"Better slow down!" I shouted and Mr. Canada pulled both engine throttle sticks back hard. Bali-Hai settled down like a good girl in a straight line and forgivingly allowed us to begin navigating a very narrow channel bordered on the left by a rocky sea-wall and to the right by a huge concrete shipping port where construction and other such materials were unloaded. There were about three half-sunken, derelict boats tied to the wall on our right and some workmen walking around moving materials and shipping containers. We putted slowly now through the channel which was about forty feet wide. Ahead of us I saw some small, colorful buoys that appeared to be tied to the center of the channel.

"Is that the center marker?" He asked as he moved his head to the left and right nervously.

"Here? I doubt it. Slow WAY down." I said as I moved to the bow to see why the little buoys were there.

"Usually, it means something is submerged so go to the right. Quickly!" I ordered him now. This was no time to fool around. I heard some of the men on the huge concrete dock yell something and I looked but could not make out what they were saying. I got right on top of the bow just in time to see a huge, submerged boat that lay directly in front of us.

"Full reverse!" I yelled. "Full reverse NOW!"

But he was not quick enough. There was really not enough time. Thank God we were just cruising along below ten knots because we now hit the submerged boat with the bow.

"Trim up the engines, NOW!" I shouted and he began trimming them up as fast as he could but one propeller still hit the boat hard, bending it beyond use. For some reason, Mr. Canada killed both engines, turning the keys to the full off position. We now floated slowly out of control, the light wind was unfortunately beginning to pick up and push our boat towards the rocky sea wall.

"What now?" He asked.

"Give her to me!" I snapped and pushed him off the bench seat. In less than fifteen seconds we'd be washing up on the leeward shore and we'd never get this thing home. I checked the props. One was mangled, the other was fine. As I dropped the good engine, I pulled the other one completely out using the buttons on the throttle levers. Bali-Hai's electronics whined and then I sparked the good engine just as it submerged, the engine bubbling as it went down.

She was now angled almost directly towards the sea wall as we were being blown that direction. In an instant, I decided that just one engine would not get us going backwards quickly enough to avoid hitting the wall. It was then that I also realized that I had no clue which way the tide was moving. I could not chance going against wind and waves with just one prop

140

backwards, so I whipped the wheel hard to the left and gunned the one good engine. She leapt forward towards the sea wall which made both of us curse loudly but then her one good prop grabbed and her rear end swung right so hard that I had to spin the wheel the other way to avoid over steering her stern into the wall.

"Now, where was that damn boat?" I asked myself aloud.

It was dead ahead of us so we'd have to either hit it again or hug the sea wall and hope that we'd skirt the edge of the vessel, which we did and just barely. We looked left as we passed the huge, white corpse of a boat about forty feet long and only submerged about two feet in the middle. We crept out of the channel, avoiding looking up at the men on the concrete wall at the far end of the channel who talked loudly to each other about the two idiots in the boat.

I slowly drove her back to the open sea and then I gave her back to Mr. Canada. He took the wheel and we cruised slowly along silently for a few minutes.

"What the hell was that?" He finally asked.

"That was your Bahamian tax dollar at work." I said. "That thing has obviously been there for a while."

"Close call, eh?" He laughed.

"Close?" I asked. "Actually, you're going to want to trim the bow up a bit. We may have a hole in the front end and we don't want to sink. One of your props is shot so let's use the other engine to get her home gently and tie her up so we can get our masks and dive to see the damage."

He agreed with a nod and we headed back to Sandyport. Getting her back through the channel entrance and finally tied up safely took some work but we managed. We grabbed a mask that was on board Bali-Hai and jumped into the water to see the hull.

141

Fortunately, there was just a good scratch but no holes. However, the prop and the lower part of the engine were trashed.

"That'll cost a bit." He laughed.

I tried to laugh but just wondered what the heck he was thinking. All I could think was "what a shame." She was such a beauty. She needed a new daddy.

CHAPTER ELEVEN
Watered Down

I needed a drink of water. Like a lot of people, we kept a five gallon water bottle in the kitchen with a small, plastic pump affixed to the top. We paid about $30 for the poorly-made but supposedly reusable little water pump at the local hardware, leather goods, and car insurance store. I pumped out a glass of water, kind of like they used to do on that old TV show "Little House on the Prairie". Granted, this was not a well, but it felt similar. It felt like I had gone back in time.

If you thought bottled water was popular where you live, it was a downright necessity for most people throughout the Caribbean. The water in the Bahamas was pretty much non-potable. It would not kill you, but most people can't drink it unless they grew up here. It's OK to bathe in as you can mask the slightly foul odor with soap or shampoo, but to be able to drink it took time and most people just don't bother.

If you put a glass of pure water next to a glass of the stuff that came out of the pipes in the Bahamas, the Bahamian water would be the one that smells like a big glass of egg farts. The saltiness and sulfur smell would make you race to the water purification store and invest thousands into a water filtration system like many wealthy people did, or you would do like we did and just drink bottled water.

When we lived there, over 2/3 of the entire population of the Bahamas lived on New Providence and there was no way that rather small island could satisfy the thirst of over two hundred thousand people. Most water was shipped to our island from neighboring Andros Island where there were many fresh water springs. Andros was sparsely populated and had become the drinking fountain of the Bahamas. From our beach we could see the large water transport ship as it made the daily trip to and from our island bringing many millions of gallons of water to be stored and used. The name of the ship that carried the water appeared to be "Titas", which I guessed was Latin for "very long hose". Turns out it was just a river in Bangladesh.

There was some strange irony here; a tanker that would normally carry some kind of fossil fuel was burning many thousands of gallons of the same to transport something that naturally fell from the sky. Perhaps irony was not the correct word. "Commerce" or "capitalism" might be better words. It was my guess that the government might have had something to do with this archaic but profitable system. The water transport ship made Nassau, Bahamas a little like the desert paradise of Las Vegas. Without a lot of delivered water, both of these beached whales would dry up and suffocate under the weight of their own blubber.

For some reason, Nassau had not re-adopted the use of cisterns to capture and store rainwater. I was told that many years ago cisterns were the norm. It seemed clear that the "greening" of the Bahamas was many years away, but it would have to happen or the place could literally dry up. Imagine how much water would be shipped from Andros if diesel fuel was suddenly $10-15 a gallon. Or if diesel fuel was not available for a few weeks due to a war or some political sabre rattling. People would be burning palm trees to desalinate seawater. Speaking of greening, when we

144

all wise up and get off fossil fuels, imagine how much fun it would be to sell water to Saudi Arabia. And they would buy it too. That or drink their oil. But for now, we'll keep buying their oil so we can ship our water back and forth and they can buy another dozen palaces and fill their pools with Lamborghinis and virgins.

Carrying a half dozen five gallon bottles of water from the store to the car and then from the car to the house was not fun. A gallon of water weighed almost eight and a half pounds so these bottles weighed almost forty-two pounds each. Six bottles topped two-hundred and fifty pounds of water that needed to be picked up weekly. And no genius had yet developed a five-gallon bottle with a handle yet, so you needed the grip of a steel worker to carry them. If I drove alone, our car was almost too small to hold more than six bottles, and here we were again with the fossil fueled vehicle transporting water.

People talked about all the minerals in water. Well, Bahamian water was loaded with irony.

We tried a water delivery service for a while. It was nice not having to schlep the heavy five-gallon bottles from the store, but the service was as unreliable as most things around there. Heck, it took over an hour to get a Domino's pizza delivered and their store was less than a quarter mile away. The drivers always got lost even though:

1. The drivers all grew up there.
2. The name of our building was on a big sign outside on the only main road; the same road as the Domino's place.
3. Our building was frigging ORANGE. How do you miss that?

*Why didn't we just go pick up the pizza ourselves? On a Friday night, oh come on...that would require effort AND sobriety! Two things sorely lacking in the Bahamas, especially among the chubby, white expats that dot the beach.

After too many missed water deliveries, we decided to just pony up the extra fifty cents per bottle and buy it ourselves. That's right it's cheaper to have the water delivered than to buy it at the store. I figured the reason for this was the water delivery company gave you a bulk rate discount if you bought a book of coupons. But getting the water delivered on the scheduled time and date was like winning the lottery, so the coupons you bought were about as worthless as a lottery ticket. I think the water delivery company knew this. I suppose they figured they could save money by just not delivering the water. And it worked!

In my opinion, we were going backwards. De-evolving. When I was a kid, we just turned a handle and fresh water came out of the tap. We drank pure water from a garden hose and it was wonderful. Now we must travel a considerable distance to the store to get the same thing that was once cheap and pure. And unless you bought a large amount of water, you would pay more per gallon than you would pay for gasoline. The little bottles cost a fortune.

Imagine riding your $3,000 speed demon street bicycle, complete with your obnoxious skin-tight Lycra clothing festooned with random ads of retailers who have not sponsored you and that helmet that makes you look like a retarded unicorn. You spent too much on your bike gear, including the new must-have titanium testicle-protectant Lycra underwear so you decide you just can't afford the small bottles of water anymore. And just as you cut off another car or blow through a red light on your bike, you reached down for your *five-*

gallon water bottle for a quick swig. That would build up your arm muscles, so they'd match those great legs!

What's next? Drawing water from a hole in the ground and then carrying it home with animal skins? Balancing large clay pots on our heads? Getting people to conserve water in a nation that still tosses beer bottles and KFC wrappers everywhere you look was going to take time. Or, perhaps just a few days with no water would do it. God's version of tough love.

* * * * *

I remember the first time I saw bottled water. It was in the mid 1980's and I was living in a small house in Texas with four other college students and one of them had just come home from a trip to Europe. She had brought with her a squarish-looking plastic bottle that read, "Volvic" on the side.

"What's in the bottle?" I asked her.

"Water," she said.

"Oh. Well, what was in the bottle before?" I looked at her as I examined the bottle.

"That's what came in the bottle." She said.

"Is it some kind of Euro-canteen?" I asked. I'd just gotten out of the Army recently and the idea of some kind of disposable canteen sounded reasonable to me.

"No, silly." My wanna-be Euro-trash roomie suddenly donned her, *Oh you poor, foolish American* voice. "Everyone drinks water this way over *there*."

"What's wrong with the regular water?" I demanded.

"Nothing." She said.

"Well how much was it?"

"Oh, a dollar I think."

147

"For about a quart of water." I wrinkled my forehead hard as I stated this to make sure she got my meaning. "Really?"

"Actually, it's a *liter*." She smirked.

There was that voice again.

"Which is just over a quart." I droned flatly.

"Yeah, I guess."

"Hmmmmm. Is that the only one you got?" I asked.

"No. I have another." She chuckled. And she produced a pink and white labeled bottle. "This one is my favorite. *Evian*." She said. "It's the best."

"*Evian*. Water in a bottle. Is it purer than the other one?" I asked.

"No, I don't think so."

"Is it filtered more, cleaner?"

"Nope."

"So what's the difference?" I asked.

"It *tastes* better," she smiled.

"You know the definition of water is 'an odorless, colorless, tasteless liquid', right?" I quizzed her now. I knew this because we had drilled this intensely in the Army. Water was very important to a soldier in Texas.

"That definition sounds about right, why?" She asked.

"Oh, I don't know," I said, donning my best, *oh you poor, college-educated idiot* voice. "Why don't you just read the Evian label *backwards* and figure it out for yourself?"

* * * * *

Recently, I read that drinking water from a plastic bottle that was exposed to sunlight would cause cancer. The reaction from that? Retailers immediately began selling water bottles made of aluminum. So now we were going to *can* our water? I thought we switched to plastic because we were getting tired of all of the soda and beer empty cans littering the countryside. Soon, would learn that the metals in the cans cause cancer and we'll go back to wood containers or perhaps even back to using animal skins. I don't know about you, but right now I'm practicing balancing a huge clay pot on my head while walking long distances. Laugh now, but I'll be ahead of the curve!

* * * * *

I was sitting at my desk one afternoon emailing some friends at home when the phone rang.

"Hey Jimi." It was Mr. Canada.

"What's going on?" I asked as I stared out over the ocean through our bedroom window.

"Well…you won't believe this one." He gasped. I could tell he had something important to tell me and did not know where to start.

"The line sounds funny." I said sitting up a bit. "Are you on your cell?"

"Oh yeah. But I'm on a different cell. Bro, I'm calling you from Canada. We've been deported." He said at last. I stood up.

"What?"

"Yeah, sorry situation, eh?" He asked. "Somebody turned me in."

"Turned you in…for what?" I asked, but already kind of knew.

"My work permit was never really being processed, or it was in process but on the wrong form. I really don't have details. They came to my house and took us to jail. Then they processed us out of the country at the airport. Kicked us out within hours!" He as very upset.

"Jeez, dude. Is there anything I can do?" I wondered aloud to him.

"Actually, I need some help." He spoke softly now.

"OK, what?"

"I have a spare key to my place. There are some personal things we could not take. We only had five minutes to pack! The cops were staring at us the whole time. It was awful. My wife crying, my sons...jeez!" He began to break down.

"I'm so sorry." I did not know what else to say.

"I need you to get my spare key and go to my condo to get some personal items. I'll email you a list. The rest, take what you want. There's bicycles for the boys, toys, video games, kitchen stuff, booze, tools a barbecue...whatever we left. Take it. It's yours." He sniffed into the phone.

"Bro, you are in such a bad place. Don't think about me. Just tell me what you need and I'll get it." I said angrily. I could not believe this situation.

"And the boat."

"Bali Hai?" I asked. "What about her?"

"She's yours." He said. "Keep her. I did not have much in her anyway. She was payment for a job I never did. The keys are in the kitchen drawer. I'll send you the paperwork so you can transfer her to your name."

"I can't just take your boat, bro." I was stunned. "I'll keep her for you. Come get her later."

"We're banished! I can't come back." He said.

"You spent money on that boat. At least let me pay you that so you're not out of pocket on this." I demanded.

"Thirteen grand." He said. "I spent thirteen grand on upgrades and repairs. You're a saint." He said.

"No, I'm the luckiest man on the island. And now you're not here for me to teach to use that damn boat." I laughed.

"Probably for the best." He chuckled. "I'm a better passenger than skipper."

He and I worked out the details and I made sure he got his personal items; mostly photos, documents and some jewelry. He transferred the boat to me as promised. I had no truck to pull it, no dock to store it and had to take the money out of savings but it was not a deal I could turn down.

My luck was hot. I asked our pastor where to park the boat and he said I could use his dock in Sandyport. The trailer was stored in Lyford Caye with the rich and famous so I'd have to deal with that later. I got a boat for next to nothing and a free, safe place to dock her that was literally five minutes from our home. I decided to parlay my sudden lucky streak into the purchase of a car.

CHAPTER TWELVE
We've Got You Covered

With Jake in school and Beth back in California for a short trip, I seriously set out to find a car for us. I had found a man who was in the Japanese auto import business who said he could get me a Honda CR-V for about nine grand. It had a lot of extras and was right-hand drive (RHD). I was excited to drive a RHD vehicle as I'd never done it before. The Bahamas had retained much of its British heritage, and although now independent, it was still part of the Commonwealth and they still drove on the left side of the road.

A RHD car made sense here, and seemed so *foreign*, which was something that drew me for some reason to a new piece to our adventure I guess. A RHD car paid for with the local colorful money just made being here so much more exciting, like you were really more than just a couple hundred miles away from the USA. If only they spoke a different language then the entire foreign country thing would be complete. Well, truthfully they did speak English in a manner that was pretty difficult to understand.

For the purposes of this story, we'll call the car guy "Pat". Pat was to be my indoctrination into the world of how business was sometimes handled in the Bahamas. Let's just say that I had a lot to learn.

Initially, I asked Pat if I could pay for the car with my credit card. Another one of my Ralph Kramden type of schemes had me thinking that if I used my JetBlue

152

AMEX card that I'd rack up valuable travel miles. I had the money for the car, but since we traveled so much it made sense to at least try to get miles any way I could.

"I gotta charge you three percent." He said.

In the Bahamas, many businesses charged an extra fee to use a credit card to offset the fee they paid to the credit card company. It felt like they were being extremely petty, especially when you were paying ten dollars for a hamburger, four for a soda, and a mandatory 15% tip regardless of if the food comes today, tomorrow or never. Stores in the USA built in the cost of using a credit card to the price of the item, but at least they were sneaky about it so you were not reminded that you were being charged.

"Three percent sounds fair. Where can we do this?" I asked.

"Well I got no card machine right now." He admitted.

"So the whole credit card thing is moot."

"What?" He asked.

"Never mind." I said. "How can I use my card if you don't have a machine?"

"I got a friend." He explained. "Maybe we can run the card troo him."

This began to feel just a bit shady, but Pat assured me that his friend was a respectable dentist with a professional practice. For a small fee, he'd allow me to pay for the car with my card.

Again, the whole reason I wanted to pay this way in the first place was to get airline miles on my Jet Blue AMEX. Since we planned to fly back and forth to the USA so much, I wanted to get as many miles as I could. But now, I was beginning to understand why most people don't hassle with airline miles. Especially considering the "black out" restrictions the airlines imposed on the actual usage of the miles.

Just my luck; it turned out that whenever I wanted to fly was a black out period.

* * * * *

"How about if I fly the next day?" I asked the friendly JetBlue agent.

"Sorry, that day is not available." She said.

"Well, my schedule is pretty flexible. How about the *next* day?" I hoped she had something.

"Sorry."

"Are there any days available that week?" I asked.

"Hmmmm, I don't see any. Well, wait a minute. How about this: you fly out on the red-eye Tuesday night, your wife could follow you the next day at 6 AM and meet you at JFK Airport in New York, since you'll have a 12 hour layover anyway and your son can fly directly to Fort Lauderdale and then on to San Francisco International where he can wait for you to arrive." She explained.

"You realize my son is only 7 years old, right?" I asked.

"Oh yes, he's a True Blue member. We have his information right here." She replied.

"Then how the heck is he to travel alone? And do you really think that other itinerary for my wife and I is reasonable?" I asked.

"Sir, I'm simply trying to accommodate your complicated schedule." She snapped.

"How complicated is it to fly across the country?" I asked. "We do it all the time."

"Well, the restrictions you've placed on us…"

"Restrictions I've placed on YOU." I said. "I'm just trying to use my miles to buy a trip. Isn't that what they're for?"

"I suppose. But it's easier to just give them to family members as gifts." She said.

"If I gave this gift to someone in my family, they'd never speak to me again."

"Perhaps you could give them to your in-laws?" She quipped.

* * * * *

I was to follow Pat in my rental car to the dentist's office. Pat drove ahead of me in his Cadillac, and I followed as closely as I could as he sped through residential neighborhoods at ambulance speeds. I floored my little Suzuki and I could hear the two squirrels under the hood cursing at me. I think one cursed at me in Spanish! Funny, I expected Japanese.

"Sorry, guys. We've got to get to the dentist, pronto!" I said and punched the gas again, whipping the two squirrels onward.

Finally, we stopped in a small parking lot and entered a one-story office building. The air-conditioning was running on "artic" in there and my skin immediately goosed up. *Why did they like it so damn cold in this country?*

"Jeez, you guys like it cold." I said to Pat.

"Yeah, nice eh?" He grinned. "It's like Alaska, right?"

"Nobody likes Alaska." I said. "Even Eskimo's wear thick clothes and build a fire because it's COLD."

"I like it." He said. "I'm chillin'." Suddenly, I wished I'd never heard that word.

155

Freezing AC was a status symbol, I guessed. He leaned on the counter and spoke to the attendant through two inches of scratched-up bulletproof Lucite. This dentist office was not like any I had seen at home. A few minutes later his friend came out wearing what appeared to pajamas and he had his face covered with a medical face mask. He looked a bit like Michael Jackson in court.

"So yoummff wanna pay card ummfff car and den ummmfff small fee, OK? He said. His voice was muffled through the mask and his accent only added to my confusion. I had to guess that he understood what we were doing.

"Sure." I said.

He motioned to a small ATM style machine. He began to tell me how to use it, but I assured him that I'd already taken the course at 7-11. I punched in the digits, pulled the tape, signed it and gave it to him.

"I'll need a copy of that." I snapped as I reached for the paper.

"Ummmfff copy machine not..." He mumbled and motioned with his hands.

No copy machine either? OK, fine. Even through his mask, I understood that the machine was broken.

Of course.

I would have to get a copy from my card company. I had charged fifty percent of the price of the car, plus three percent with the rest to be paid upon delivery. Pat initialed the contract he'd brought with him and we agreed to settle up once the car arrived from Japan.

Japan also drove on the wrong side of the road and to the delight of Bahamian auto importers, Japan required its residents to sell their cars once they are about ten years old. I suppose this was one of the ways they insured that Toyota kept selling those Camrys.

The cars were generally in great running order and good cosmetic condition as well. The only thing was the names were different. A Camry was a "Dove". A Corolla was a "Party". And I think a Celica was an "Ashtray" or something. In any case, the cars were just fine to drive for another ten years.

I was sure the importers made a large percentage on the cars, but when compared to the price of a new car on the island, it still made sense to buy a used Japanese import.

Once back in the car my cell phone rang. It was Beth.

"Is everything OK." She asked. "You sound stressed."

I lied and said that everything was fine. The little voice in my head was trying to speak but for some reason I kept ignoring him. I could not tell if my instincts were correct here because everything was done in such an odd way. Was it me or was it the place? I did not want to be suspect of everyone just because they did things differently. It was a constant battle in my mind as I tried to "go with the flow".

Pat and I had entered into a contract that outlined the details of the vehicle, total price and approximate delivery date. Pat assured me that the car would arrive in about two weeks from Japan.

Pat was a pretty big guy, but he was soft spoken. We were very civil in the beginning, even friendly with each other. But, when he did not deliver the CR-V on time I got pretty annoyed as I had already made arrangements to turn in my rental car. I left messages at his office but I did not hear back from him. I had to keep calling him and was not looking forward to the conversation once we finally spoke.

"Pat, you said the car would be in my hands yesterday. I've been trying to reach you and left a bunch of messages. What's the deal?" I asked when he finally answered his cell phone.

"We've had some problems with the shipper." He explained.

"Pat, I understand that things happen, but I'd really appreciate it if you'd keep me in the loop. When do you now intend on delivering the car?" I asked.

"I don't understand it. My shipper is usually right on time. For some reason the car did not get on the right boat. He say the car will be here in a few days." Pat explained.

"Do shippers normally *estimate* a delivery time? I mean doesn't the boat make the same trip all the time? It seems they would have a pretty clear idea of when they'd be here." I said.

"He say the car here on next Friday."

"Well, this being Friday makes *next* Friday sounds more like a week than a few days." I growled.

"Right, um-hmm. A week then."

And now, I was beginning to feel the old runaround warming up its legs for the race.

"You know, Pat. This rental car is really costing me. If I knew you could not deliver on time I would have bought elsewhere." I said.

"No, it'll be here. And don't worry about the rental. I'll pay for the extra days." He said.

Well, that was nice. Perhaps I had been a little hasty with him. Here he was in a tight situation and in order to keep me happy he would pay for extra rental car days. I felt badly. Was I being the ugly American?

"Well, thanks Pat." I smiled a bit. "I appreciate that." I hung up the phone and felt much better about the whole situation. Even the little voice in my head felt ashamed for doubting the integrity of this guy. The little voice left but promised to be back.

Two weeks later, Pat and I had a similar conversation on the phone. Both the little voice in my head and I had been cursing Pat for many days.

"Told ya!" The little voice said, almost smugly, as if he wanted this to happen.

"The car is on the loading dock downtown. It's *here*." He assured me.

"That's great. So if it's here, why can't I drive it?" I was just about out of patience.

"There's a problem with the import papers. The man there says I can't get it out until we fix the problem." Pats voice trailed off a bit as he said this.

"Problem?" What the hell was he talking about now? The little voice in my head was just shaking his head, apparently in an attempt to silence the little voice in his head.

"I told you so." The little voice said. I actually considered hitting myself in the head to shut him up.

"What is the REAL problem, Pat?"

"Ummm, I don't have enough money to pay the duty and get it released." He finally told the truth.

"So, the real problem with the import papers is the fact that you're broke? Is this normal? Don't you handle this kind of thing all the time?"

"No, no not normal at all. This very unusual. Very unusual." And then he was quiet. He almost sounded sad. Before I allowed myself to feel sorry for him, I had to work this out.

"Okay....Pat, I'm not sure what to do here. I'd like to take just the car, pay you off, and be done but I'm not comfortable with this situation. As a matter of fact, I think I'd like to get my money back and just move on." I said.

159

"Well I can probably get the car out today." He quickly offered a solution.

But, I now knew that he would say just about anything to assuage me and then move on to the next lie. I realized that this deal was now on damage control and I needed to minimize my losses and get out quickly. Now there was a new voice in my head. It sounded like Ben Kenobi saying, *"Don't examine your feelings! You are an idiot and a sucker! Use force. This is not the car you want!"*

"Meet me down at the dock." Pat said.

"When?"

"In two hours."

"Let me get this straight. I meet you at the dock in two hours and we can get the car. Then I pay you the balance, we say good-bye, and I drive the car home. That's the plan, right?" I illustrated what I expected quickly.

"Right."

I'd been at this for weeks now and the prospect of being done with this guy was very appealing. There was now a chorus of voices in my head and they were all screaming for me to get out of this deal, but I did not listen. Obi Wan Kenobi just sighed and the runaround man prepared for a marathon, while the little voice just sobbed.

"OK, Pat. My son and I will meet you there at 4 o'clock." And we hung up.

I did not know if I was happy or not. Pat had strung me along for some time now. The only reason I believed I had any chance of this working at all was because he did have a legitimate car lot in the middle of the island. I'd seen it. He couldn't be a complete crook, could he? I mean, he *was* a used car salesman. Aren't they all honest?

160

"I'm screwed." I said out loud. Obi Wan patted my shoulder and shook his head.

The downtown dock where tourists disembarked from the cruise ships was called Prince George Wharf. A lot of cargo got dropped off at nearby Arawak Caye. We were close to the "Fish Fry" where native food and drinks may be purchased in small restaurants, endearingly called "shacks", which was what they used to be until the government cleaned up the place, put in running water, bathrooms and a paved road. Now tourists and locals alike frequented the place. As I said before, it was nice, but I missed the old Fish Fry where it was mostly locals playing dominoes and laughing deep into the evening. It was a lot more rugged with no bathroom, a muddy strip for a road, and some of the conch shacks resembled little more than a plywood lean-to. But we sure had fun. I sat and reminisced, looking up at the very place Beth and I had sat when we decided to live here, as we waited for Pat to show up.

"Daddy, do we get our new car today?" Jake asked.

"I sure hope so, son." I smiled at him as I answered.

I rubbed my hand along the back of his sweaty neck. He looked at me and smiled one of those life-changing smiles that only a child has. If I could just hang out with him for the rest of my life... how calm and content I'd be. Jake was the center of the universe for me and in that universe everything was perfect. He was a proof to me that Heaven existed. If Heaven was like Jake, sign me up.

When Pat was twenty minutes late, I called him with my cell phone. When he was thirty, forty and then forty-five minutes late, I kept calling him. He kept assuring me that he was stuck in traffic and would be there as soon as he could. Something I can't figure out about Bahamians and traffic is this: how can you drive the same road your whole life, every day, and never learn to account for the same traffic problems? If a drive took ten minutes without traffic and thirty with traffic, why don't they allow thirty minutes during rush hour? There was no answer. They just don't. So if a Bahamian told you he'll be there in ten minutes, triple that if there was traffic. I think they expected you to do the math. Or, they were just not used to dealing with uptight American time freaks like me.

When Pat finally showed up, he was very cool about the whole thing. I wish I could say the same for me. Jake and I had been waiting at the Fish Fry for forty-five minutes and I was miffed. Pat just rolled down his window half-way and motioned for me to follow him.

We drove out to the back of the Fish Fry where the cargo ships unloaded and Pat stopped his truck. He rolled down his window again.

"There it is." He said. "The silver one."

I looked over in the direction he pointed and there beyond a chain-link fence topped with razor wire was a silver CR-V. Could it be that we were actually going to be done soon?

"Well, let's go get her, man." I opened my door and urged Pat to get moving.

Pat shook his head, "Too late." He said. "Dock man is gone by now."

"Then what the hell are we doing here, Pat?"

"I hoped he'd be staying late." Pat's lame explanation was the last straw.

At this point the only reason I did not go off on the man was because I had Jake with me and I noticed that Pat had a youngster in his cab.

"He'll be here tomorrow." Pat said.

"If he's not here, and if I don't drive away in that car tomorrow, we're done." I said and we sped off.

And this time, I meant it. No more excuses. I finally had enough.

On the way home, I was doing all I could to keep from losing it. It felt like a bait and switch con but deep down I knew the guy was not that bright. He was just a really bad businessman. I was to learn that this was common here (just like at home). While there were many very professional people here, there were just as many that had no business being in business. There were two ways to find your way through this: one was by trial and error, but that could be immensely frustrating and expensive. The second way was to do things the way the locals did and that was through social networking.

Every local knew where to get everything they needed. They knew who the good folks were and they surely knew the crooks. The best thing you could do was make some good local friends and use their contacts. Locals were always willing to direct you to the correct person and it seemed that if they didn't know the correct person they knew who did. It was a much better way to get things done than using the Yellow Pages, believe me.

The problem was, I was still so new that I had no good contacts to lean upon yet.

I was beginning to dislike my new home, somehow blaming the whole island for the actions of one dumb man. I knew what I was feeling was wrong. I was making up a rule book in my mind and I kept thinking about rule number one: living here certainly was different than visiting.

After we got home, I looked at a folder on my laptop where I had been keeping little thoughts and copies of

163

any email I sent back home, which was more than just a few sentences. I found a description of island life that I had sent to my mother recently.

* * * * *

Outside I hear the gentle buzzing of the motorboats in the distance every now and then. There are people laughing and having fun on vacation. I hear the thump of some party music in the distance as it rebounds back at us from Sandals Island. The warmth of the late afternoon sun chides me to lower the east shades and head outside to watch the sun drop lower in the sky.

I have friendly neighbors that stop by to offer me a beer and we wash away the day as we watch the sun go down. As we wait for the colors of sunset to form, I have time for daily sandy football games with Jake letting me be the quarterback. He runs tirelessly and we play so long I swear he's a bit taller when we quit for the day.

Lately, my favorite thing is to sit on the sea wall and let the wind blow the wave spray up onto my face as I close my eyes. Then I let the sun sizzle the moisture off my face leaving only the salty footprints of a thousand misty little drops.

* * * * *

After reading that email, I was not so angry at the world. It reminded me of the happier moments that made up a day here. I decided to just try to calm down and move forward. I was letting the bad business practices of one man get me down on the whole country. I decided to stop that right then. Many expats came here and thought that they would either force this island to change or just complain until it did. But they were wrong. These people had their own way of doing things and no amount of foreigners would get them to do a thing differently, even if it made sense. They too had their pride. And pride made fools of us all.

I would give Pat one last chance. I tried to look at it in a Zen way: either it would work out or it would not. I tried to accept this mindset and move forward. In the end, I would have a car some way. I wondered if Pat had any idea how much trouble he caused me? I was sure he did not and that this was all just a storm in my own head. I needed to get ahold of myself and work this out like a man. An old friend of mine back home used to say that now that we were older we were playing by "big boy rules." I guess I needed to start acting like a big boy.

Unfortunately, I never heard back from Pat about the car. I'd paid $4,500 plus 3% for all of this trouble. I had left a message on Pat's voicemail telling him some lies about the big, bad fraud department at American Express. I tried to get him to believe that the jack-booted storm troopers from the American Credit Card Army would soon be at his door, but he never called me back.

I called my credit card company for help, but had to leave a message. I kept calling and finally got someone to listen to my story. When I finally received a phone call back from my credit card company saying that the charge for the car had gone through, and that the signature on the receipt had been verified as mine.

"Well, that was a big waste of time." I said. "I never said the card was stolen. I told you I signed it."

"It's company procedure to do our *own* investigation." The customer service rep snidely replied.

165

"So what recourse do I have now that my money is gone and I have no car?"

"You may request a refund from the vendor."

"Really? Wow, I had not thought of that! No kidding? It's that easy? Here, I've been wasting all of your time." I began to get sarcastic.

"If the vendor refuses to refund your payment, then I'd suggest contacting local law enforcement." The rep apparently was reading from his script for when the customer becomes a sarcastic asshole.

The man droned on and on about international law and credit card policies but I was lost in my own head. Where did they find these people? What were the requirements to get this job anyway? Perhaps if you were too stable for the US Post Office and not yet quite inept enough for the Department of Motor Vehicles, you could start out in telephone customer service. And after a few years in customer service, if you were truly awful enough, you might someday graduate to that loftiest of goals for those with none: working for the federal government.

Where was the friendly, attractive lady that helped the man on vacation that I had seen on the commercial?

* * * * *

"Hello... I've been robbed! We're vacationing at the top of Mt. Everest and someone took my wallet." The distraught man in the commercial said. He hugged a tree as the wind and snow whipped at his meager coat and scarf.

"No problem, Mr. Smith." The attractive, yet non-sexy woman said. *"We've got you covered."*

"But, I'm afraid the robber may go on a shopping spree with my card. There are yak and mukluk dealers just 20 miles down the hill. Who knows what they will buy?" The man replied.

"We'll either reverse or cover all those charges, Mr. Smith. Now, I'm sending a helicopter evac team to air drop another card for you right now. It should be there in about five minutes. And as a courtesy for all of your trouble, I'll send along one of our spa kits for you."

"But we're at the top of a mountain. A very high... well, actually it is the *highest* mountain in the world." He said.

"We've got an air-droppable, portable spa complete with attendants and a hot tub to ease your neck tension." She explained.

"How did you know I had neck tension? Wait...I hear a helicopter! There's the parachute. How can you afford to do all of this?" The man exclaimed with joy.

"Have you ever looked at the APR on your monthly statement, sir?

"Ummm, no. Not really."

"No one does." They both share a chuckle. "And frankly, I wouldn't recommend it!" More chuckles together as the man reaches out to open the package containing his new card, snow and wind still whipping by but now the sun peaks out its loving face and smiles on the man, if only for a moment.

"You enjoy your spa treatment! And please, let us know if there are any problems with the new card. Remember sir, at American Express, *we've got you covered!*"

* * * * *

"So, what you're telling me is that in the three days since I contacted you about this all you've done is verify that the signature on the receipt was indeed mine?" I groaned into the phone.

"Well, we also cancelled your card for you."

"Why did you do that?" I barked.

"To avoid further fraudulent charges."

"But you just said that you verified that I made the purchase."

"Yes sir. And apparently we need to protect you from yourself. Have a nice day." He said and hung up.

After a few days and a few messages, I realized that I was probably screwed. And right about the time I was going to consider cheering myself up for only having put up half the money... I had an idea: the dentist in the Michael Jackson mask. Perhaps I could lean on him.

* * * * *

"And if I don't get a full refund immediately, I'm prepared to go the distance on this." I said this to the dentist over the phone. I wanted to sound menacing; yet professional and polite. I also needed to be a bit vague as none of my threats were real.

"I'm really not involved in this. I just did a favor for you." He said.

"A favor...I'm afraid that favors don't require payment, sir! And as you may remember, you charged me three percent to use your machine. That makes you an accessory. A dentist involved in credit card fraud. All those years in college...such a shame!" I pouted for his future.

Wow, that almost sounded convincing. I guess I should keep watching Law and Order.

168

JAMES P. RENO III

"Look, I don't' want any trouble." He said.

"You're a dentist, right?"

"Yes."

"I will add that my neighbor is with the ministry of health here in Nassau." I grinned. I'd never even met my neighbor, but I had been told he worked with the government in some capacity. "Now, I don't want to have to inform him that a local dentist is making money on the side running credit cards for a local crook in a car scam operation, but I will if you don't help me here." This idea just came to me and I went with it.

"OK, OK. I'll call Pat." He said. "Please, don't call anyone about this."

"Call him now." I whispered. "I'll wait for your call."

Within ten minutes the phone rang.

"I can have your money for you tomorrow." Pat said.

"Hey Pat, you fucking crook! Great to hear from you! Didn't you get all my messages from the last few days?" I laughed at the man now. No more deals.

Silence. This is the BBS over the phone.

"Call me tomorrow by nine and I'll meet you. And don't forget, you owe me two grand for the rental car too." I reminded him of his earlier promise.

The next day I agreed to meet Pat in the parking lot of a local bank. I was more than just a little nervous, but determined to settle this situation and move on. Pat showed up and told me he would go make the withdrawal.

As I waited in the car, I imagined him holding the place up, running outside and tossing me a bag of money. But I reminded myself that although he was a crook, he was more of a con man than anything else. He was no bank robber. I was beginning to wish I had a gun. But I had been told that the local police REALLY

169

frowned on gun play outside banks. It made them jumpy.

Pat came out of the bank with a thick white envelope full of cash. He handed it to me through my car window. After counting out the money he'd handed me in an envelope, I noticed it was short.

"Where's the money you promised to pay for my rental car?" I asked.

"Oh, I can't pay for that now." He growled at me like a huge bear.

"After all this, I'm not surprised."

"I just need you to sign this release saying you're paid in full." He said handing me a piece of paper.

"I'm afraid my pen is all out of ink."

"I've got a pen here." He reached for his pocket.

"Then you sign it. I'm out of here." I said and drove away.

* * * * *

With the Pat ordeal over with, I decided to stash the money in the condo and take my son to the mall to play some video games with him. I took a note from the envelope and we headed for the arcade at the mall. I asked the guy behind the counter if he could break a hundred and he did. We played for an hour or so, and then got a bite to eat before going back home. I had to hide the cash in the house as we did not have a bank account here. As "tourists" (which we were because we had not yet settled our residency paperwork), we were not allowed to get a bank account. We had money sequestered in various places around the condo and I made a list of how much was hidden in each spot.

A week or so later, Jake and I were back at the mall playing video games at the same place we always visited on Fridays after school: Mr. Pretzels. The manager walked directly up to me and appeared to have a very clear purpose.

"I need to speak with you." She said. She sounded very serious. Her voice did not blend well with all the silly noises and sounds the video games produced. And her stature did not match the attitude she was lofting up my direction, either.

"OK, what can I do for you?" I asked and tried not to grin. The arcade was just not the place to get shaken down by some random manager that stood about four foot six inches tall. With her "Mr. Pretzel's" name tag and the mall-cop attitude, this was beginning to seem funny.

"You were here last week?" She asked. Her face was now deadly serious.

"We're here about once a week or so, yes." I said and grinned a bit.

"You gave that boy over there a hundred dollar bill? This is not a laughing matter, sir!" She snapped at me.

I looked to where she was pointing and saw a very sheepish look on the boy. He worked there and had broken the hundred for me.

"I believe that's him. What's this all about?" I asked. I was not grinning anymore.

"That bill turned out to be counterfeit. He should have checked it with our scanner, but didn't." She said.

"Well, what do you want me to do? The bill was obviously passed to me. I'm not a counterfeiter." I said indignantly.

"Someone has to do something about this." She said.

"Perhaps you should contact your bank. I'm sure customer service there can deal with this. They're always so helpful in the States. I'm sure they'll be more

171

than willing to assist you here." I said. "Now, unless you want to call a cop or something, we're leaving."

"Fine." She growled at us as we passed.

She stood aside and let us go. As we walked out of the mall, I kept expecting one of the menacing-looking police officers carrying the bamboo stick with the shiny little piece of silver on the end to arrest me, but no one did. I was glad. Mall cops back home were wimps. The ones here looked like the Special Forces. Believe me, a huge black man with a Caribbean accent, a khaki uniform, a bamboo stick, dark sunglasses, a beret and big white teeth can be very intimidating. They make scary movies about such encounters. James Bond almost was almost killed by some guys that looked exactly like that.

On the drive home, I felt badly for the kid at the arcade. He probably got a good tongue-lashing from his boss for his mistake. But I believed the manager would either turn in the money to the bank and get it replaced, or just dump it on to the next person. Counterfeit money was really just a game of musical chairs anyway. I had noticed a lot of shops in town having signs saying they don't take one hundred dollar bills. Apparently, there had been an increase in the counterfeiting of that particular denomination recently. It was just like at home.

I wondered how many of those hundred dollar bills that I had stashed at home were not real and for a moment I wondered if Pat had given me a stack of them. I wondered if his entrance into the bank was just for show and that perhaps he had the bad money in his pocket the whole time.

But then, I thought better of it. Pat was not that clever. He probably was not even really a crook. I still believed he was just a bad businessman, and that if I gave him another six months he just might be able to deliver a car.

I hoped to never see or talk to Pat again, but a week later he phoned.

"I got that CR-V." He said with a warm voice.

"Good for you. Why are you telling me?" I quickly got on the defensive.

"I thought you might still want it." He said.

"Pat, I will not buy a car from you in this lifetime." I promised with a very clear and sincere voice.

"Really? Why not?" He sounded hurt and confused.

"Wait, do me a favor. I was just kidding. Hang on to the car. I'll pick it up from you in a week, OK?" I laughed.

"Well, do you know anyone who might want to buy it?" He asked.

"Are you kidding me?" I chuckled "You can't be seriously asking me this?"

"Well, do you?" He asked.

"Well, now that you ask. I do know someone that is looking for a car exactly like the one you have." I said with a serious tone.

"You do?" He asked.

"Yes, I do. I'll get back to you." I hung up.

Now he could wait for my call.

CHAPTER THIRTEEN
Rose Island

Some friends we'd made at Jake's school introduced us to so many of their friends that I'd never need to consult the phone book for anything ever again. Finally, we were getting plugged in. I even got a job working for one of their friends at his commercial roofing company. It wasn't much and the work was hard (more on that later.) But it was something that could lead to something else and I really liked the owner of the company. My boss at the commercial roofing company was a wonderful Scottish man we'll call Larry.

I had met Larry at a boating party on Rose Island. Some friends of ours had invited us to meet them and some other friends who had boats for a day on the beach at a local island about 30 minutes from Nassau called Rose Island.

Rose Island is a small place with beautiful beaches on its north side that the local party boats took tourists to get a feel for an uninhabited Caribbean island. The problem was that the huge double-decker ferry-type boats blasted their music so loud as they emptied hundreds of tourists onto the beach that the entire "eco-island" style trip was completely ruined. The DJ on the ferry shouted through the PA constantly as the drunk tourists had rump-shaker contests on the beach, downing gallons of cheap rum punch that they would most assuredly throw up on the way back to the cruise ship. The tourists always left hundreds of clear plastic cups and Marlboro Light cigarette butts all over the beach. It was such a shame.

Luckily, the ferry boat operators only took the tourists to the western most tip of the island, leaving the rest of the sliver of land to the locals with boats and the actual inhabitants of the island who lived much farther east on Rose Island.

Bali Hai seemed to be in great spirits today as she sped along with me, Beth, Jake and my mother-in-law, Clarice, who was visiting us for a couple of weeks. If you had never trusted your life to a boat, then a boat was just a vehicle. But when you had taken a boat out far beyond the safety of the shoreline, a boat (especially an older boat) had a personality and even a spirit that you could sense as you guided her. Bali Hai was about ten years old and there were days when she was cranky and I was not sure if we'd make it back. And there were days when she just purred and I hammered the throttle for hours. This may sound strange, but you could feel the boat and almost sense its health. Well, I could anyway.

We passed the western tip of Rose Island and saw the huge ferry vomiting up a load of tourists all over the beautiful beach there, and I pressed the throttle a bit harder to get past this spot. As we headed a few minutes further east along the shoreline, we began to see dozens of small boats like ours tied up to the beach, evenly spaced, their bows faced away from the island.

Due to the number of boats there, I had just realized that we would have a tough time finding our friends.

"Do we have any idea what their boat looks like?" I asked Beth.

"They said it was white and about thirty feet long." Beth said.

That narrowed it down to about 90% of the boats on the beach. Kind of like the Metallica concert-goer who tells his pals to meet him on the main floor.

"I'll be the skinny guy with long hair wearing a black shirt." He says.

"We'll find it." Clarice said. She stood up and began looking.

My mother-in-law was in her seventies, so I slowed way down as we scanned the beach. She was trying to help, but had no idea what we were looking for. We began to look for our friends on the beach rather than the boat itself, and after just a few minutes we saw some ladies waving their hats at us. Luckily, they had spotted us.

Pulling into the beach and flipping the boat 180 degrees was a bit tricky. There were people, kids and dogs EVERYWHERE in the water. I had about thirty-five feet of space within which I had to spin our thirty-one foot boat. Luckily, there was very little wind and wave action and three guys I knew came out to assist me in anchoring and tying up.

I headed the boat toward the beach and tried to gauge how deep the water was by the nearby people standing in the water. It appeared to be about waist deep. Bali Hai drew just two feet of water with the engines trimmed up, but trimming the engines this way gave me less control over the boat and in docking situations. With so many people nearby, control was crucial.

It was tough to see everything around a boat this size with people and boats so close, so I had Beth and

Clarice watch the bow and stern as I began to rotate the boat on its axis using the two engines against each other – one engine running forward and the other running in reverse. This was something I had practiced many times in the marina so I was fairly confident, but performing in front of so many other men always made my blood pressure go up. You never wanted to be "that guy" who screwed up the whole thing. You just tried to appear confident, silently talking yourself through the whole thing, keeping calm so you didn't overdo anything, and realizing that you were really not enjoying any of it.

I gave the bowline with an anchor to my friend Aussie, who swam it offshore with his swim fins and securely anchored it in some rocks. Another friend ran the stern line to the shore and tied it to some bushes as I adjusted both engines back and forth trying to maintain our position. I thanked God that I had enough line and that those guys were there to help so I didn't have to bump into neighboring boats and apologize.

It felt like the entire beach was watching as I spun the boat into place. My forehead was sweating and my movements were quick and deliberate. I did my best to appear like I did this every day, smiling and nodding at my pals. Beth, Jake and Clarice all looked at me with wondering eyes. They wanted to know if it was OK to exit the boat and head to the beach. They would never understand just how difficult it could be to make something like that look easy. As a daddy and husband, it was my job to try to make it look easy. It wasn't. Finally, I felt the anchors were secure and the boat was in a good position between the other boats. I cut the engines, pulled them completely out of the water, and waited just a moment longer to insure we were secure.

"It's OK." I said. Beth smiled and kissed my cheek. "Bring the cooler." She said.

It was always a bit of a let-down when I had to switch from confident boat captain to obedient pack mule, but I began carrying all of our stuff to the shore. It's part of my husband role. My pals all helped out so it was quick work. They were at the "we're-kind-of buzzed-and-enthusiastic-to-help" state of drunkenness and all of them actually appeared disappointed when we were finished unloading the boat. I looked back at Bali Hai as she bounced lightly in the small waves. She was larger and nicer than most of the boats on the shore. How did I get so lucky?

At our age, outings were merely a reason to drink and eat in a different location. Everyone was in bathing suits and almost all were in the water doing the "Bahamian Bob", one hand always dry from holding a beer or plastic cup, as we stood chest-deep in the water talking to each other. The group was mostly white Bahamians and expats, but there were a lot of others there too. People of many colors managed to make and keep friends on this island. The color lines were blurry but still there.

"Jimi, this is my friend Brent... my pal George... my cousin Vince...."

The introductions were constant. I would never remember them all. I wondered if I could get one of those underwater writing pads that they use on dive trips to keep notes. Wet handshake, friendly nod, Bahamian Bob, and admire the boats as we floated together. There were so many new people here and they all seemed to know each other. I'd need a little more time to get comfortable with all of them.

On the beach, my buddy Aussie and his pal Brent were playing with a skim board (a short surf board,

178

about a half inch thick tossed sideways along the shoreline to jump on and hydroplane the thin layer of water that lies there). I had grown up skim boarding for years in Santa Cruz and grinned as they fell on their rumps again and again. They would run on the beach along the shoreline and toss the board into the shallow water, and then jump onto the board only to slip off and fall.

"Jimi, you're a surfer. What the hell is wrong with this thing?" Brent asked me as I walked up to them.

"You haven't had enough to drink." I said.

"Or too much." Aussie said. He looked down at a large red mark on the rear of his thigh where he had fallen hard. "That'll swell up nicely by tomorrow."

Aussie's confusing accent continued to intrigue me. There were so many people like this in the Caribbean. They were all travelers. With his Guinness accent having been blended with rum, Brent sported an accent that was based in either Irish or Scottish, I could not be sure, as he too had lived in the Caribbean for a long time.

"Let me see that thing." I said, reaching for the board.

Brent handed it to me and it almost slipped out of my hand.

"Well, here's your problem." I continued. "You've got no wax on the board."

Both of them looked at me like I had suggested that they put cheese on a patio.

"Guys. You've seen surfboards, right? Surf movies? Well, remember them *waxing up the boards*?" I made a circular motion on the board as I quizzed them.

"And the wax makes it more grippy! I see!" Brent said, smiling.

179

"Where do we get this wax? Will candles work?" Aussie asked.

"It might. It would be better than nothing, but board wax can probably be bought wherever you got this board." I said.

"Like to give it a go?" Brent asked me.

"Me? Noooo. It's a long haul back to Doctor's Hospital and I don't need my big ass cracking up here on this beach." I said.

They kept on me so I had to give it a try. I gave it a small toss and jumped on gently enough to get a small ride. They were impressed. I was happy to keep my body in one piece. At forty, skim boards were like num-chucks: wood designed to harm you.

I went back to where our umbrella was set up, our multi-colored umbrella that came with the boat. Our multi-colored umbrella that shouted "GLAAD to be here!" Who picked that thing? Oh yeah, the Canadian. Well, I'd have to give him some grief for his color choice, but I'd have to compliment him on his open-mindedness and confidence in his masculinity.

Beth had set up our small lunch and was enjoying a Kalik beer.

"Want some food, baby?" She asked.

Since arriving here, I'd probably put on thirty pounds. Sure, why not. I already felt like a beached whale in my swimsuit, but if I drank enough I'll get comfortable in my own skin again. What a vicious circle.

Beth had brought along some meats, cheeses, hot dogs, nuts, fruit, muffins, etc. Lots of snacks to be had! Bahamians swore by Kentucky Fried Chicken and most just brought two cases of beer, a bottle or two of champagne, and a huge bucket of KFC. There were

180

lots of chicken bones on the bottom of the ocean alone the shore of Rose Island.

"KFC never tasted better." Aussie said as he tore in to a leg.

"Have some." His wife, Jenny said to me.

I grabbed a piece and took a bite. They were right. The KFC tasted different out here. I likened it to how a cold Coke tasted after doing yard work in the hot sun for three hours. If you waited long enough, anything tasted pretty good.

Jenny was Australian and was from Perth. Aussie had met her while in Australia and brought her back to Nassau. Their two boys were both born on the island. The older one was Jake's classmate, and he had apparently introduced Jake to a big gang of boys here on Rose Island. The boys were now taking turns leaping off the bow of a large white boat. A huge, hairy man was shouting encouragement as the boys stepped over the edge of the bow and dropped into the water.

"C'mon lad. It's OK, mate. It's not as far as it looks. Give it a go!" He was saying. The huge man was Bahamian Bobbing with a beer in his huge hand that looked like a shot glass in a baseball mitt. He looked friendly enough so I waded out into the sea, dry hand holding my Kalik, other hand offering him a cold one.

"Awwww, thanks, mate." He said as he downed the last of his other seemingly miniature beer. Man, this guy was big. Without insulting him, I'd say that his accent most closely resembled Shrek, but was a lot thicker and more difficult to understand.

"No worries." I said and extended my hand. "I'm Jimi."

"Larry." He said, shaking my hand.

"Giving my son diving lessons, I see." I said, looking up at Jake as he pondered jumping off the boat.

"He's a great lad." Larry said. "A bit cautious of jumping, though."

"This is all new to him." I explained. "Go ahead, Jake." I yelled up to him. "I'll be right here for you." Jake had his little life vest on and looked down at me.

Come on, son. You can do it. He stepped off the boat slowly and finally let go, dropping into the water. I let him bob underwater a bit and then reached out to him. He swam up to me.

"I did it, Daddy!" He shouted.

Yes you did, I thought to myself, but just nodded at him the way guys do. I hugged him, gave him a swat on the butt and let him paddle ashore where the kids were lining up to take another turn jumping off the boat. Jake made me proud of him about 100 times every day. To me, he was the perfect child. Even his shortcomings (which were few) were endearing to me, probably because he got them from me. We worked on correcting them together.

My Kalik was finally kicking in and I felt chatty, so I began talking to Larry about boats. The white boat the kids were jumping off of was his. It was a nice cabin-cruiser type boat as opposed to the open bow style of Bali Hai, but about the same length. I told him that I had no place to keep the trailer and that the yacht club master over at Lyford Caye was anxious for me to get it out of his storage area. He mentioned that he might be interested in buying the trailer. I never planned on taking Bali Hai out of the water and could not pull her with our little CR-V anyway. We made a deal to meet and take a look at the trailer together. He offered in the deal that if I ever needed to use the trailer that he'd let me use one of his trucks to pull her out. I smiled. This guy was thoughtful and kind.

We packed up to leave around 4 PM as the wind shifted and the mosquitoes that lived on Rose Island began to make their presence felt. Clarice couldn't swim and needed help getting back into the boat. I made a mental note to ask her about this situation. Who grew up in California on the coast and never learned how to swim?

The wind shift had caused the waves to pick up just enough for the boat to move up and down, making boarding on the swim ladder dangerous for a seventy-year-old woman. Larry, Aussie, Brent and I all assisted her as she climbed aboard. At one point, Larry had to just put his huge hand on her rear end to help her get in. Larry and I just grinned a bit at each other. It had to be done. And Clarice got a mild thrill.

* * * * *

Larry and I made an arrangement to meet at the storage area to look at the trailer, so I got the harbor master to come out and unlock the gate for us. Larry looked at the trailer for about five minutes before agreeing to buy it from me.

"How much do you need, mate?" He asked.

I had not given this any thought. I had no idea how much a used boat trailer was worth. It needed new leaf springs, the crank jack did not work properly, the four tires needed replacing, and there was some rust.

"Man, I don't know. Whatever is fair." I said. I'd gotten such a good deal that I could afford to be cavalier and I wanted to make a good impression on my new friend.

"How about a thousand?" He asked.

183

"Sounds fine." I said.

I really did not care what he offered and I was thinking more like $500, but I generally short-change myself in situations like this so his offer was most likely right. He made arrangements to pick it up with the harbor master and said he had to speed off to a job.

I drove home, relieved that the trailer was off of my hands. I did not even know I owned it until the Canadian had reminded me in one of his emails long after I'd bought Bali Hai. So now, I was only $12,000 into my boat after paying $13,000 to the Canadian and selling the trailer for $1,000. The boat was worth around $30,000, so this would officially be the only time anyone in the world made money on a boat purchase. I made a note to call the people at Guinness, the book not the beer.

That was how I met Larry and we became fast friends. He later invited us to a barbeque at his house and our wives got along very well. Our sons were the same age and played together like old pals. It all just felt like a really good fit. We began going to dinner together and Larry introduced us to everyone everywhere we went. It seemed they knew a lot of people on the island. Getting plugged in like this was similar to being accepted by the cool kids at school.

It was not long that Larry and his wife approached me and offered me a job, or at least a look at a job. They wanted to see if I wanted a position with their company so I'd really not be officially working. They knew I was looking for work at Club Caribe, and said that they could hire me until I got a position at the new resort project. If I was hired, it paid only $200.00 per day (tax free), but it could be something, a foot in the door on the island, and it would make me feel good to be working again. They were offering me a "look" at a possible job, not a job just yet. It was something. I gladly accepted. Finally, a way to get started working here. I could not believe my luck. I was eager to begin.

* * * * *

It was odd to me that Bahamians kept such pitched roofs. There was no snow so I wondered why were their roofs so steep? LARRY began to point out different jobs he had done as we drove by them in his truck on my first day at work. They used rolled metal and fabricated it into long, flat pieces that they repeated again and again to cover the roof. Being from California, I was only able to stand the heat and humidity on the island when I was in our pool; I realized that I would probably turn into a puddle of Jimi on one of these hot tin roofs. I would have to get used to it somehow.

"Wear trainers." Larry said. "Trainers allow you to feel the changes in the roof. Boots have hard bottoms. You can't feel shite! Trainers bend and you can feel the roof as you walk. Trust me on this, mate."

The first thing I had to do was look up what a "trainer" was. Turns out it was a tennis shoe, as we called them back home. At least people my age called them tennis shoes, whether you played tennis in them or not. One of my old pals back in California originally from the east coast called them "sneakers", but then again he also called a pizza a "pie." As the world becomes smaller, perhaps we would all agree on a term for shoes that you wore in a gym when exercising, but for now I'd have to call them "trainers".

British people called "boots" what we called "cleats". I learned this at one of Jake's soccer games when a man complimented me on my son's "boots". I

185

had a lot to learn about shoes in general in my adopted home. It was, after all, once a part of Britain. English here sounded very little like what we Americans spoke. I wished we could all just get along and wear flip-flops... or thongs, sandals, slippers... whatever!

Larry was climbing up the ladder part of a scaffolding to the top of a new market, and I assumed I was to follow him. The roof was about fifteen feet above the ground. Larry never gave me actual instructions so I just followed him, hoping to figure out this new job along the way. Larry went up the scaffolding very quickly, which surprised me. He was a really big man and couple years older than I was, but he moved quickly in everything he did and when at work he appeared much younger than his actual age.

Once on top of the roof of that old market, I had that "I belonged" feeling again. I had shopped at this store for many years. Beth and I shopped here the first time when we honeymooned in Cable Beach back in 1995. To be standing on top of this roof now with my new employer, grounded me in a way I couldn't really describe, but it felt like I'd just passed a mile marker. A major change in my life that felt good. It somehow validated this nutty move we had made and made it seem like it might stop feeling like a dream sometime soon.

Larry had two employees on top of the roof that were busily making some changes to the facade and the decorative edge. It seemed that everything they did involve cutting, bending, and applying rolled metal to the roof and their hands showed it. They did not wear gloves and they did not have proper tools for their work. They were working men similar to the Mexican guys I worked with back home at my father's commercial pipe-fitting company. They were clever and did the best they could with what they had, but they really were just jobsite-trained laborers with little skill or knowledge about the job as a big picture. Larry guided them in almost everything they did.

Larry did not introduce me to the guys there, nor did he speak to me about anything. I just stood there and tried to look important. Being white and obviously foreign, I'm sure the guys on the roof wondered who I was and what I was doing with Larry, but he let all of them wonder. At one point, Larry mentioned that he needed something.

"I've got some better cutters in my truck." He told one of the guys.

I saw this as an opportunity.

"I'll go get them." I said.

"Good. They're in the right side box." He said.

I climbed down the ladder and already began sweating. It was typically warm and sticky out, and the most exercise I had gotten lately had been at the air-conditioned gym I was a member of, so actually "doing something" made my body react in a way that I did not like. I was out of shape.

I got to the truck and opened up the box he spoke of to find a complete mess of tools and materials, all of which looked completely foreign to me. I fished around and found three different sheet metal hand cutters, and I decided to just bring them all so I would not have to keep going back and forth. When I got to the ladder one of the guys was looking down at me.

"Toss it up." He said.

Having worked as a commercial fire sprinkler pipe fitter for years with my father, I was skilled at tossing things upwards to my father on the scissor lift.

"Which one do you want?" I asked and showed him the three I had brought.

187

"Da one wit da yellow handle, mon." He said.

I put the tool in my right hand and flattened out my fingers, palm up. I gave the tool a very flat toss so that it almost hovered right in front of the man's face as he reached out to grab it.

"Good trow!" He said.

I made a check mark smile in my mind. Some things you never forgot. I then climbed back up the scaffolding only to have Larry meet me at the top and say that we needed to leave. Back down the scaffolding, sweating and feeling parts of my body that I'd forgotten I had. We headed for his truck.

"We've got a sales call to make." He said.

Now this is something I could do well. I had worked in sales for years and was sure I could apply some charm here. I looked forward to meeting the prospective client.

We drove east to a neighborhood I never had a reason to visit and stopped at a vacant lot at the end of a court that backed to the sea. Larry spoke to a Bahamian man for a few minutes, while I walked around a bit, looking at the site. Shortly thereafter a man and woman in their forties pulled up in a Mercedes and approached us.

"Good morning." Larry said.

These must be the customers, I thought.

"Good morning." The man grinned through tightly clenched teeth holding a cigarette. He wore aviator shades and a ball cap that read NY on the front. He was about forty and reeked of East Coast US cockiness. His wife took her time getting out of the car. She was about a hundred pounds overweight, wore long black hair and was dressed for the beach. I wish they all could be California girls.

188

Larry introduced me, but did not say why I was there to any of us, so I just stood there trying to look official while he explained the different types of roofing products he offered, the costs involved, and the time it took to install each to the couple. He gave them some color brochures and a card and after about twenty minutes, we left. I thought to myself, "I could do that."

"They break ground soon." Larry said. "This is the type of thing I need help with, estimating jobs, reading plans, and meeting with clients."

"I've done this type of work before." I said. "From my construction background, I can read plans and I did a lot of sales, estimating and bidding for my father, too."

"I also need help running crews. Making sure they get on site on time, have the tools and materials they need, and understand what they have to do that day." Larry explained.

"Well, I ran jobs for years. I was a journeyman pipefitter and a job foreman. I've run a lot of crews and done some big projects." I said, and now I realized that although I had thought I was already employed that I was apparently still applying for the job, which was only now actually being explained to me. Still, it sounded like something I could do. I did have a lot of jobsite experience and was a foreman at a very young age. I really could handle this quite easily.

Larry had about five different trucks. One had a crane for loading the heavy spools of rolled metal and other materials, another had a dump bed and others were just full-size Dodge and Ford work trucks. He took me to his storage yard, which was really just about a half-acre of flat land that was fenced in by ten-foot high chain link fence. There were several large metal shipping containers, about ten feet high by forty feet long, that he kept his materials and tools in, an old boat

189

on a trailer, a derelict Jeep Wrangler, and some other junk lying here and there. He gave me the keys to an older Dodge pickup.

"Here, you can use this truck." He said. Now this was a surprise. I did not know I'd be getting a company vehicle without being hired.

He tossed me the keys.

"OK, thanks." I said.

"Meet me here at the yard tomorrow at 7 AM." He said.

I knew what time we started work. Now we were getting somewhere. Asking what time we stopped work seemed a bit petty at this moment, so I did not ask. If it was anything like I suspected, quitting time would vary depending on how the job was going. This was not something I liked, but it was how things went in construction.

I drove home to our condo from the yard and was elated. This was certainly not the job I'd imagined I'd be doing here and I knew very little about roofing, but I had a possible job and a company truck. Soon, perhaps I would be earning money here in the Bahamas and I'd get a work permit. This made me begin to disconnect with the USA. It felt kind of like when you first moved out of your parent's home. You feel lonely for them and scared to death that you wouldn't be able to pay your rent and feed yourself, but at the same time the sense of pride and independence was unmatched. My own independence was beginning to make me feel like I was "home", instead of just visiting.

The dreamer was beginning to stir and awaken. I began to get a sense of permanency and realized that if this worked out, I'd become one of those expats that we met all the time. I would no longer just be the glorified tourist. I was actually on my way to becoming Bahamian in some way.

CHAPTER FOURTEEN
The High and Lows of Working on Rooftops

The next day at work I went to the yard, but Larry was nowhere to be found. I called him on my cell and he said to meet him at his house as we had a job to go and bid. I was a little miffed that he changed our meeting place and forgot to tell me, but I realized that this was going to be part of working for someone else. It had been a long time since I had depended on anyone to tell me what to do during the workday and it was going to take some getting used to.

Driving in the early morning traffic, which was substantial, felt good for some reason. I guess that since I had been a beach bum for a while now that it really felt surprisingly good to have an actual purpose in life instead of just leisure and personal pursuits. I now understood why most retired people began working again. They became bored. Americans have always been industrious people. We were more like worker-bees than butterflies, and we felt best when completing a task of some kind. We loved to relax and have fun, but it felt better to do so once we had earned the right to do so.

Larry and I drove downtown together in his truck. We were headed for a job at the cruise ship terminal in the heart of the tourist area.

"Did you get that paperwork together for me to fill out for my work permit? I'd like to get that started

192

ASAP." I asked Larry as we bounced along the small Bahamian road in his Ford F-250.

"She's putting it together for you. We've got a temporary one done already." He said.

"She" was his wife. He often referred to her as "she", "her", or "the lady."

"So, I'll be OK to work soon?" I asked.

"For the time being you're fine. You're not working. No worries, mate." He nodded at me as he watched the traffic and skillfully navigated the road in his huge truck.

I wondered if he was telling me the whole truth. I wondered if what he meant was that we needed to feel this relationship out a bit more before he felt the need to actually apply and pay for my work permit. These permits were very difficult to get and cost about $30,000.00 so I understood his hesitation, but realized that I was working in a very gray area for now. If questioned, we would just have to work it out and tell (whomever) that I was simply observing him in some capacity, not actually working. That might sound like BS but it was true. A few names dropped and possibly a few hundred bucks, and this explanation would surely suffice. But, I still worried constantly about being deported for working without a permit. I put it out of my mind telling myself that many people did this, which was true, but I would feel much better once my paperwork was legitimate. In typical over-do-it fashion, here I was trying to get a work permit before I had a job. I remembered Mr. Canada and shivered. I'd rather be too cautious when it came to working in the Bahamas than face deportation and banishment from the island.

* * * * *

The Canadians had been deported this way. That day, when Mr. Canada called to ask me if I wanted to buy Bali-Hai was because they had been deported. He said that the police came to their condo and told them they had ten minutes to pack some personal things and that they were going to be out-processed immediately. They were taken to the local jail (a very nasty place I've described before, but imagine having your blonde wife and two young sons, one seven and one five, in there with you...not good.) After a few hours in jail, they were taken to the airport and told to book the first flight out of the country, to anywhere. Luckily, they found a direct flight to Canada that cost them a fortune to book as it was literally a last minute ticket, but they made it home. He'd given me the details of their story later in an email. That scenario played out in the back of my mind constantly as I worked for Larry. The Canadians were not only told to leave, they were banished for good. This might be a "bummer" for them, but I owned property here. We had a condo that we paid cash for, now we had a boat and a car, and we had lots of personal items to include in a house full of new furniture and electronics. It would be very difficult on me to be banished from the island.

We missed the Canadians, but their misfortune and hurry to leave had gotten me a beautiful boat for $13,000.00 which was an unbelievable price for such a beauty. It was all he wanted and all I could take out of savings at the time. I figured that Mr. Canada took that low sum as he was worried his boss might come try to repossess the boat. This was a small detail Mr. Canada told me after we had agreed on our deal. He had not been properly paid, so he sold the boat to me and his SUV to a friend from work. However, the boss wanted both the boat and the SUV back. Quick paperwork and hiding the boat for a few weeks kept the boss' temper from doing something he'd regret. Mr. Canada told me the boss had threatened some awful things if he did not get the boat back but I took that chance. She was legally mine and after a while the threat faded. We did not take Bali Hai out for a maiden voyage until all of this nonsense was behind us. But there is no standard waiting period for nutty people to relax so I made sure I was not alone and had some sort of weapon on board the first five or six times we were on Bali Hai.

* * * * * *

Larry parked his truck in the parking lot where Beth and I had once had a huge argument after leaving our attorney's downtown office one day when we were still mired in escrow hell. I shot a mean glance up towards their building. I still owed them some kind of payback for how utterly useless yet expensive that attorney was, but God was surely watching me and I suddenly felt guilty for even thinking of revenge. What a tightrope I walked as a Christian man. Now I got to feel guilty for some attorney screwing me over and me wanting a pound of flesh.

As we rounded the corner and walked in front of the stately British Colonial Hotel, the throngs of tourists began to crowd the sidewalk and the roads became jammed with the many buses, taxis, and delivery trucks that rule the roads at this hour of the day. The energy in the air was electrified with the bustling commerce and the excited visitors.

I felt a huge sense of belonging, knowing that I had walked these streets for many years as a visitor and had felt the exact things that these people felt. They were enjoying the wonder of a new place, the thrill of discovering future favorite things, the balmy climate, and the friendly locals. It all felt like a distant memory to me now as we quickly strode, navigating our way through all of the swim-suited merriment dressed in our jeans and work-shirts. We surely stuck out but in a very good way. We belonged here. "Almost" working here gave me such a rush of status that I felt my back straighten, my gaze focused narrowly on our destination and my step was deliberate as I politely made my way past these mortals. Superman was on his way to some place very important. Please…step aside.

I had many of these unforgettable "moments" when we lived on the island. This moment ranks in the top five.

After going through some pretty heavy post-9/11 security, we were inside the huge cruise ship terminal and it seemed like one big party. There were small shops everywhere selling everything from scooter rentals to jewelry, clothing, excursions and trips, daiquiris, and everything a tourist would need.

There were people everywhere and it was difficult to keep up with Larry as he rammed his way forward. The wave of people parted in front of the big man, allowing me to cruise along behind him like a remora to feed off the droppings of the predator shark above. At another security check, we told the man we needed to get out onto the actual ship dock area and had to surrender our driver's licenses.

"This one not local." The officer said.

Uh-oh.

"His local not processed yet, mon. He stay wit me. No worries." Larry said in his adopted island-speak that told the officer he was local and could be trusted.

"I keep the licenses." He said.

"No worries, mon." Larry said. "We be back in turdy minutes."

Now we walked alongside the behemoth cruise ships toward our destination. Prince Charles Wharf could dock up to five of these horizontal high-rises at a time and often did. To me, they always looked like tall, white hotels that had decided to lie down for a while. The hum of their engines made the dock vibrate as we walked. We entered a building, went up some stairs and began looking at a vacant tourist area on the second floor.

"The government is transforming this whole area." Larry said. "They need to expand and upgrade the whole building to fit more tourists."

"That was pretty crowded down there." I said.

"That was nothing." He said.

* * * * *

And I kind of expected him to say that. Why is it that people always downplay the present to a newcomer in order to somehow magnify the past? When I used to surf in Santa Cruz, California (where I grew up), I'd paddle out on my board and see someone I knew floating on his board, eyes fixated on the horizon watching for the next set of waves to roll in.

"How's it breaking today?" I would ask.

"Been alright, but you should have been here *yesterday*." He would always say.

And even if I said, "But I *was* here yesterday. Actually, I was here with you."

He'd then say, "Oh no, I meant the day before."

"Yeah, you must have."

It's that way with everything.

You can go to the Super Bowl with ninety-five thousand other people, not a seat to spare in the largest dome in the world and even have the Jumbo-Tron screen reading:

"LARGEST ATTENDENCE IN HISTORY!"
"90,326 FANS IN ATTENDANCE HERE TODAY!"
"NOT JUST HERE, BUT ANYWHERE!"
"SERIOUSLY, THIS A FRIGGING RECORD!"

And some dumb fan will surely say, "Ohhh, this is *nothing*. Last year it was *really* crowded!" It never fails.

* * * * *

"Larry, it was shoulder to shoulder back there. How could it get any more crowded unless people head surf?" I asked. He kind of ignored me. Good thing. I did not want to have to explain what "head surfing" was anyway.

"You should see this place in the high season." He said. "*Pandemonium*. Right, now this area here is all going to change so we need to measure it and put together a bid for a whole new roof."

He handed me the "dumb end" of his tape and told me to stand still, while he walked away, measuring walls, taking notes and making calculations. He never really explained anything to me and I felt a bit childish. Was I supposed to keep asking him or would he eventually just tell me what he was doing? I wondered how I was going to be able to do this on my own.

Back in the truck, Larry handed me some paperwork to read while we headed back to his house. I studied some crude sketches of a rooftop and attempted to take in everything I saw.

198

"I need you to take your truck and my big ladder to an old friend's house. You'll need to get on top of their house, survey the existing roof and take new measurements for materials." He said.

The whole thing sounded pretty simple. Finally, I would be given a chance to prove myself on a real job. I was finally getting a tryout.

CHAPTER FIFTEEN
Tickle Berry Don't Make You Laugh, Mon

As I drove very slowly through some of the smallest streets I'd ever seen, narrowly missing the parked cars along the road, I peered at each house for the address Larry had given me. The roads were so narrow in some places that I was sure I'd knock mirrors with some of the parked cars on this street. Every minute or so another car would come up behind me, or ahead of me, and I'd have to find a place to pull into so they could get by. I wished Larry had given me a smaller truck or I'd brought my Honda Cr-V. Driving this big vehicle was making me sweat so badly that I was almost slipping around on the bench seat.

According to a surrey driver I'd met once, the reason there were signs on the roads here that said things like "Dual Carriageway" was because the roads were originally built for "carriages", not Dodge Ram 2500 trucks. Most of the property lines were drawn and the buildings were put up back before larger vehicles used the roadways. Most of the out islands in the Bahamas were either dirt and sand roads, and most of the roads on New Providence (where most Bahamians actually live) were tiny, paved roads with potholes everywhere. Driving on the island could be quite dangerous.

Add to all of the above, the fact that they drove on the other side of the road, seemingly allowed drinking while driving, there was always a general lack of police presence on the roads. Add that to the fact that every young Bahamian man drove a motorcycle, pulling wheelies at sixty miles per hour everywhere he went, or an oversized SUV, or a very fast imported tuner car. It all added up to absolute mayhem on the roads.

No wonder Beth preferred to have me drive.

I looked down at the sheet Larry had given me and frowned. Who the heck names their house "Tickle Berry"? I wondered if the English understood just how silly some of their words sounded to Americans?

The tradition of named houses instead of actual numbered addresses was one of those charming little things that I had loved about the Bahamas as a tourist. As a workman trying to find a jobsite, it maddened me. I'm sure it was cute to have a named house when there were 500 people living here, but now that there were over 200,000, not only was it not cute but apparently all of the good names had been taken.

Tickle Berry? Please.

Larry's directions were typical for a local. Locals always forgot that you had no point of reference, so when they told you that a place was easy to find and they used reference points that meant nothing to you, it was easy to get lost.

"Let's see....." I said aloud to myself. This was something I often did when I was particularly nervous and needed encouragement.

"He said left at the old red house, then three blocks to the tingum tree (whatever that is), then stop, get out of the truck, spin three times, then down another block to the pork store, a sharp left at the Amended First Baptist Church of the Newly Rediscovered Faith of the Recently Re-Converted. (Many Bahamian churches had very long names and apparently, this church had a few locations, so I was not to confuse it with the original one but to look for the *Amended* First Baptist Church of the... oh man was I lost.)

Time was ticking by and I needed to get this job done and meet Larry back at his place to go to another job. I hated auditioning but it was necessary. I sweated and my heart began to speed up. I calmed myself and looked at the directions again as an older man walked by, probably sensing my distress.

"Can I help you, brother?" He asked. He was about sixty-five, thin, gray, and wearing an orangish suit complete with a fedora.

At home, he would be a pimp. Here he was just a man on his way to church on a Thursday. People here went to church a lot. He was extremely clean and smelled of nice cologne with not a drop of sweat on his face. It was 236 degrees outside. He was wearing wool and walking in direct sunlight so intense that in an apparent suicide a cat walked right up to a dog with a sign that read, "Screw it, I give up."

Even in this heat, the man seemed to feel as comfortable as I felt sweaty, nervous, and confused.

"Actually, I'm lost." I said.

"You can't be lost unless you don't know where you are or where you're going." The man said.

So odd he was not sweating. I panted similarly to the dog nearby who had thrown the cat over his shoulder like a coat and was trotting away.

"Do you know either of these things, young man?" He asked, smiling a bit. "I'm sure I can guide you. I've lived here forever."

He seemed nice enough and I surely needed his help, but his fortune cookie wisdom was really irking me right now. I wanted to ask him if that suit came in lavender, but thought better of it and did not want to be rude just because I was overheated and frustrated. And why ask a stupid question? If it came in orange, it probably came in lavender.

"I'm going to the Tickle Berry house. It's supposed to be on this street but…." I began to explain but he cut me off, gently waving a large black Bible in his hand.

"Tickle Berry is just up here on the right. It's the house with the red flowers in front. You have to walk to the left side and get the maid as the folks ain't home right now. Just follow the music." He said.

I sat in my truck and just stared. *"Follow the music"*? Did he really just give me directions that included *"follow the music"*? I smiled and suddenly remembered why I moved here.

"Thank you, sir." I said. "Thank you very much."

"All the best." He said as he waved and walked away.

"All the best to you, sir." I said and watched him walk away.

I looked outside of the truck cab toward the sky and said, "Thank you for sending that angel my way, Lord…even if he was dressed like a fig newton.

Parking my big work truck was no easy feat and as I looked at Tickle Berry, I realized why Larry told me to bring the big ladder. The old Colonial house was about forty feet tall. What an odd height.

I walked past the red flowers and went around to the left when I began to hear old Bahamian gospel music. I called out politely to announce myself and to keep from frightening the maid when I heard a voice call back.

"In here." The female voice said.

I walked further along the side of the house through very lush and mature greenery on both sides, bees were buzzing in the sun as they serviced their flower route. I found an open door, which was the source of the music.

I had finally found the place.

"I'm here to look at the roof, ma'am." I said to the old Bahamian lady that was sitting at a table breaking string beans into a bowl. She wore black cat-eye glasses with a diamond neck chain and a flowered white housedress. Her skin was the color of dark chocolate and her hair was white as snow. With her sweet voice and demeanor, she reminded me of an exquisite desert of some kind.

"Mmmm-hmmm." She said and nodded. "Man said you'd be 'roun."

"OK, I'll just get started then." I said. "Thank you, ma'am."

"Mmmm-hmmm. You be careful." She said.

"I will, thank you, ma'am." I said and almost bowed as I left. Something about these people made your manners better. It was the lack of sarcasm, the gentility, and the sincerity. There was no pretense or over-thought. It was just people going about their lives, not hurting each other, and enjoying themselves. I loved them. I felt so comforted by them

It was good to be there, right there at that moment. Another golden moment, filed away to use for a smile someday.

I untied the huge extension ladder from the roof racks of the truck and carried it to the side of the house where I would look for a good place to climb. The ladder was really heavy and it dug into my shoulder and neck muscles as I carried it from the truck to the house. Although I'd carried ladders like this for years as a pipe fitter, this one seemed much heavier and clumsier. It seemed that ladders had changed a lot in the years since I'd worked in the trades, and apparently not for the better!

Maneuvering the ladder on the side of the house was very difficult as I tried to avoid damaging any of the beautiful foliage that surrounded the house. My small tool belt needed to be adjusted as my tools were pulling it down along with my jeans. I must have really looked professional at that moment struggling with the ladder, sweating like I'd just gotten out of a sauna, and having my pants slip below my hips. Every move felt uncomfortable and foreign. I'd been out of the trades for too long.

Although the house was in a neighborhood of similar homes, it was set back from the road and had some distance from its' side neighbors, so the plants that insulated it made it feel like a home in the bush that had been here for centuries. The walls looked like stone, but had to be some kind of brick with a layer of lath of some kind of concrete over the exterior. The whole place just looked and felt like a mini-castle in a mini-jungle.

Once I finally secured the ladder, I said a quick prayer before ascending the thing. It was one thing to climb a forty-foot ladder that had been tied off at the top and has someone securing the bottom. It was a very different thing to climb a forty-foot ladder that was leaning on a smooth-walled building with nothing but earth holding the bottom. I went up very slowly and cautiously, each tremor of the ladder knocking against itself only added to my discomfort. This was one of those things you're not supposed to do alone, but here I was. I thanked God for the nice woman below who could at least get help for me if I fell and broke myself on the ground.

Once at the top, I had to swing my legs over to get on top of the roof and this caused the ladder to slide to the right about fifteen feet, thankfully stopping on a tree branch. That ladder could have caused some real trouble, not to mention I'd be stuck up here without it to get back down. Before addressing the roof, I made a makeshift hook using my belt and a hammer to reach the ladder and pulled it back up. I secured the ladder with my belt to a large electrical conduit pipe and began assessing the roof. Surprisingly, the sketch Larry had given me and his notes helped a lot, so measuring the area was simple. I even took some photos and movies with my small digital camera to further explain anything my rookie eyes missed.

As I carried the ladder back to the truck, I called out the thank the maid and she said something that I missed as I was too far away and the ladder was clanking. My cell phone began to ring and I hurried to the truck, but missed the call. I really wished I could have heard what the lady had said to me as I left, but I'd missed it and had to go. Was it some piece of wisdom that would alter my life, some nicety that would better my day, or just a gracious farewell? Older Bahamians like her were one of the better things in life and when you got to be in their presence, it was best to relish the moment so I was sad I'd missed our last one.

After tying the ladder down, I looked to see if it was Larry who had called. I frowned and called him back.

"Hey Larry, I just finished with the roof here at Tickle Berry." I said into my phone.

"Right. Then what's lactation?" He asked.

"Excuse me?" I said.

"Your lactation, exactly. What is it, Jim?" He said slowly.

JAMES P. RENO III

"I don't follow you." I asked as I wiped sweat from my eyes and forehead. "Sorry, Larry. What do you need?"

We had a bad connection and a clash of accents.

"*Where are you*?" He asked impatiently.

"Oh…my LOCATION?" I said.

Why didn't he just say that in the first place?

"Yes!" He shouted.

"I'm just outside the Tickle Berry house."

"OK, when can you eat Shopping Bob?" He asked.

Jeez. I was having a terrible time understanding Larry on the phone. It was tough in person with his Shrek the Ogre accent, but on the phone, it was nearly impossible. I paused to try to think what he meant. I did not want to insult him.

"Jim!" He said loudly. "When can you eat Shopping Bob?"

"How about I just meet you at the shop?" I asked.

"That's what I've been saying all along, mate!"

"Sorry, Larry. We just have a bad connection. I'll see you there."

"Right then. And don't forget to butter your llama." He grunted and hung up.

"OK." I said and hung up, trying to figure that last one out.

CHAPTER SIXTEEN
No See Ums

It was one of those still, balmy evenings when the mosquitoes, sand flies, and "no-see-ums" usually crept up to our patio from the beach to dine on our body fluids. No-see-um was a local name for little mosquito-like flying bugs that were so small that you could not see them. They would eat you alive if you sat in the early evening in June, just after a rain with no breeze. And you would itch for days from their bites.

Usually, all it took was a gentle breeze to keep their little wings from carrying them to the human smorgasbord that was our patio and pool area. There was no breeze tonight and yet for some reason they were not present. Perhaps they were all taking the bar exam hoping to become full blown barristers.

Our Aussie friends had stopped by for a quick drink and to drop off their kids. We had agreed to babysit so they could go to an adult function of some kind. They had a great SLR Nikon camera and wanted us to take some photos of them in their prom regalia. Jenny was so dressed up that she looked completely foreign to me here in the land of flip flops and sunburns. Her black gown and spiky heels cried out for a more sophisticated island than New Providence. Manhattan perhaps? Dressed in our usual beach wear, standing next to the new glam couple, I immediately felt like I'd just shown up at a nice restaurant, but had to borrow a jacket from the smirking maître d. I began to snap some photos of

208

the attractive couple as we stood and talked inside our condo.

Jenny's husband always looked like the Crocodile Hunter to me with his requisite khaki cargo shorts, safari shirt, and thick wool socks popping out over the tops of his brown leather hiking boots. Tonight he just looked sweaty and uncomfortable in his black tuxedo. He looked like a Popsicle that was quickly melting inside a cashmere glove.

"So, Jimi... how does my man look tonight all cleaned up?" Jenny asked me, her face beaming.

"Better you than me, pal." I ribbed him a bit as the ladies talked to each other heading for our kitchen.

He grunted and frowned. When I saw him wearing that much clothing in the balmy Caribbean evening weather, I was sure it must have been punishment for some earlier crime. I cringed when I thought of the stuffy adult-party he was in for. Having to remember all those people you saw once a year, pretending to remember their names, and pretending you gave a damn about seeing them again tonight. Having to say "hello" to people he did not know or worse, did not like. All of them acting sophisticated and cool when all they really wanted to do was to burn their costumes, and watch cable, hugged up together in their jammies on the couch. I was comfy and smiling in my daily island uniform of shorts, tank top and bare feet.

Aussie tugged at his neck and sweated through his shirt. His pained expression made me feel sorry for him. I imagined him begging me to go with them.

"If you will go with us, I'll pay for a four-star dinner." Aussie said to me with a pained expression. A maître d suddenly appeared from nowhere and handed me a black jacket.

I gave the jacket back to the maître d and smirked back at him. *No thanks, Pierre. I'll keep my shorts and flip-flops.* I liked to eat, but I'd do almost anything to avoid a black-tie event.

"Now, you're sure you want to do this?" Jenny asked. Her Australian accent was sweet, but I knew that if I had to hear it every day I'd shove knitting needles into my ears.

Most accents that originated outside California annoyed me. Accents could be interesting for a short while. But after a few hours, they repelled me like a gas station bathroom. Truthfully, even an overdone California accent bothered me. For long term speech, I'm more comfortable when everyone speaks like the robots of no particular region that read the nightly news. Their practiced numb-speak narcotically comforts me as they smile through the telling of the disaster of the day, and then segued to which Hollywood star was divorcing who for who.

"I'm Tom Blankman, and that's the news."

Good night, Tom. Keep that golden voice, and that cellophane accent.

There is surely something wrong with me. But it's comfortable here. I think I'll stay.

I continually tried to assure Jenny that we'd be OK with the boys. Aussie typically had no worries about his boys. He had raised them tough and knew they would be fine. Everyone knows that Australians were hardy people. You could feed those kids sawdust and pond water, and they would still flourish.

"Don't worry guys, we'll be fine." I said.

Jenny knew that her children were lovable little monsters, and they were. I had coached the older boy who was Jake's age on the first grade soccer team at their elementary school. At a game one day, the boy devoured an entire bag of chocolate chip cookies before the starting whistle. He ran a lot faster than the other kids and scored six goals before the other team scored one. Just as I was about to add chocolate chip cookies to my pre-game ritual, I saw two kids fighting near the far edge of the field. Aussie's boy and one of the Bahamian girls on the team were going at it like two cats in a burlap bag. As I ran to the other side of the field to break up the fight, I saw Aussie's boy banging the little girls head onto the grassy field repeatedly as he pinned her to the ground sitting on her chest.

No more cookies for that kid.

The younger boy was about four and only repeated the same question again and again:

"You got any food? You got any food? You got any food?" He'd say this to Beth repeatedly.

Jenny fed them like Canadian lumberjacks, but still the little one asked for more. Maybe he had a tape worm. More like a tape *snake*.

The boys were rambunctious and definitely energized, but she did not know that they put on their best when they were around us and never gave us any trouble. They were good kids and just played with Jake until they ate themselves silly, threw up and passed out. For some reason the boys got along and never fought, but I kept my eyes on them, and the cookie jar.

"OK, well you have the cell number, the restaurant number, my sister's number… " She reached into her purse to find another number.

"Jenny, have a drink. Settle down. We'll be fine." I said.

"They've done this before, hon." Her husband Aussie said. "Would you stop worrying?" He had a mixed accent that I could not decipher. It was a cocktail of affects, a short highball glass, no ice, one part Irish, one part Bahamian, with a floater of Aussie.

* * * * *

He had told me that he was born in the Bahamas, but was of Irish descent so he had dual-citizenship. He'd gone to school in Ireland and had the stereotypical stories of being beaten by the nuns in Irish Catholic School, which had (of course) made him another recovering Catholic. One of his parents was Australian and he'd lived there for a while as a child and young man. He had met Jenny there in his twenties; she was a bartender and he was a bartendee. Somehow he'd convinced her to move back to the Bahamas with him. This was easy and simple when you were both in your twenties and both so damn good looking.

It was common to hear blended accents here. Many people moved here from all over the world and had spent their lives traveling, living in different countries.

We had befriended a guy named "C" who came in on a ship and stayed with a friend for a few months. C had traveled so much that his was the most blended accent we'd ever heard. His own voice sounded confused. We were never sure if it was a put-on he could not maintain, or if his accent just naturally vacillated between an English accent, some kind of island accent, and a Canadian accent.

"Where do you come from?" I asked him one day trying to conclude my wonder about his speech pattern.

"I'm originally from Calgary. I've lived all over Europe, sailed all of the seas, and seen most of the planet. I've been all over the world, man. I've become a blend. I guess I'm a different kind of citizen. I'm a resident of the planet Earth." He proclaimed.

No shit.

I talked to Mr. Texas about the new guy and asked for his opinion.

"What's with the way this guy talks? What's his story?" I asked.

"That's easy." Mr. Texas said. "He's an *asshole*."

* * * * *

Jenny tried to assure us that she trusted us, but still looked worried. I could tell that she was not concerned about her kids. She was afraid her boys would eat all of our cookies and burn down our house. Aussie was sure they would carve a path of destruction through our home, but for some reason he seemed OK with this.

"Let me get you those earrings. Come on." Beth led Jenny into our bedroom and the girls laughed about something as they left.

Aussie and I were old enough to know that there were no earrings and that this was simply fem-speak for *"I don't really have anything to tell you. But we have to do this every so often to keep the men wondering."*

We knew this but we still wanted to know what the heck they were talking about in there.

"So... when will you tell us where you're working, mate?" Aussie asked and smiled at me as I handed him another beer. He had downed the first one quickly in an attempt to cool himself from the inside out.

It was very muggy out tonight and there was little to no breeze. We chose to sit at the indoor bar instead of out on the patio. The slow-spin fan overhead made Casablanca shadows on the walls and squeaked a little. We clinked bottles and drank together. No words, no toast. We toasted the way guys do, in silence and with a nod. It's something women will never understand. Men communicate volumes of words with glances, gestures and postures. Sorry, ladies. You befuddled us with your ability to constantly talk so we had to create ways to communicate that did not require many words. Sometimes we would just sit and stare off into the distance, the silence only broken now and then by the sound of beer bottles opening and an occasional fart. But we're really in deep, deep thought and communicating the whole time.

"I was going to tell you guys once I thought the job would be more permanent. I didn't want to try something only to quit it and look like a flake." I said.

I had told my friends I almost had a job, but I would not say what I was doing. Truthfully, I was a bit embarrassed to tell them I was trying out to be a roofer. I was a professional back home and going back to manual labor was not only physically hard on my body, but it was tough on my ego. I was not in my twenties anymore.

"Well, I hate to burst your bubble, but once I saw the work truck out front I kind of figured it out. I've known your boss for years." He said grinning.

"Jeez, I guess I'm not a very good liar."

"Oh no, you're a *fine* liar!" He grinned. "But you can't keep secrets on this island, mate."

Backhanded compliments were difficult to emulate. They just appeared, hopefully, innocently, but still stung worse than any mosquito. They were more like a no-see-um. You don't notice even as they were biting you.

The boys had been playing outside and one of them made a loud noise. We both jerked our heads their direction, looking through the huge windows that faced the grassy garden area where they were playing.

Daddy reflex. Zero to 100 in an instant, everything checked out OK this time, so we went slowly back to our beers.

"I'd just hoped to have been hired on at Club Caribe by now. I wanted to be a part of the resort that is going to change this whole neighborhood, heck the whole northwest side of our island." I said referencing the multi-billion dollar resort still in the planning stages nearby. "What I'm doing now is more like working on a chain gang with a bunch of convicts."

* * * * *

Talking about roofing and convicts suddenly made me remember my step-father. He had worked as a roofer for a while when I was about seven or eight. He'd come home with a specially packed lunch that had gobs of tasty treats he did not eat that day. I did not question why he did not want the treats. I just took them and devoured them like any other selfish little kid. My mother told me he was "roofing", which sounded to me like he climbed houses for a living. Later I learned that he was actually on a work-release program, doing a few months in jail for theft of auto parts I believe.

My parents shielded me from that part of the story.

Back then, it was easy to convince me that the roofing job took days at a time, so he had to be away from home. To this day, I don't understand how he got to come and visit us at home to give me his lunches. But back then, I'd just drink the sugary sweet orange drink from a plastic bottle. The flavor was not like Orange Crush or Fanta, or anything I'd ever tasted. It was not carbonated and had an odd bittersweet taste.

I missed my step-father so much then. It felt so good to be with him when he came home for an hour or so, and gave me the treats from his lunch. I did not get to see my real father much in those days, so this man had to fill his shoes. Actually, my step-father could never fill my father's shoes. He just wore the costume for a few years.

My mother, my step-father and I sat on the grass in the front yard. I gorged myself on the treats he had brought home and he and mom talked for the little bit of time they had. I chewed the cookies, ate the chips and lapped up every last drop of that strange orange drink. Of the few memories I have of this time in my life, these are some of the sweetest even if they were artificially flavored.

* * * * *

"Roofing is an honest living, mate. It's something until you get the offer from Club Caribe." Aussie said reassuring me.

"Sounds like you've been talking to my new boss." I said. "That's how he explained it to me. He said I could get a work permit, too."

"Ahhh, the elusive work permit. Yes, you'll need one. But Club Caribe would probably pay for that." He said. "You should be careful. Everyone here talks too much." He said.

"Well please *try* not to tell anyone about this, OK." I said and we both laughed. We knew he'd try to keep it to himself, but would probably fail. He was Bahamian.

We watched the boys through the window as they played outside, and we sat at our free-standing bar. The beer had relaxed us and the wives had been absent just long enough for us to do something stupid. The boys looked like they were having fun, so we decided to join them in their soccer game. Aussie kicked off his shoes and socks, draped his jacket over the back of one of our chairs, unclipped his bow tie, and we went outside.

They boys were playing soccer on the small patch of grass just outside our place. It was only about forty feet long by twenty feet wide, and was bordered by our building and the property line fence. The sea-wall patio was to the north and a line of bushes was to the south. Some idiot had seen fit to place concrete stepping stones along a makeshift path that lined the building. They were about eighteen inches square, three inches thick, and had been placed on top of the grass instead of properly setting them in the ground. Since they had been painted white, they offered no protection from slippage when wet, and since they were not dug into the grass one had to hop from one to the other, stubbing a toe almost every time. This cheap "upgrade" reeked of the former owners and I made a mental note to remove them ASAP.

The boys were not bothered by the stepping stones or the short playing field. They were playing for the World Cup out here and ran quickly by us, shooting goals and cheering. The boys had little ball control, so I had to fish the ball out of the sea a few times after it went over the sea wall. I was now wet from the waist down and Aussie had sweated completely through his crisp white shirt. We all had sand and grass stains on our feet but we played on. The boys yelled with glee now that the two daddies were out here sharing their fun. They ganged up on us and began to beat us pretty soundly.

Within minutes, all five of us were sweaty, dirty, and I'd stubbed a toe on the stepping stone so there was some blood, too. Add the beers to it and you had a perfect Bahamian cocktail: sand, sweat, beer and blood. But we soon learned our game was not timed well.

"Aussie! Look at you now!" Jenny said as she and Beth came outside. They both looked so clean and pretty.

We were panting and wiping sweat from our foreheads. The women were glowing that pure cleanliness that men only experience when they are young and in the military. The women looked so clean and pure that I thought I saw some hummingbirds attempting to extract nectar from their ears. Was that a harp I heard in the distance?

The women did not approve, and they made this clear by wrinkling their foreheads like drawn Roman shades.

"Guess it's time to go, mate!" Aussie said to me.

Aussie freshened up in our bathroom and I gave him a fresh shirt. It wasn't a tuxedo shirt so his tie looked kind of funny, but he did not care. He washed up quickly in our sink before they left. They thanked us a tenth time before finally leaving.

"We are going to be so late!" Jenny said to her husband as they walked out of our condo, down the tiled hallway towards the main door, her heels clicking and echoing as they walked.

Beth and I watched them as they left.

"Take your time. No reason to hurry back, OK?" I said to them and they waved again.

"His hair will never dry." Beth said, making note of the humid weather.

"I know. Good thing he has very short hair." I said.

"Go change your shorts. You're a mess!" Beth said.

I hugged her and she squealed a bit but hugged me back.

We went back to watching the boys as they played together on the grass and silently wished the same wish we always wished together again. We wished we had more children. We sat on the sea wall and watched the boys play in the sticky night air. I forgot all about the mosquitos and no-see-ums on this night, and by the grace of God, tonight they forgot about us too.

CHAPTER SEVENTEEN
Black Tar And Black Nails

I was following Larry's truck in my truck as he sped through traffic. We were on our way to look at an old church and he said he had his whole crew meeting us there, so I'd finally get to meet the guys. Perhaps this would be my final tryout.

We were in the "all-business" section of the inner island where the cruise ships and daiquiri shacks were nowhere to be seen. The hotels at the edge of the island were all built of concrete and brick, and this part of the island was where those items were made and stored. As a tourist lounging in a beach chair, you would never see that the island actually was a living, working place and there were generations of families that have made their living here, one brick at a time. There was a rich history in this country going back centuries. And while most of us don't travel far beyond the beach when we visit places that advertise "sun and fun", it could be very grounding to see places like this. Truthfully, grounding or not, it was always relieving to go back to my condo on the sea at the end of each day.

We pulled into a grassy area and parked our trucks. We got out and I followed Larry toward a large church that must have been a hundred years old. It had a roof that was pitched at such a steep angle that we'd need a helicopter, some rappelling gear, or at least a good scaffolding to work this job. I had a feeling we would get none of these things. Man, it was going to be hot today. I imagined the TV news that night:

"Two Nassau workmen burst into flames today as they worked to replace the roof on a local church. Film at eleven."

Bahamians were tough people and they had long ago gotten used to making do with what they had. For this job, they would probably just use track cleats or a lot of Velcro. They'd never admit they needed more.

A group of about fifteen men surrounded Larry as we got closer to the building. They were all Bahamian, all in their twenties and thirties, and not one of them dressed properly for a roofing job. The all just wore t-shirts, jeans and trainers. Where were the overalls, the boots, the thick Ben Davis shirts that I remembered from my construction experience? These guys looked like a bunch of men that had just walked in off the street. Some of the more menacing looking ones appeared as if they'd just walked out of The Fox Hill prison on the southwest side of the island.

"This is Jim. He's with us here today." Larry nodded at me and I nodded to the men who remained expressionless.

"If Jim says something that means it came from me so treat him right." Larry said and I nodded to the men trying to look somber, but approachable. OK, this WAS a tryout.

The group of men either looked at the ground or just stared blankly at me as Larry made the introduction. Being a man was tough sometimes. Why couldn't we all just sit down for a while, have a beer or two and get to know each other? No, that would have to wait until after we had all sized each other up, poked at each

221

other with some verbal barbs for a few days, and tested each other on the job site. Who set these man-rules up, anyway? A lot of them were really stupid, so I'm guessing it was men who made them.

Larry had not said much about what I'd actually be doing for him. The whole thing had really been a guessing game for me so now I guessed I'd been given some level of authority over his crew. For now, they did not need to know I was just a stand in for Larry. The men seemed to accept this without comment, but I was sure they had an opinion.

Larry then called out for someone named "Fishy" who was apparently his senior man and the two walked toward the building together, leaving me behind. I wondered just when Larry was actually going to attempt to make me feel like I belonged here, but I decided to just follow them and try to insert myself somewhere and learn what we were doing as we went along.

The plan for today was simple: rip off the existing copper roofing material, separate the actual copper from the rest of the tar and nails, load the copper into my truck, and for me to bring the copper to the metal scrap yard to be weighed. I was to take the money to the Lady afterwards and then check back in with Larry. Larry took off and I was left with the crew. He gave me no instructions or guidance. Not knowing just how to start this project, I went to Fishy and spoke with him.

"So, where are our tools?" I asked.

"We got some hammers, pry-bars and wood." He said.

"OK, let's get started." I said.

We handed out the tools to the men from a large wooden box that was on site. Each man took a tool and headed for the roof. There was a small walking area on the second floor that they used to begin tearing the material off, and then they began attaching two-by-fours sideways to the roof to use as foot holds as they worked their way upwards. There was no reason or organization to the work. The men just used what they had and shouted at each other all day. They talked constantly. They talked loudly. They talked so much that the staccato of a dozen hammers hitting the roof was actually a bit soothing. It was difficult to make out most of what they said as the accents were so thick, but what I could hear was mostly just street talk and jabbing at each other with insults.

I had learned to just accept this on job sites before. It was part of the usual B.S. that men did to puff themselves up. I always preferred to be a bit quieter so people had to wonder if I was simple, nuts or just plain dangerous. Either way, it worked and most men did not mess with me. The truth was, I was never very clever with words in those situations. I tended to freeze up or say something very stupid that I regretted later. It was never like the movies where Arnie or Sly said something clever and then pommeled the bad guy. Not for me. But I could fight pretty well and had long ago chosen to be the strong, silent type. Better that than say something dumb.

I had learned on job sites back home (and in the Army) that the best way to handle situations like this was to lay back. You just minded your own business. Eventually someone would challenge you. When this happened you had to respond very quickly and decisively. If a physical altercation arose from the verbal jabs, you had to beat down your adversary so quickly and violently that the others took it as a warning.

Working on some construction sites was a lot like being in prison. I've had this confirmed by more than just a few who had experience in both places. The

Army could be a lot like that too. These places were all men and I guess they were still governed by the "Big Boy Rules". No lefty PC stuff here. It was the law of the jungle. I hated it, really hated it, but somehow fit in. Luckily, I was big. At 6'1", 240 pounds, most guys just figured I was more trouble than I was worth.

About ten of the men worked diligently at hacking away at the hard copper roofing, bending and tearing it off with their bare hands. The rest of the workers gathered up the material the first group tossed down to the ground, and began tearing the tar and gunny-sack-like cloth material away from the copper.

I was still trying to figure out what I should be doing here, other than watching these guys work when I noticed that the sun was very high in the sky and the men were sweating profusely. I found where Larry had left an Igloo water container and cups, but there was no water, so I quickly drove my truck to a local market and got a bunch of ice and two five gallon bottles of water. I put the ice and one of the bottles into the Igloo and told the men to get a drink when they were thirsty. All at once the work came to a halt and they all came down from the roof and began drinking from the Igloo. They struggled for position at the cooler and I thought a fight might break out. Eventually they all sat down in the small shade the edge of the roof offered and leaned their backs against the wall of the church. After about ten minutes, I wondered if this was going to be a "union-fifteen", which back home meant about a thirty minute break and I began to think of the Bahamian phrase for "get your lazy asses back on that roof" when Fishy noticed me and must have read my mind.

"Git you lazy mudda-fuckin' body up off dat groun, boy!" He shouted at the men.

Oh yes, perhaps those were the words I guess I was thinking of too. The men grunted and slowly climbed back up on the roof and began tearing at the material again. The men moved very slowly and it seemed to me that the work was not going quickly enough. I'd never removed copper from a steep roof before so I decided to grab a hammer and climb the roof to see what we were doing. I wanted to set the pace for them and get them moving. All of the men looked at me, and I realized that I was probably doing something wrong but acting like the slave master in the cotton field was not my style. I have always led by example on the job site, so I began to tear into the copper roof with my hammer.

It took one minute for me to realize that this was very hard work. It took several strikes with the hammer just to bend the metal and get it to tear. I could almost feel the men chuckling at the fat white boy. The copper was about as thick as a penny but had been rolled in long sheets to cover the roof, and was probably fifty or more years old. The claw of the hammer helped to make the tear bigger, until you had a chunk of copper to pull off but the cloth and tar held the metal like an old friend and made it very hard to remove. The tar broke off in very small, hard chunks and created a black dust in the air that I was sure would kill us all someday. My fingers began to get nicked and bled in a few places as I worked. I needed some gloves. We all did.

Reluctantly, I climbed back down to call Larry on my cell. He said there was a supply store nearby where I could sign for what I needed. I was getting better at understanding him. But rather than take his directions, I grabbed the smallest worker and had him ride with me. With his guidance, we got to the store quickly and I purchased twenty pairs of gloves and headed back to distribute them to the men on site.

I handed the gloves out to the men back on the site, and they took them from me like hungry dogs. They used them immediately and things seemed to go along just a little bit faster. I put on a pair and jumped on the roof and hammered again just quickly enough to get a small piece of old tar in my eye. It was small but felt like a huge rock. Nice move. I was rinsing the tar from my eye at the Igloo drinking container when Fishy came up to me.

"Dem gloves a good idea but dey gon tear quick, mon." He said.

"Then we'll get more, Fishy." I said.

He smiled, nodded and walked off. I was not sure if I was winning these guys over or if they just thought I was a fool, but I figured I'd just be genuine and work hard. The rest was not up to me. These things took time.

I began to help tear the cloth and tar from the copper and pile it into my truck. It saddened me to feel just how weak my body had become. I struggled to tear the metal free and watched as the others seemed to do it more easily. I was no longer the twenty-something pipe-fitter I once was. I was a forty-something desk jockey. How sad I was to admit this to myself, but I did. Then, I fought it. To compensate, I turned my actions up to "sprint" level, while the others were set at "jog", our speed now remaining equal, but my effort had tripled. I would sleep well tonight! I still move slowly compared to the men around me. They were in perfect health, stronger and more fit than I'd probably ever been and yet they lived on KFC, rice and beer. Getting older sucked but being the weak white guy on the job sucked even more.

Larry had told me that the copper was very valuable. I was reminded of this as I began to see a group of men sitting at the edge of the church property watching us work.

"Dey gon come take the metal if we don get it out soon." The little guy said to me as we tore at the roofing.

The group of men stared at the truck like it was their payday.

"They'll come and just take it?" I squinted at the men through the bright sun and prodded him. That would be bad.

"We can stop dem, but it be a fight." He said.

"A fight, eh?" I counted my men and looked at the men eyeballing our copper. It was close to even... what the heck was I thinking? "OK, let's get this load out of here. You know where the metal drop off place is?" I asked him.

"I do, mon. It be by my cousin place."

"Go tell Fishy we gone." I said. Hmmm, that was weird. My accent was changing. Well, it was inevitable I guess.

We had to drive right by the group of men as we left the site, my truck suspension was sagging from the weight of the copper. The men stared right at me, but did nothing. The truck was so heavy. It groaned under the load. I had to turn very slowly and wondered if we had put too much weight on the rear. Each small bump made the whole load lurch up and down. I had to drive very slowly off the church property. So much for my quick getaway, these guys could have taken us down as we crept by. Now I knew what a small fish feels like when it swims by a group of sharks. I felt relieved as we drove onto the main road and down the busy street. Crowds and traffic never felt so good.

227

We drove through the middle part of the island, through ghetto after ghetto with my new guide giving me directions. After driving past the same shopping area twice, I asked him if he was lost.

"No, mon." He said staring ahead with "been to prison" eyes. I decided to try to make friends.

"What's your name, bro?"

"Sniper." He said. "Sniper MacIntosh."

"Nice to meet you, *Sniper*." I said and we shook hands.

"Now, Sniper. Are we lost?" I asked.

"No, mon. We jus lookin." He said.

"Lookin for what?"

"Lookin ta see if da man dere." He said.

"So the place is nearby?"

"Ya mon, it right dere." He said and pointed to a small street that led off the main road.

"Why don't we just drive in there and see if they can help us out with this copper?" I asked.

"OK." He said. "If that's wha choo wan."

I didn't even bother to ask why we didn't do this in the first place. Larry once told me that the thing a Bahamian man hates the most was if you let him know you think he was stupid. You could get killed for this so I was careful, even with this small guy that appeared to be about nineteen and about a hundred pounds soaking wet. His name *was* "Sniper." Most people on this island were armed with a gun or a knife, so it was best to remain friends if you could. I carefully turned off the main road.

The metal scrap yard was more like some guy's small house with a big yard full of junk. There were dogs everywhere. Rottweilers, German Shepherds (in this heat?), and feral semi-wild dogs called "Potcakes", all looking menacingly at us as we pulled up. There

228

was a very old bus on one side of the yard, which looked like it was someone's home, and a very large tow-truck/wrecker that was held up on wooden four-by-fours. There was a metal-frame shed about twenty by forty feet that held other junk. From the rear of the lot, we saw some blue smoke that was rose upwards from an arc welder. Instead of a welder's mask, the user had three pair of dark sunglasses on to shield his eyes from the bright light. Having burned my corneas once while helping my father use a welder as a young man, I cringed at the pain the man was surely in for later this evening. Even a tough guy could burn his corneas.

We parked the truck, got out without a word and Sniper walked ahead of me, leading the way. I had hoped for some kind of pre-game chat but there was none. I tried to look as nonchalant as possible as I followed him closely, trying to look like we were walking together, instead of me following him. The nuances among men were very subtle and I needed to look calm, potentially dangerous (but non-threatening), confident and as if I came here every day. I had to feign a comfort level that I did not possess.

Suddenly, a man quickly walked by us with a pistol in one hand, talking loudly into a cell phone in his other hand. He was headed toward the small home where the women were sweeping what appeared to be a dirt floor. The women laughed loudly and swept away. Jeez! What the heck was I doing here? This scene was right out of a thriller movie where the oblivious American steps into the third world where there were lots of sweaty dark guys with glowing white teeth and rusty machetes. I did not belong there. I had to pretend that I did.

There was very loud music coming from the home and the women were dancing, eating chicken, and

229

drinking beer as they swept. Sweeping a dirt floor always confused me. There was just more dirt, right? I decided to think about that later. The loud laughter fell out of the home like witches around a black pot, or at least that might describe why the hair on my neck was standing straight up. The fat ladies in the house provided the evil laughter that completed the background for my nightmare.

The man with the gun and the phone yelled something at the women and they yelled back. He walked away from the house and in a moment I saw him speed away in an older Cadillac that did not look like it was safe for travel on public roads, to say the least. It appeared to have come from the Mad Max movie set complete with chicken wire for a wind screen, large, knobby tires, and what appeared to be a 50 caliber machine gun on the top. Maybe that was just a makeshift antenna. Maybe my mind was playing tricks on me.

"Come on, mon." Sniper said from ahead of me.

Apparently I had stopped walking and had not noticed. I began walking again and we approached the arc welder area. Sniper tugged on the welding man's arm (something I would never have done) and the man stopped to look at him.

"Copper." Sniper said.

"Wha?" The man yelled over the loud music.

"Copper!" Sniper shouted.

"Well den, unload da shit, boy! Why you tuggin' on me?" The man yelled and he turned back to his work.

"Excuse me, sir." I said and the man looked at me like a disease.

"What choo neet?" He asked, staring through my eyeballs and right into my mind. The smoke from the welder began to clear as we looked at each other. He

230

held the welding rod still as he stared at me. It looked like a sinister stick held by a hellish conductor.

"Where is the scale and how much do you pay per pound?" I asked. The man grunted and tossed his tools down.

"Where ya truck?" He asked.

I pointed and he walked over, circled it a few times, and then walked back.

"Six hundred." He said.

I looked at Sniper who nodded.

"OK, fine. Where you want it at?" I asked and noticed my accent slipping again.

The man laughed, "Do it look like it matta?" He laughed loudly and the men near him laughed too. I have never taken being laughed at very well.

"No, sir." I said. *"It really does not look like it matters at all."* Then his face straightened.

"What choo mean b' dat?" He asked.

Sniper cringed.

"Just agreeing with choo, mon. I gotta make a call to my boss to make sure it's right." I said reaching for my cell phone. There goes my accent again.

Sniper shook his head with small jerks at me.

I looked at my phone.

"Looks like I got no minutes." I said. "I'll call him later." I had plenty of time left on my monthly cell plan to use my phone but I was getting the feeling that my confident, tough white-boy act was only going to get me so far. If I really pissed these guys off, I might end up in a hole somewhere.

"Sniper, let's unload." I said and we walked back to the truck. All I wanted to do was get out of there.

"He don't let no one make no calls from his yard." Sniper whispered under his breath as we walked towards the truck.

"Yeah, I got that." I replied quietly. "Let's just get this done."

We unloaded the copper as quickly as we could; all the while, one of the large women was watching us from a picnic table in front of the house. Perhaps her job was to insure we only put copper on the ground and not bricks or other filler.

When we were done, I sent Sniper to get the money from the man, but he came back to say that we had to follow the man to the bank. We waited a few minutes and then he sped by us in a brand new black Range Rover waving for us to follow.

At a nearby Scotia Bank, the man went inside to make a withdrawal. He was gone twenty minutes when my cell phone rang. It was Larry.

"Jim, how long does glue burn?" He asked.

I began the deciphering process. This was an easy one.

"When will I return?" I asked.

"Right." He said.

"We're getting the money right now. The man is in the bank and we'll head back once he comes out with it. He's been twenty minutes already." I said.

"What such nugget?" He asked.

"We got $600." I said. I was getting better at this.

"Right then! Das a hula hoop or I amscray." He said.

"It's more than I expected, too." I was guessing on this one. He had lost me again.

"Right, well poop scoop watching the house get cleaner, OK?" He asked.

"Right, sure." I said. I had no idea what he wanted, but would drop the money off at his house with the Lady for safe keeping and then have her call him for me for my next assignment. She could translate.

232

The man came out of the bank and handed me the money in an envelope.

"Wanna coun it?" He asked.

"I trust you." I said. "Thanks. See you again real soon."

The man just nodded and apparently appreciated my gesture. I figured I'd be seeing him again soon and wanted to make an impression. As soon as he was gone in his SUV, I counted it. It was all there. On the way back, we stopped at Larry's house and gave the money to the Wife.

"I'll trust you that it's all here." She said semi-jokingly, but her comment did not sound or feel much like a joke, or a compliment. I knew I was done with this tryout and whether I had passed or not, this was not for me.

I told Larry of my decision on the jobsite the next day. He understood and took it much better than I did. Later that week, he stopped by our condo with two cases of Kalik and a check for $400. I took it as a gesture of friendship. He did not have to do that, but he did. He was a class act. He still is.

CHAPTER EIGHTEEN
Along Came A Brit

It was a Saturday, pretty early in the morning. Beth usually liked to sleep in a bit, but I had always been up before the sun. Jake was surely asleep in his bed, but I'd check on him anyway. So I did not wake her, I quietly pulled back the drapes and opened up the house to look out at the sea when I saw a stranger sitting on top of our sea wall, looking at the pool. He was a tall man with short brown hair. He was smoking, wearing flip flops and swim trunks. He was Caucasian, but was very tan. I walked out to the pool to greet him, something I always did when I saw a stranger on our property. Living on the first floor made us easy prey for bad guys, so anytime I saw someone I did not know I confronted them. Burglaries, even in our neighborhood, were common. Why so much of "paradise" was located in the third world never made sense to me, but it was reality. Oh yeah…that's why Hawaii was so expensive.

I peeked in on Jake, still fast asleep in his bed, and headed for the patio.

The man introduced himself as John. He was English. After I talked to him, it turned out he was very English. Poor guy, because he looked (and smelled) like he was suffering from a force 10 hangover.

"Did a right tour of the local pubs and casino last night with some blokes from the office." He said in his charming English accent. "I believe it was half four by the time head hit pillow. Though I feel like hell now, I

234

suppose one must do this now and then for the client."
He rubbed his glassy, red eyes.

We talked for a while. His accent did not pelt my
ears like so many I'd heard. His was real and pedigree.
He was born and raised in England. He had spent
some time in the Army where he was something called
a "para" which meant he jumped out of airplanes in the
Army, but that it was a special group so I was intrigued.
I'd always wanted to be a Ranger in the Army but
breaking my left arm five separate times as a kid made
me unacceptable. I let him know this.

"Oh...so you're a craphat." He said with a straight
face.

"I'm sorry." I looked at him with my eyebrows
furled.

"Forgive me! I take too many things for granted."
He laughed. "You don't know what a craphat is!"

"I'm getting the idea." I said sourly.

"Well, it's no issue, mate. We all need men on the
ground." He said and I could tell he meant it so I let it
go.

He was going through a divorce. But apparently he
had been at this for some time.

"She wants the divorce, she can bloody pay for it."
He said. "I'm in no hurry to remarry and no one is
cueing up to take her of my hands. It's been years now.
Lovely woman."

John said he hated soccer and loved rugby.

"Most Americans don't get soccer." I said. "22
guys running for an hour and a half with the final score
of 1-0? There should be a "yawn-meter" on your TV
when a soccer game come on. If you rack up too many
yawns, the TV should just turn itself off."

"Bloody soccer. Hooligans." John said with
disgust.

He talked and smoked incessantly. He had good stories, one story leading into another. Within thirty minutes of meeting him, I knew where he worked, what he did for a living, his marital status, his salary, and the full details of his compensation package at work. He communicated more in an hour that I could have fit into an entire day. He talked a lot, but he spoke well, cramming a lot of information into each tale. He seemed to know a lot about the world, too. After an hour talking to John, you felt like you just took a history course. The man was very interesting from the start.

"I've rented that apartment there over the garden on the second floor." He said. "I'm a QS at Club Caribe." This tidbit got my attention.

"What's a QS?" I asked.

"Right, you Yanks don't use QS's." He said. "Oh, sorry. That was rude."

"What? You mean the *'Yank'* crack?" I asked.

"Yes. I don't mean it in a negative way." He said.

"Oh, that's fine. But we prefer 'rebel' or 'traitor'." I said smiling.

He grinned and chuckled a bit.

"Right." He laughed.

We understood each other's humor.

"Well, my American cousin, a QS is a 'Quantity Surveyor'. Kind of like if an accountant and an engineer mated and had a child. Assuming anyone would date an accountant or an engineer. Me being a little of both." He said.

"And assuming those robotic, technical people were actually interested in sex. Kind of like if a DMV worker and a postal worker getting together." I said, but John did not get it.

"Both are low-level government employees." I said and he nodded his head.

"To be fair, I'm an appraiser. And the joke on us is that if you fail the personality test at the DMV or post office, you become an appraiser."

"Right. Well. If my project manager comes to me with a big change in say, the light fixtures on a hotel project, it's my job to figure out how much the change will cost so the owner can determine if he's willing to pay for the change. There's a lot more to it, but that's the gist." He said.

"I've been trying to get an interview with Club Caribe for almost a year now." I said.

"No luck?" He asked.

"Zip. Most of the people working at Club Caribe act like it's the Secret Service. You'd think they were guarding nuclear launch codes over there instead of just building another weight-gain facility for American tourists. Getting to meet the people in charge of hiring has been impossible." I grunted.

"They're probably just protecting their jobs by keeping you out. You're a threat to them. *Tossers*! I'm sure I can introduce you to my bosses. What's your specialty?" He asked.

"I grew up working for my father's fire sprinkler business. We did a lot of commercial work. Does that count?" I asked him hopefully.

"Can you read engineering plans and blueprints?" He asked.

"Absolutely."

"Can you count to one thousand?"

"Forward and backwards." I said.

"Then you qualify!" He laughed. "There are junior QS partners at my firm that can't spell their bloody name and have never stepped foot on a construction site. You'll run circles around those wankers! That and you're a veteran! Our group down here is in desperate need of someone with your specialty. No one here knows a bloody thing about fire sprinklers." He said.

I wasted almost a year of networking just trying to get an interview and this Brit falls from the sky and lands on my patio. This was shaping up to be a fantastic Saturday.

As John continued to talk, I saw that we had a lot in common. We were both ex-Army, both liked rum on the weekend, both lived in the same building now, and apparently both wanted to work for the same company. Our conversation flowed easily from the start. It looked like we were going to be friends.

After John left, I headed down to the beach and looked out over the dead flat morning sea. I watched my toes in the sand as the clear, warm water floated over them. The ocean was gin bottle clear and felt to be about eighty degrees. I stood there at the water's edge and gave thanks to God for my place in the world. I was living my dream, but I always wondered when I'd wake up and the dream would feel more normal. Up to now, I felt like I was living someone else's life, and I was skulking about hoping no one would find me out and send me home.

I'd wanted this so badly for so long. I remembered the last day of a vacation we took here a few years ago. I had gotten up very early and set up my old Sony movie camera and tripod on the beach in front of the Radisson hotel to record the sunrise. I entered the scene the camera filmed, walked around on the beach, picked up shells, watched the water, some early beach walking people went by... I recorded for an hour, so I could watch it when we got home. I even planned on having it play in the background on my TV so it would help me feel like I was still there.

While I never really did just play the tape in the

background, I was never your normal, average tourist. I was obsessed.

For years, I'd tried to imagine our lives here on this island and now we were here. And what kept me from totally enjoying the experience was my fear that without work, all of this would end soon. It seemed cosmically incorrect for us to have come this far, to have lived the dream this long for it to actually end. It felt like a trip to the doctor's office to find out I had an incurable disease. I felt like I had to make every moment count now because the moments were numbered.

I was once told that the moment you realize that you will one day die was the moment that childhood ends. I was not ready to accept that this journey had an expiration date.

No expat looked forward to going back to the hard-shoed, dry-cleaned, 8-5 we had left behind.

For some reason, I thought of that movie, "Nine to Five." That's only eight hours. Who the heck only works eight hours? And they got an hour for lunch, didn't they? I couldn't remember. I could barely even admit I saw that dumb movie, but I could still sing the words to the title song. No wonder my memory was shot. I'd used it up on some really worthless items like this, some commercial jingles, and some Boy George lyrics that crept into my brain after being repeatedly pelted with his heavy rotation songs in the 80's.

One day after dropping Jake off at school, I went to the market to get some eggs and grits, and I found myself looking at the locals forlornly.

"I would miss you." I said in my heart. I looked at them in as if I'd never see them again, wanting to burn their mannerisms into my memory. I watched them do the same things they'd done all this time, and for some reason it all felt precious to me.

I waited in the breakfast to go line at the market and watched the thirty or so customers ahead of me. The one woman behind the counter was apparently engrossed in a conversation with a good friend. This would take a while. It usually did, but today I did not mind.

I waited patiently in the parking lot for the owner of a huge Ford F-350 pick-up truck who had parked behind me to come out of the store. He'd blocked me in, but today it did not bother me when he finally came out, saw my predicament, and just smiled and waved in my direction.

I waited for a guy who had stopped his car in the middle of the street, holding up traffic, so he could talk to someone. This happened a lot in the Bahamas. I watched them and patiently waited.

I got home, already sweating, but not wanting to turn on the AC as utilities cost a fortune and our AC condenser was terribly inefficient. My wife slept on the couch. She had been working on California time. She was enjoying her mid-morning nap after the rush to get our son off to school. I ate my 2,000 calorie Bahamian "light" breakfast that was making me have to up my pant size about once a week.

As I always did, I checked in on my investments online. The stock market continued to fall. I read more news about the downward spiral of the US economy. My company was not getting any orders in this terrible market. I watched as our investment portfolio was cut in half and all of the equity we had in our home disappeared.

"What the heck are they doing back there?" I asked myself. I looked out the window at the ocean and whispered to myself.

"SHIT."

Being on an extended vacation in the Caribbean was not a good idea when the world around you was beginning to fail. The Bahamas had no real gross national product outside of tourism. When the tourists couldn't afford to visit, the Bahamas suffered.

"When da US get a cough, da Bahamas get da flu." A friend told me once.

There were many people on this island that liked to think of themselves as businessmen and bankers, but the truth was that the money was not made here, it came here. When the money steadily came here the contractor could build, the banker could shuffle the money around and the government could tax imported goods until a sandwich costs $26.00. But it was obvious that when the tourist money stopped coming in that this place would grind to a halt pretty quickly. When the rich folks got tired of the escalating crimes of the jobless, the whole island would begin to depopulate of its part-time residents. Then the working expats would have to leave in search of opportunities elsewhere. The Bahamas would resemble a half-deflated balloon left over from a big party the night before, tied to a chair not able to hit the ceiling anymore but still above the floor.

These thoughts went through my head as I allowed my mind to spin the whole situation into one big negative. Why had we paid cash for this place instead of just kept on renting? We had $650,000 tied up in this place! Perhaps not a lot to the folks out in Lyford Caye, but it was a bundle to this beach kid from a modest upbringing. As I watched the stock market tumble from its peak at just over 14,000, I consoled myself with the reality that we probably would have lost a ton of money in the market anyway. At least we still owned the condo, even if the value had dropped.

241

I decided that if I was to survive here that I had to quit second-guessing our moves. Even if the market completely crashed and there was rampant crime on the streets, we'd still own this place on the beach. Money in the market had a habit of vanishing into thin air. I remembered giving my money manager $25,000 once when I wanted to spend the same on a 1962 Corvette. The money I gave him disappeared the next day while I drove passed that Corvette for months. That stuck with me for years.

I felt better knowing that while the value of our place here in the Bahamas had certainly fallen, at least we were not in the same boat as many people we knew who had completely lost their 401K's in the market downturn. That's the nice thing about brick and mortar; it may go down in value, but at least you could still live there or rent the place. You did not have to drive passed it every day and wonder what happened.

* * * * *

I saw John again as I sat in our Honda waiting for the electronic gate to our parking lot to open. I was driving to get some groceries. He was standing just outside the gate near the roadside in the early evening wearing a tight, knit black sweater, slacks and hard leather shoes. I stared at him and shook my head. Why was he wearing that in this heat? It was almost 90 degrees and muggy as a locker room after a football game.

"Hey bro, where ya' goin'?" I asked him.

He stared at me for a moment. He'd never seen me in the Honda before and squinted to see who was driving.

242

"Ahhh, hallo there mate." He said. "I'm off to a paaaawwty." His English accent was the playful sort, the kind I liked. I could not tell if he was overdoing it for effect or if he just really enjoyed being English. Maybe he'd imbibed some Blue Sapphire before leaving his condo. He mentioned liking rum and gin.

"Gin. It's so *English*." He said matter-of-factly. It tasted like pine trees to me but after a few gins, anyone could adopt a comfortable English accent, couldn't they?

"Need a lift?" I asked. *Or a change of clothes*, I thought to myself.

"Oh no, mate. I'm just waiting for the bus. No worries." He said.

I had known some English people in the past and I already knew that when you wanted to do them a favor you had to ask at least three times before they might accept. The Brits are a strong bunch of people. They punched far above their weight class and did not get where they were by asking for help from others, even when it might had been wise to do so.

"Well I'm apparently heading the same way you are, bro. Jump in and I'll drop you off." I pushed him a bit.

"Oh no, it's really no distance. I'm just popping over to the Sandyport subdivision." He said as he pointed the wrong way. "The bus should be along shortly."

"Sandyport is the other way and the jitneys stop running at six pm." I said. "It's dark out, there are no sidewalks or proper streetlights and the people here drive like they're in a race."

"Is that right?" He asked, his face twisting just a bit.

"Most drivers here have a cell phone in one hand and a cocktail in the other. Walking this road at night is

243

not a good idea. Sure you won't come with?" I asked again.

"Cocktail in one, phone in the other... right. Well, I suppose if it's not too much trouble." He said this as he opened the front door on the left side and got in.

"Is this an *English* Honda?" He asked.

I learned that English people believe the world was England-centric. To them, all things were either related to England or were invented there.

"No, but I bought it here from a Bahamian guy who is a Japanese car importer. The Japanese drive on the wrong side just like you guys do and the guy I bought it from did *speak English*. It should be comfortable for you." I teased him.

"Rather." He said and adjusted his seat and belt. "Nice stereo, mate. And the AC blows quite icy, indeed." He noted the different amenities inside the small SUV.

"Thanks. Who's party?" I asked.

"Oh some knobber from the office. I really wish I didn't have to go, but one must show courtesy to the chaps upstairs." He said. "Mind if I smoke?"

"Not at all. I just need to pick up a rack of beer, some ice and a couple other things at the roundy up ahead. Then I'll drop you off at Sandyport." I nodded at him.

"Perfect." He said. Then he looked at me quizzically. "How many beers are in a 'rack' and what is a 'roundy'?" He asked.

"Sorry, I sometimes make up words hoping that they'll catch on. A rack is a flat or a case. It's 24 beers." I said.

"Does it matter if it's bottles or cans?" He asked.

"No. And a roundy is a roundabout. I'm sure you're familiar with those." I said.

"Oh yes. Driving in London can make your head spin with the *roundies*, the traffic and all the people dodging in and out of the roads. It's good fun, though." He grinned.

"Driving here is not so much fun. I never thought I'd live to miss the freeways back home in California."

"Are you from California?" He asked.

"Born and raised." I said as I pulled into the liquor store. "Need anything?"

"I might come in to catch a box of fags." He answered as he opened the door.

"You might want to rephrase that while you're here, pal." I said grinning.

"Oh, the 'fags' part. Right. Downright militant about the gays here aren't they?" He asked. He was well-groomed, in good shape and well, the accent. Some people might think he was gay.

"Well, they almost turned Rosie O'Donnel's gay cruise ship away. There were protesters everywhere downtown. Bad move too. Gay people know how to live and they are not afraid to spend money. The Bahamas probably lost millions in gay tourist dollars with that move." I said, fishing to see if he was gay.

"Probably because they can afford it. Most don't have kids. And with two incomes, hey why not?" He raised his shoulders and eyebrows as he spoke.

He referred to gays as "they", so he was probably straight.

Many gay people I knew were very clever and full of life. They lived on the fringe and seemed to grow stronger from the negativity they experienced. Some even seemed to thrive on it. It made them hard sometimes but they tried to keep a smile on their face. I felt sorry for them. But, parties where there were some gay guys always seemed to be just a little more fun.

And there were never fist fights at gay parties. I'm not gay myself. But after living in San Francisco for many years, I could speak "Restaurant Gay."

We left the store for Sandyport and John began to tell me more than I ever wanted to know about cooking paella. He went through every step and detail. I was grateful that Sandyport was only a few blocks away. I had to roll my window down as he was wearing about a quart of very strong cologne. For some reason, the mixture of him telling me how to cook a spicy fish meal, the strong smelling cologne, and his smoking cigarettes three at a time was making me a bit nauseous.

"Then aaaaaaaftaaaa you've shelled the crawfish… He went on describing his paella recipe, step by step.

Maybe he *was* gay. But I loved him. He was great.

We saw John a just few times over the next few weeks, usually as he came and left for work. Once in a while we'd wave at him and chat a bit as he sat on his patio smoking. A few times I saw him at the pool and we would talk briefly. He was apparently very busy during the day and disappeared at night. One time we saw him, he was with an attractive woman about his age, which I guessed to be in the mid-forties. We greeted them as they quickly walked past us in the first floor hallway area near our door. It looked like John had a visitor.

One day I saw John and one of his co-workers talking on his patio upstairs as Jake and I played football on the grass next to our condo. I yelled up to ask if they wanted a beer.

"Sounds good, mate." John said. "This is Mongo." He pointed to the man with him as they both stood up and leaned over on the railing to look down at me.

"Pleased to meet you." Mongo said. His accent was even more dashing than John's.

I suddenly felt like I was at a proper boarding school wearing tight tweed shorts. Mongo seemed to speak without his teeth separating from each other, barely moving his jaw. He was very English. It was great fun listening to how they spoke.

"Nice to meet you, too." I said. "I'll get the beer." I went into the kitchen through the side door and fetched two icy canned beers. I went back out and asked if they'd like me to toss them up or if they'd like to come down. They decided they'd come down, so I put the beers back in the fridge. About ten minutes later they came down in their swim trunks with towels and sunglasses.

"I'll get the beer." I said and went into our condo.

"Nice place you've got here, mate." John said as he peered inside our side patio door into the kitchen.

"Like to take a look?" I asked.

"Love to." He said and they came inside the kitchen.

I cracked each can open and handed them their drinks. We toasted.

"Cheers." John said.

"Cheers." Mongo said and he looked around. "Two or three bedrooms?" He asked.

"Two." I said. "All fourteen units have two beds and two baths."

"Very nice. And what a view." Mongo walked into the main living area and looked at the sea. The view made him smile like it did to everyone.

"That's why we live here." I said. "I didn't want a condo but houses on the beach are just too spendy."

"Where can I smoke?" John asked.

"On the back patio, follow me." I said and led them outside. We all sat down and looked at the beautiful pool and sea. When I got to show someone else for the first time it felt new to me as well. We had a panoramic view of the ocean. It was stunning. We all took it in for a moment and I looked for the ashtray for John.

"I'll join you." I said. "Excuse me, I have to get my smokes."

"You smoke?" John asked.

"Not all of the time." I said. "I'm a social smoker." I went inside and got my pack of Millport Menthols from the freezer. They were the cheaper brand that tasted nowhere near a Marlboro Menthol, but after a few beers I did not care. Beth and I only smoked when we drank so we usually smoked the cheap brand. I went back outside and sat down again.

"You keep your fags in the fridge?" Mongo asked.

"Well, we usually keep our fags in the closet… *until they are ready to come out*." I said with a smile.

Crickets.

Neither seemed to get my reference.

"Yeah, we keep them in the fridge." I grunted.

"Don't they tend to taste a bit like mutton or pork?" John asked. Both Englishmen seemed very concerned.

"We keep them in plastic bags in the freezer to avoid that smell."

Blank faces stared at me.

"It's keeps food smells out of the smokes and is supposed to make them stay fresher longer."

More blank faces.

"You see, we don't smoke them that quickly… only when we drink." I explained.

"Ohhhhhh, OK." John said and they both seemed satisfied now.

I wasn't sure if there was a dialect barrier between us or if Mongo was suffering from some jet lag. I'd have to be more clear and direct when I spoke to them.

"Mongo got robbed out front the other night." John said as calmly as if he had told me that Mongo had gotten a bad haircut.

"It's true. No big deal." Mongo said.

"Bollocks! He held him up at gunpoint and took all he had." John laughed.

"What?" I almost shouted. This came out of nowhere.

"Yes, took my watch and keys. Sorry bastard. I only had about ten quid on me." Mongo said calmly and smiled.

"Yeah, that'll show 'em." I said sarcastically. Again, blank faces. "What I mean to say is.... weren't you afraid? Didn't that just scare the piss out of you? What did the guy wear? Are the police after the guy?"

"I'm a little bothered for sure. It happened quickly so I was quite shocked at the moment. He had a black ski mask on. I'm sure the police are doing their best." Mongo quipped.

"Their best being not much." John chimed in.

No one, even the new arrivals, had much faith in the local police. The word from the locals was that their police were poorly paid, under-trained, brutal and corrupt. I had never had any dealings with the police, so I could not verify this rumor. Expats were warned to steer clear of them, unless you had a good contact within the force that could help you if you ever got tangled up. I'd met some very nice local police, but the constant rumors I heard from the locals made me wary of them.

How the hell did things get like this? Weren't the police supposed to be the ones you could trust? I did not like the local police at home in California and frowned every time I saw an officer. In my opinion, it took a certain personality type to become a cop. Some took the job to make up for being picked on in high school. Many liked their job for the excitement, but there were surely many who were just good people that wanted to help society. At least, I hoped so. They do a job I don't want, so I had to admire them at the same time. I saw them as a necessary evil right up there with a standing federal Army, car insurance, and attorneys.

"Well, I didn't give the police much to go on. The bloke was very average for a local. A black man, about 5'8" tall, medium build, wearing all black head to toe, and brandishing a rusty old revolver. At least he could have robbed me with a proper firearm." Mongo said.

"Right. Or at the very least he could have given you a right sock to the face." John added.

"That would have been much better." Mongo agreed.

"Why would you want to be hit?" I asked.

"Oh, he'd have gotten paid leave for months if he'd been properly attacked." John explained.

"I could have worked it into years off with the right psychiatrist." Mongo said dreamily. "Post-traumatic disorder vacation."

"As it is now, he'll be lucky to get six weeks off for suffering the incident." John said.

This reminded me that they came from the land of socialized medicine. If he got a punch to the face, he'd be off to Disneyland with the family. If he got a pistol-whipping, he could semi-retire. If he'd been shot (and lived), he should go thank the guy because he would probably never have to work again. I wondered if their way was better than the American way of paying for insurance that usually did not cover you. The trick many people played on our system was to have no insurance. Hospitals could not turn you away if you were dying.

"Mongo, I am truly sorry that this happened to you. And I intend to insure that something like this never happens again." Not only was I looking for a phone booth where I could change into my super hero costume, I was truly feeling embarrassment for my building. I suddenly felt bad and paranoid that we lived here. It happened often when something like this occurred. The regret-coaster crested a hill and down we went again.

Back in California, there were neighborhoods you simply avoided. And nicer neighborhoods had boundaries. Here, where we were all crowded onto this little island and all beaches were public, such boundaries were not as evident. Sure, there were gated communities like ours, some with guards at the gate and on patrol. The problem was that the gates were sometimes maintained by people related to the ones that robbed you. I'd heard of a recent caper where the security guard was actually the burglar. Just like at home, most security guards just napped in their booths and let anyone walk right in.

* * * * *

"Excuse me sir, what is your business here in Conchy-Town?" The security guard asked the man walking up the gate. The man had a machete in one hand and a shotgun slung over his back.

"I'm here fer da gardening at the Smith house." The man said.

"That explains the machete, but what about dat gun?" Asked the guard.

"Don't you remember me, mon?" The man said. "It's your cousin, Michael Hendricks."

251

"Ohhhhh, hey brudda. How's the body?" The guard laughed as he hugged the man.

"All is well, all is well." The man said. "How you mudda?"

"Goot, goot. We all goot." The guard chuckled.

"Alright, I gotta be getting' to woik." The man says. "You be safe."

"God bless." The guard said and passed the man through. And then, "Oh hey, wait. What about the gun?"

"Oh, it be mine." The man said.

"Oh, OK." The guard chuckled and they both waved again.

* * * * *

I got through the guard gates at Sandyport and even parked my boat there for years without ever living there. No guard ever asked me for I.D. or if I lived there. They just waived me through. Of course, it probably paid to be white and look like I belonged inside one of the gated communities where most of the expats huddled together, afraid of the dark people outside.

I despised these little "bubble" communities. The expat men went to work, the expat women stayed home and gossiped about each other, and they all avoided black Bahamians and the danger that lurked just outside their worthless gate.

Perhaps they thought if there was a problem that they'd just call the police. But the only police presence one ever felt here was the crisp white-shirted officers that patrolled the tourist area downtown in an effort to make the visitors feel safe. In a strange cultural twist, the male officers walking the beat were mostly all very thin. Many of the women 'beat' officers were usually so fat that they dwarfed their male counterparts. They walked around the downtown area looking official, but harmless. When something really criminal happened, they immediately called for backup on their radios and the real police, the ones in the dark blue uniforms, berets and boots, showed up in their squad cars carrying clubs and guns.

The real cops were the menacing looking men that carried varnished, thin bamboo sticks about 30" long with shiny metal tips on both ends. Their faces were always sweat-shiny. They wore mirrored aviators and black berets. I had always wondered why the beret looks tough on a man in uniform, but put the same hat on a guy reading in a Berkeley book store and he became a wimpy conscientious objector. Again, I was reminded of how James Bond would deal with these guys. I believe he would upshift his Aston Martin and just leave. Smart man.

The well-armed, jack-booted, bad-ass beret-cops were not used properly though. On Friday nights when traffic was heavy, they'd set up road blocks at roundies to check vehicle registration window stickers, instead of busting all of the drug dealers that hung out at hotel bars.

I remembered having an open Kalik in the Honda as I passed through one of these traffic road blocks for the first time. I figured I was busted and planned to stay the night in the hell-jail I'd heard about. The cop just looked at the window sticker and waived me through. Thank God, I thought to myself. The cop acted deadly serious; but as I looked at his uniform, I had to stifle a laugh. For some reason people in this country avoided sewing their patches onto their uniforms. Officials and school kids here all wore uniforms with the patches hanging on a single safety-pin. Before long, the patches were all rolled up and looked like salami and cheese on a hors d' oeuvres plate. I'm no uniform snob but jeez, how much time does it take to sew on a patch?

* * * * *

As our visit wound down to its conclusion, I invited John and Mongo to take a ride on Bali Hai with us sometime. They both said they'd love to go. We finished our beers and they said they were headed for the casino bar where there was live music. They invited me, but I passed and decided to stay home and take a cool swim with Jake and Beth instead.

* * * * *

"Daddy, I can swim!" Jake said.

"Swim?" I asked him as we played together in the pool. "Show me." Beth sat on the edge and smiled at us.

"Well, you have to hold me and throw me." He said.

"Throw you?"

"Yes. That way I can dart the wall." He explained. I looked up at Beth who just raised her eyebrows and shook her head.

"OK, can you dart underwater?" I asked Jake.

"Of course, Daddy!" He laughed. "Push me!"

"Let me mark the wall of the pool first." I walked to the wall of the shallow end and pointed to the wall.

"Is that the 'bull-eye', Daddy?" Jake asked.

"That's it. Ten points if you hit it underwater."

"OK, ready." He said and I went to him and held him in the water horizontally.

"One, two…three!" I said and pushed him through

the water. He pumped his little arms under the surface and kicked as he slowly made his way. His fingers touched the wall of the shallow end and he came up gasping for air.

"Did I do it, Daddy?" He yelled out as I grabbed him. He was still just a little too short to stand even in the shallow end.

"Yes, you made it!" I shouted and lifted him up above me. He laughed and we repeated this game for another half hour before he tired. We counted the points he added up, sometimes just off the mark for eight or nine points, but mainly right on the 'bull-eye' for ten. I looked up at my wife and she gave me that reassuring look that wives sometimes give that makes a husband know that he is in his place.

Here, somewhere between the middle of a tryout job and an introduction to a possible job, with the whole of the US economy falling apart, our little family grounded me. My beautiful wife and son pulled me down from my constant worry. Being with them reminded me of why we were here. They made me feel happy I was alive and I looked up and thanked God. It did not matter where, as long as I was with them. And I was so glad that He reminded me of this right when I needed it most. Thank you.

CHAPTER NINETEEN
London Calling

When I contacted the other owners in our building to discuss the recent robbery, most of them shrugged it off.

"But the man was almost shot." I said. "Having a gun pointed at a guest on our grounds is not acceptable."

"What can we do?" asked Duff, my upstairs neighbor.

Duff and I had never really gotten along and I had kept a friendly distance. He'd made some comments about American beer being akin to having sex in a canoe... *fucking close to water.* I usually just ignored him, but secretly hoped he would cross the line so I could knock him out. We crossed swords at owner's meetings, a place he did not belong as he was not an owner but a tenant. However, he was sent to represent the real owner, his boss. Suffice to day, we did not like each other from the start and neither of us knew why. I continued to dislike him because his humor was rude and he was a bit cocky. I think he did not like me because I was American, and I probably exude all of the qualities that a Scot might find offensive in an American. Just to rile him up, I once told him that I would have a tough time finding Scotland on a map, and that I sometimes got Scotland confused with Ireland. He didn't like that. I knew he wouldn't. I made it clear I could find *him*, though.

"I think we should look into getting a security guard." I said.

"We've tried that before." Duff quacked. "The guards are expensive, sleep on the job or they may just rob you themselves. And besides, they're not armed and the robber is. So what's the point?"

He made a lot of sense. But I never just gave up because a task was difficult. Duff was not a leader. He was some sort of administrative servant for a local builder, a real "can't do" kind of guy. I knew there was no way I'd get him to ask his owner to help pay for the extra cost of a guard. But, he was moving out soon, so perhaps that would be a step in the right direction with different attitudes at the building meetings.

The other owners were not keen on the idea of a security guard either. My "can-do" attitude would not sway them. The people in my building could be very cheap sometimes, even though most of them appeared wealthy. I figured that one of us would have to be robbed, hurt, or killed before something would be done. I just hoped it would not be anyone I cared about. I liked most of the people in our building. But working with them on any project was always problematic.

* * * * *

John and Mongo invited me to meet them down at the Cricket Club to watch a game of rugby.

"It's on Sunday so we can have a 'full-English'." John said.

"What's a 'full-English'?" I asked.

"It's a *proper* breakfast." He said, as if what the rest of the world ate was improper. Englishmen still believe that the world revolved around them. I suppose it was a memory that was difficult to release now that

257

they had given most of the world away and 90% of the people in London spoke a foreign tongue. I decided to play along.

"Well, you'll have to teach me about rugby." I laughed. "It just looks like a bunch of dudes playing keep-away with a pregnant football to me."

"No worries, mate." He said.

After church, John and I drove in his tiny Suzuki SUV to the Cricket Club. As I sat down, his "truck" felt like it was just a bit larger than a box of wooden matches. I crammed myself in, folded my knees under my chin into a yoga pose, and sweated as I struggled to find the seat belt.

"Roomy little wagon, eh mate?" John smiled.

And by English standards it probably was quite roomy. But for an American, this was the kind of vehicle you might tow behind an RV when you were retired and visiting all the states you'd missed when you were younger. He turned on the radio and played some local noise through his tiny speakers full blast. It was just loud enough to make whatever he was saying impossible to understand, so I just nodded and chuckled when he did as we bounced down the road.

I had been visiting the Cricket Club for many years and knew the owners intimately. The wife and kids had been to our five-year vow renewal on Cable Beach. They were great people and ran a very popular little British pub that had good British food and Euro-centric sports on the TV's. And, true to the name, they had a cricket field out front where people played games regularly.

We walked inside and the place was packed to the walls with about fifty or sixty men in a room that would comfortably hold thirty. They all sat at the small round tables or lined the walls holding their pints of beer.

Mongo had saved a table for us and we sat near a wall. John ordered two full-English breakfasts and two Stella Artois pints. Stella was skunk beer to me, but he loved it. I was taught to never drink beer that came in a green bottle.

"Now mate! You will learn some proper *English*." He said as he lit a smoke, smiling.

I did not point out that Stella Artois was a Belgian beer. John beamed. He was in his element. The Brits here were all very loud and they shouted at the TV as soon as the game began. Like anything new, rugby looked confusing to me until John gave me the basic rules. He leaned closely, so I could hear him over the yells of the other men and he kept teaching me the rules. Mongo chimed in here and there to correct John, and the two of them would argue for a minute. Then after a while, it began to make sense.

We had already downed three pints of Stella before our breakfast arrived. With the huge amount of people in this place, the kitchen became jammed up quickly. The one waitress serving all of us was Bahamian and she was typically slow, so it was just over an hour before our food arrived. I was not bothered. I was getting mildly drunk, enthusiastic about rugby, and having a great time with my new friend.

A full English breakfast was huge. It came on an over-sized plate and consisted of toast, eggs, baked beans, tomatoes, bacon, sausage, mushrooms and a few other things I couldn't remember. Somehow we crammed three of these huge plates, three pints of beer, and a full ashtray onto a table no larger than one of the tiny tires on John's SUV. We began devouring the food ravenously.

"One of these will hold you all day." John said.

"Maybe they should call it a 'full *Englishman*.'" I

said.

"Ahhhh, very good." John said flicking his ash thoughtfully and then shouting at the game again. "Come on, you plonker! Hold on to the bloody ball!"

I was happy to get some food into my body as being in the noisy, crowded, smoky pub, and imbibing so much beer made me dizzy. John never wavered. A bit of the Brit Grit I'd heard so much about.

England was playing France, so the crowd was particularly excited. There were no Frenchmen here and if there were a war might have broken out (again). England finally won the game and the men all cheered. They had yelled and cursed throughout the game like drunk sailors, but when it was finally over they shook hands and muttered around a bit, while they quietly paid their tabs and quickly left. Kind of like if a big group of people were dancing in a club and the music suddenly stopped and the lights all came on. You suddenly noticed that you had been wiggling your butt and shaking your arms in the air... which suddenly made no sense. The yelling had stopped quickly and most of the men left right after the game ended.

It felt very much like watching an important football game at home, but the air of danger was missing. Many sports bars at home had something in the air that reeked of a fight breaking out at any time. American sports fans could really be assholes to each other. This was different. I told John about this as we began to make our exit after the end of the game.

"Well mate, that's because rugby is a hooligan's game played by gentlemen." He said.

"What about soccer? It seems like there are always mob fights at those games in Europe." I inquired, really wanting to learn.

"That's because soccer is the opposite of rugby.

It's a gentlemen's game played by hooligans." He said as we walked out of the Cricket Club, again, as if everyone already knew this and I was a child of the world just now being taught.

"Well, how do you feel about football?" I asked.

"Do you mean 'soccer' or 'American football'?" He asked.

American football? Hmmm, I'd heard that before. I knew that the rest of the world called 'soccer' 'football' and they wondered why we called our game 'football' when the foot only touches the ball on four specific plays in the game. My research revealed that our football evolved in the 1800's having been brought back from England by American students that had studied abroad and learned to play rugby. Some rules and ideas on how to play the game changed over time, and we have modern football now being very different from rugby.

Ask any Brit what they think of our football versus their rugby, and one of the first things they would say was that American football was weak because of all the padding the players wore. What my British cousins forget was that in American football we had full-speed, head-on collisions that rugby does not have as they do not use the forward pass. It had been said that rugby was a "contact" sport. Well, so was dancing. (OK, a rib to my English cousin, John). Football was a "collision" sport.

While I have learned to really enjoy rugby, comparing it to football was like comparing soccer to lacrosse. They were different sports, each having equally interesting rules of play and outstanding athletes. I liked both and arguing about which was "better" was a task better left to fools. A real "sportsman" appreciated all sports and belittled none.

261

"I like American football very much." John said. "But it's got way too many commercial adverts."

OK, he had me there.

"It gives you a chance to use the men's room after drinking too many pints." I laughed.

"Hmmm. I usually do that at half-time." He said.

"Right, with every other over-served gent in the place." I laughed.

"You've got a good point!" He smiled. "Perhaps an advert/piss break would be helpful."

I liked the way he was willing to give and take when conversing. He was a very fun and congenial man.

We headed back to our building. For some reason, John grabbed two beers and switched on the TV to watch more sports. I was right on the edge of sleepy from too much food and also just a little drunk, but apparently we would push on.

Beth was in California on business and Jake was having a sleepover at a school friends' house, so I invited Miss Beena from upstairs to come down for a visit. We opened the house up to the outside and turned on the TV to watch a football game. Miss Beena was a woman from Florida who lived on the third floor. She had become good friends with us and she came to many of our barbeques, dinners and parties. She and the Texans were staples in our Bahamian diet.

"What should I bring?" She asked.

"A bucket, a sponge and some aspirin." I said. "John looks ill."

John was fine and he just shook his head and grinned at me.

"Bring the boy a blanket, Beena." He shouted so she could hear him. "I think he's going down for a kip."

"I have some pizza in the fridge." She groaned.

"Careful. Pizza makes John a bit *chatty*." I yelled

so he could hear in the next room.

"What?" John said innocently.

"Pizza or nothing." She whined. She was almost always having to work on the weekend at home so I knew she dreaded, but would accept, my invitation to watch football.

"I don't' know. I'm already pretty tired. Oh yeah, I'm still unemployed. I guess I'll just take tomorrow off, again. What about you? How's the job of *yours*" I asked.

"Ass." She said. "See you in five."

"What's the matter? Miss Beena got a little weekend work to do again?" I laughed at her. "At least you have a job."

Miss Beena worked at Club Caribe and had tried to get me introduced to the right people for an interview, but so far had not been successful. I liked to tease her about how worthless her "great contacts" had been so far.

We watched the game and had a few laughs. John mentioned to Miss Beena that we'd been watching rugby at the Cricket Club.

"I love rugby." She said. "Some friends of mine play in Florida."

"We should catch a game together sometime." John said.

"There is a league here on the island." I offered quickly.

"Just a bunch of chubby expats bumping into each other." John said. "I mean we should go see a *proper* rugby game, in England."

"Sounds great." I said.

He grinned widely and the wheels were set in motion. I had no idea, but John had been given two tickets for a very important rugby game in England and had not decided who he wanted to take. He asked Miss Beena to look up flights to London on her laptop.

I was feeling every drop of the beers from earlier and a trip to London was suddenly sounding like a very good idea. Before I realized what I was doing, John offered the extra ticket to me and Miss Beena had reserved a flight to London on Virgin Air. I handed her my wallet to get my credit card to pay for the flight online when suddenly someone said...

"I wonder if this will be OK with Beth?"

"*Oh, she'll be just fine!*" The little voice chimed in and we all agreed. Well, if the little voice said it was OK... I guess I'd go for it!

I would only be in London for four days. Beth took trips to California of seven to ten days regularly. Miss Beena would keep her company and help with Jake. Within thirty minutes, I had booked my first trip to London, received approval from two people who had zero authority, but I did have the stamp of approval from the little voice. As I sat there and thought about what I'd just done, already feeling buyer's remorse, I hoped that when the clouds cleared that I'd still feel just as eager as I had earlier.

"One more thing, mate... " John said.

"What's that?" I asked.

"I got you a meeting with my boss in London. I've told him a lot and he's keen on meeting you." He grinned.

John worked for a QS company that was based in London, but did work all over the world. I quickly remembered: a QS was a Quantity Surveyor, which was kind of like a cross between an engineer and an accountant, two breeds that had been banished from procreating in the United States many years ago. It seemed that their children were too boring to move so they died as infants. I was in.

"Why didn't you say anything about this before?" I asked.

"Hey ho, I guess I wanted to see if you were serious about going." He grinned widely, very satisfied with my reaction to his secret.

I realized that he had no idea just how much I wanted to work at Club Caribe. Getting a job with his company would be fantastic. They paid well, had a great compensation package for living abroad. According to Mongo, who had kids, they would even pay for Jake's schooling. This job would be the bridge from glorified tourist to working expat. It would establish us here like concrete. We could put little hand impressions and a penny for a date that marked the day we truly escaped.

"Thank you." I said. "You have no idea how great this is."

"It's just rugby, mate." He said grinning.

British people got uncomfortable if you made a big deal out of a favor they had done. He had set me up. The favor he was doing me could change the direction of my life for a few years. I would find a way to thank him someday.

"*See, I told ya!*" The little voice said. I kicked him out and went to bed smiling.

* * * * *

I was reminded that I had married the right woman when she came home from California, and I mentioned to her that I was leaving for London in two days.

"A rugby game?" She asked. "All the way to London for a game?"

"Well, there is more to it than that." I said.

265

"What?" She asked.

"Why not come out to the beach with me? I'll tell you there."

She liked surprises, but like most of us she liked them a lot more once she knew the surprise was a good one. We walked out the patio door, across the grass, and to the pool patio area to the sea wall.

"John got me an interview with his firm in London. I may get a job at Club Caribe." I said after we sat.

"Oh my God!" She said. "How wonderful!" She hugged me and then went right into wife mode.

"It's real Winter there, not like here, so we'll have to get you some warm clothes, a suit, some shoes... " She began listing things out loud.

"We've got a couple days. We'll pull it together. I've got to work on my resume with John and study up on their company." I explained.

And then I paused and said, "Hey, you're right. I don't have any real shoes, do I?"

"Just flip-flops." She laughed. "But they have bottle openers on the sole just in case you have beers with someone!"

We both laughed out loud at the ridiculous way we now lived compared to the "real" world. We hugged each other tightly. The California boy turned island expat was headed for the old Blighty. It seemed that things might work out and I allowed myself to be completely hopeful for a good outcome. No matter how hard I tried to act cool, I was still feeling pensive. John seemed pretty sure the job was mine. Beth did not hide the fact that she was thrilled. I needed to get on this happy train with the others.

We began to pack my bags with the few warm clothes we had brought from California for trips to the East Coast. I sifted through some dress clothes I'd

266

bought in Florida, in case I had a job interview on the island. I did not have a suit, but I did have slacks, dress shirts and ties. I'd buy a pair of hard-soled leather shoes and talk to John about needing a jacket. I also set up a dinner meeting at our place, so we could discuss what I'd need to know about the company for the interview, what to expect, and who I was to meet. John and Mongo said they'd bring some study materials for me and they would also look over my resume one more time.

I did all I could to prepare. I memorized everything I could find online about the company's history as I prepared for my interview. I practiced interview questions with John, Mongo and Beth for hours, and finally felt that I could pull this off. I modeled three different outfits for Beth, but we decided to pack them all. Beth put everything she thought I might need and somehow we managed to get all of it into one large suitcase and a backpack. The rugby game never entered my mind. I focused on the job interview that could make it possible for us to remain here. Rugby was a bonus.

John's flight was a day before mine, so we dropped him off at the airport.

"See you tomorrow." He said smiling. "In *England*."

"Tomorrow?" Well it'll be something like that. What about the time change? More like two days. I think I arrive the following morning sometime." I thought out loud.

"No worries, mate. I've got your itinerary and will pick you up at the airport." John said. We shook hands and he turned to walk off towards the British Airways desk.

"See you in *England*." I said to myself as I walked

267

back to my Honda. I was headed for England for the first time in my life. The thought of this trip was making me giddy like a kid. I was genuinely excited.

The next day, Beth drove me to the Nassau airport. I wore jeans, tennis shoes (trainers, whatever) and a Hawaiian shirt. This was about as dressed as I had been in a long time. The socks on my feet felt odd and my toes sweated.

"You're quiet." Beth poked at me.

"I wish you were going."

"Me too. But you have to do this alone. I understand." She said as she rubbed my knee. "You'll do fine."

"The interview is not for a couple of days. I'm actually only there for four days, can you believe it?" I frowned. "Such a long trip, so far away...for four frigging days."

"It's a short trip, for sure. But you'll cram a lot into it." She smiled.

"I'll take tons of pictures for you. I have to admit, it's going to be fun. The last time I was in Europe was when I lived in Paris and that was almost fifteen years ago. Man, time flies!" I said as I thought back to the days when I was in my mid-twenties and had gotten a modeling job in San Francisco that turned into a six-month stay in Paris. That part of my life, before I had met Beth, seemed like someone else. The memories were mine but they felt removed now, kind of like a movie I'd seen.

She kissed me at the airport. The airport traffic cop frowned as we parked in the drop-off zone for a minute too long.

"You'd better go." I said. "I'll call you as soon as I can."

"I love you. Be safe."

"I will. Love you. Bye."

I walked away from her and tried not to look back, but I could not help it. She waved and blew kisses to me. Again I was reminded of how lucky I was to be with this woman. I waved back and then turned towards the airport. I felt the sidewalk beneath my feet knowing that these were the first steps of a very long journey. I looked back at her once more and waved, and then went into the airport terminal.

Nassau International Airport was a relatively small building as compared to the amount of traffic it handled. The ceiling was unnecessarily tall, which did nothing for the acoustics. The unintelligible announcements were fairly constant and echoed throughout the interior. The place was always excessively crowded with nowhere to sit, and the noise level fell somewhere between a freeway and a firecracker. I imagined being able to meet the engineer of this building and then giving him a smack in the face, but he was surely dead by now. The island had simply outgrown the space.

After going through the ticket line, the luggage search, the customs area, the interview room, another security check, a vision test, and a rectal exam, I was typically annoyed. All this security, x-ray equipment, uniforms and weapons, and still most of these so-called security officers couldn't find their ass with a guide and a GPS. One really large lady guard just sat on a stool and glared at people as they put their luggage on the carousel. She was eating from a red and white box of chicken and appeared to be very good at it.

I'm not a cruel person, so here's Rodney Dangerfield:

"She was so fat her farts weighed two pounds."

269

How had she passed the physical test when she had to lean to the left to be able to find her gun on the right? Sorry, I think I had already mentioned how much I like authority.

I went to the airport bar. Beth and I had downed many "let's just have one more Kalik" beers over the years as we sadly ended another of our Bahamian vacations. We would film each other with our over-sized movie camera and laugh, oblivious of anyone around us.

The small bar had one of the crankiest bartenders on the island. I hated that bar. I bartended throughout college, so it really irked me to see guys like that making any money at all. "Everybody plays guitar, everybody tends bar." I had heard many years ago. In my experience, most people do both very poorly. I sure hoped that bartender could play guitar. He had six people holding cash in their hands, signaling thirst, and he moved behind the bar like he was wearing snow skis. He never smiled or said anything. He just looked at you when he was ready to serve you and grunted a bit after you ordered. I thought I'd play with him a little.

"Hi, can I get a Ramos Fizz?" I asked.

He just continued to stare at me.

"Singapore Sling?"

He still stared.

"Grasshopper?"

Glassy eyes with an expressionless face.

"Pink Squirrel?"

Still as an English soldier standing guard.

"Rusty Nail?"

A statue faced me.

"OK, I'll just have a beer." I said.

He cocked his head just an inch.

"A Kalik." I clarified for him.

270

Heavy sigh combined with a slight head shake.

"Kalik *Light*." I said and he bent forward, and pulled a bottle from the cooler in front of him. He opened it and set it down in front of me.

"Eight dollars." He said.

Wow, he *can* speak. I put a one hundred dollar bill on the bar and stared back at him. We began again.

"What, no change?" I said smiling.

He looked down at the floor and frowned, shaking his head with disgust.

"Did you get bad news today?" I asked.

* * * * *

I was flying from Nassau to Newark, New Jersey on Continental Airlines and from there I would switch to Virgin Atlantic for the jump across the pond to Heathrow International Airport. I'd heard great things about Virgin Air and was excited to take that leg of the trip. I had to listen very carefully for my flight announcement as the high ceilings in this building combined with the announcer (who apparently was speaking through a cat's ass) made it nearly impossible to understand anything spoken into the P.A. system.

Today, I was feeling very different. I was leaving my adopted home to fly to London to interview for a job back on my adopted home. This was all very cosmopolitan for this small-town beach kid. At home, you just drove and applied for the job you found in the newspaper. Here, there was some serious traveling to be done.

I would need to get some rest on the red-eye flight if I was going to be worth anything when I landed. I was not good at sleeping on planes as they were just too small. At 6'1" and 245 lbs., the seats in coach barely held me, and the ones in first class were comfortable, but not enough to sleep. Add to that, instead of even trying to sleep, I would bring a dazzling array of electronic gadgets to amuse myself. The trip would not involve a nap, but I'd sure feel dreamy when I arrived.

CHAPTER TWENTY
Across The Pond

The flight up to Newark was uneventful and only took about three hours. In Newark, first I purchased some British Sterling Pounds at a currency kiosk. I knew that in England, unlike the Bahamas, they would not just accept US currency. I would have to use their money. I then headed for the Virgin Atlantic terminal and checked in at the ticket counter.

"Good day, sir." The pretty young English woman behind the counter greeted me with an accent that bordered on delicious. And I loved it when people said, "*Good day*."

"Good day." I said, trying not to appear intoxicated. I was not drunk, I was tired. There were many phases of tired that resembled drunkenness. I was somewhere between "flirty" and "sleepy".

She looked at my passport and checked my itinerary. "I see we have you booked in our Economy class." She said as she made a bit of a pouty face.

"Would you be interested in upgrading to our *Premium* Economy class?" She asked.

* * * * *

This reminded me of when my brother Eric was selling cars and was trying to explain why adding some pinstripe paint, fake leather seats, and an FM stereo in a Ford Mustang II made it the "LX" version.

"What does LX mean?" I asked.

"Luxury, of course." He said and grinned his big salesman smile.

"But, it's the same car with some lame upgrades." I accused him as if he was responsible.

"Oh, I assure you that this LX version is a far cry from the original. For example, the LX has seats that adjust."

"And the regular one?" I asked?

"Well, they adjust…but the LX seats adjust further and have lumbar support." He explained.

"What else?"

"The LX version has heated seats, heated mirrors and a heated ashtray."

"A heated ashtray?" I stumbled on this amenity. "Who the heck needs that?"

"No one, sadly." He made a sad face and answered sincerely. "But with all the wiring to the seats, mirrors and through the dash…the ashtray naturally heats up. So, we sell it. I mean who wants to smoke a cold cigarette?" He raised his eyebrows as he made this point.

"Actually, I keep mine in the fridge."

"Right, but most people smoke a lot more regularly than you do. Actually, I've never understood how you never became a bonified smoker." He looked at me suspiciously.

"I look at it this way: sometimes breathing smoke and drinking poison sounds like a great idea. Then I wake up the next day, feeling like hell and need a break from both. How people smoke every day, much less drink every day, I've never understood." I explained.

"Well, they do. And most people enjoy their cigarettes nice and toasty from our little ashtray heater." He smiled.

"Still sounds like BS to me."

"That's because it is." He admitted. "People are stupid and we capitalize on it. Imagine two nice pair of running shoes, both pretty much the same in every way, except one has a white swoosh on the side. People will pay double for the one with the swoosh because it's been sold to them as superior."

"Too bad both shoes were probably made by the same kid in Bangladesh." I said.

Eric nodded. "Same kid probably made the Ford Mustang, too. It's his fault the damn ashtray heats up."

* * * * *

I had hoped that Premium Economy was more than just a price hike.

I had hoped that Premium Economy was more than just a price hike. I asked the friendly lady at the ticket counter what the difference between the classes really meant.

"We have three classes available for you today, sir. We have Economy, Premium Economy and Upper class." She said and showed me a list of amenities from each level of service.

From the description in the brochure, it appeared that they had what we would call Coach, First Class and "WOW!" class. The WOW, or Upper Class as she called it, provided a private sleep chamber complete with pajamas, a bar with real barstools, a private chef, live entertainment, a shooting range, a fly-fishing pond and a bowling alley. You could get a massage, a haircut, go rock-climbing and finish a master's degree all in the same flight.

I was very interested in the Upper Class level of service and she said there was plenty of room, but when she pulled out the credit application, I figured it might be a bit too much for this trip.

"Maybe another time." I said.

I upgraded to the Premium class, which turned out to be like a very nice first class seat with top notch service. I liked Virgin Atlantic! This was much better than American Airlines, which had a first class section that felt like sitting at a Greyhound Bus station. The coach class on American felt like the bathroom at the Greyhound Bus station, and the bathrooms on American resembled a port-a-john on a construction site in Guatemala. I've always thought that to be allowed to have the name "American" on anything that it should require a certain level of service. What an embarrassment.

I settled in to my seat and was given a pre-departure cocktail, while I browsed through the entertainment system. Then, before my first cocktail was gone, I was given another pre-departure cocktail. Well! What service! I'd better be careful or I'd just pass out on this flight.

While I perused the high-tech entertainment system, a third cocktail was handed to me but I turned it down. It was then that I noticed and immediately loved the fact that they had different entry doors, so the different levels of service did not have to glare at each other as they boarded the plane. I had never understood why airlines had the first class people board, give you a glass of champagne, only to then have the coach people board. It's not fun having two hundred strangers glare at you, elbowing you, and bumping their carry-on luggage into your head as they passed. This airline did it right! But, I must say I watched with envy as the three gentlemen headed forward to the Upper Class area. *Snobs*!

The cabin was not full, so I rocked my seat backwards to test how far it reclined. It was nice, but not enough for sleeping. The beautiful young flight attendants fluttered around like butterflies, smiling the entire time and appearing very pleasant. I'm not a sexist, but having pretty females as flight attendants sure felt like a bonus to me. I'd much rather be served on a plane by Barbie than by Ken. Ken can fly the damn thing. Or, perhaps Barbie's butch female cousin "Pat" could be the pilot. I really don't care. Again, I'm not a sexist. But I am a heterosexual male. There's a difference. And being served by all these Barbie types was just fine with me. Either way, I knew that I was going to enjoy this flight, and I settled in for the long ride.

* * * * *

For me, being an American traveling to England for the first time felt a bit like returning home. This was where our forefathers lived and this was the land they left for a better life. This was the country we had to fight for our independence. While we share a mutual respect now, I could not help but feel like I did when I went back to my father's house after serving in the Army. The boy that had left his home at eighteen had changed while in the military. The man that returned years later was different. As I headed for England, I remembered that I was not a traitor or a rebel like they considered our Founding Fathers. I was an American. Proud as I was, I would still do my best to be a grateful guest, and act as politely as possible.

After getting my bag, and wandering through the rushed mouse maze of crowded corridors that made up the Heathrow Airport, I found my way to the security area exit and there stood John, just beyond the gated area, grinning and snapping my photograph.

"Good morning, mate!" He said. "You look a bit bleary."

"Oh thanks. Well, I was able to catch a movie on the plane but mostly just enjoyed the great food and a short snooze." I said.

We walked in a very hurried manner to the car lot in a light rain.

"Has the weather been bad since you arrived?" I asked John as we hurriedly waked.

"What weather? This is English sunshine, mate."

Before I knew it we were racing along on the M-5 motorway doing close to ninety miles per hour.

"Welcome to England!" John said as he skillfully darted his rented VW Golf in and out of traffic on the busy freeway.

"This is the M-5 I told you about." He said this as if it was supposed to frighten me. He forgot that I was from California and that just a mile and a half from my house there were twelve lanes of freeway that I drove daily.

"Wow." I said and tried to sound enthusiastic.

There were three or four lanes on each side, a concrete wall in the middle, and of course everything was backwards with us driving on the left with John sitting on the right side of the car. The average speed seemed to be about 80 MPH, but every now and then some nice car would fly by us at 120 plus. It seemed that everyone drove either gas-sipping clown cars or behemoth cargo trucks. A Jaguar or Mercedes would fly by every so often. I tried to enjoy my first impressions of this foreign land, but my jet-lag was fogging my memory lens and holding down my excitement meter.

278

John soon exited the freeway and now we sped down tiny country lanes through lush, green rolling hills dotted with fat sheep. John appeared to think we were in a rally race as he jammed through the gears and raced along narrow roads built for a Roman chariot.

Finally, we turned into a parking lot for a small place called The Cock Inn. At that moment, I was convinced that John was completely comfortable with his manhood. Back home, I didn't visit places in San Francisco like the Cock Pit, Man Hole, or The Ram Rod because the names just turned me off. This place was called "The Cock Inn". Had I been alone, I would have just driven by this place.

It turned out that The Cock Inn was simply named after a rooster and it was a small, country pub. I soon learned that many old English pubs had silly names. The English were playful people, but most of the pubs were hundreds of years old so the words used then had much different meanings now. Even with this in mind, I still had a good laugh when we walked through London one day past a pub called the "Bung Hole."

We sat down by the fireplace in some very comfortable chairs and John bought my first "jar" of London Pride Bitter.

"It's not beer or ale, mate. It's 'bitter', which is an old version of beer. It was kept cellar-cool in kegs below the pub and hand-pumped up bar by the barman." He explained as I watched the barman work a decorative lever that apparently pumped the liquid up some tubes from the cellar.

"OK, I'll give it a try." I said.

He grinned widely so I knew I was in for some kind of surprise. What I tasted was something akin to a dark beer that had been left on the kitchen counter overnight and had lost its carbonation. It was cool, but not cold.

"I think this one is broken." I said.

John laughed so loudly that the patrons at the bar looked over. It was then that I noticed there was not music or much sound in the pub. It was oddly quiet with just the crackling fire making pops now and then.

"It's not 'broken' mate. That's how it's supposed to taste." He said, still chuckling.

"But it's flat." I explained.

"Right."

"How come you're not having one?" I asked as I sniffed the glass again.

"Oh, well that stuff gives me the farts." He laughed.

I figured that I'd give the bitter another try and after I'd finished the jar I ordered another.

"Uh-oh, it's going to be a rough ride home." John laughed.

"Just roll down the window if you have to, this stuff is weird but for some reason I like it." I smiled. Perhaps it was because I was in England in a pub with my English pal sitting by a crackling fire and looking out the window at the English countryside... or perhaps I actually liked the stuff. I did not care. This was a new experience and I was literally drinking it in.

I was giddy from jet-lag and traveling and could have used a nap, but John was having none of it. He immediately took me on a whirlwind tour of the countryside where he grew up in East Sussex. We passed the Queen's horse racing track, a national park, looked out over a battlefield from a vista point, went by his old house, and many other places before he finally drove me to our hotel. It was fun, but the bitter and the jet lag had me ready to trade my good watch for a cheap pillow.

We stayed at a small inn outside London near the Salford's train station. John quickly checked me in and helped me with my luggage to my room.

"Thanks, John. I wasn't sure how much longer I could wear these underwear." I said.

"Oh yes. Very nice, I'm sure." He grimaced. "You should relax, clean up and rest a bit. There is a restaurant and pub downstairs."

"Are you taking off?" I asked.

"I've got to go meet some pals for dinner tonight so get some rest. You saw the train station, right?" He asked and I nodded my head, but was really not sure.

"It's called 'Salfords'. Just walk up there tomorrow morning and take the train to Victoria Station. Give yourself about 45 minutes for the trip. I'll meet you there at nine to show you London." John explained and he left me alone in my small room.

My jet lag made me a bit overwhelmed with all that he had just shown me and told me, so I wrote down the time and names of the stations he had mentioned. I looked out the window of my room to see a huge green meadow with horses nibbling at the grass. This was not what I had expected at all. I thought we'd be staying in London, not the country. But this was cheaper and it was a cozy, clean room.

After taking a shower in the tiny bathroom with the even tinier shower and bathtub, I looked around the room to see that there was no phone. I needed to call Beth, so I walked down to the check-in desk and the lady there told me that the nearest pay phone was across the street at a restaurant. I walked outside into the night and looked around. It was very odd to have horses and green pastures outside the window in my room and just a short walk away from the hotel there was four lanes of busy traffic. It was literally freezing outside with a pretty brisk wind that carried little pieces of ice that stung my cheeks. I remembered just how difficult it was to use a phone in Paris and figured that this would be just as difficult, so I decided that I'd try to call her in the morning from London.

Back in the room, I tried to figure out how to connect my laptop to the hotel Wi-Fi, but had no luck so I could not email her either. I was getting drowsy and the clock said 8 PM, so I figured I'd lasted long enough on my first of four days here. There were only three channels on the TV, so it was easy to find something boring that quickly put me to sleep. I cannot recommend falling to sleep with a documentary about Attila the Hun playing in the background, but there was really nothing else on the TV.

The next day I awoke to my cell phone alarm, quickly showered, and left for the train station. It was below freezing outside and I was thankful that Beth had packed a long coat, scarf, hat and gloves for me, but it was not enough. The winter weather in England was something I had never experienced before. The sky was grey and there was a constant drizzle of freezing rain. My Caribbean blood was too thin for this kind of weather. I was shaking and my hands were numbing quickly. I would have to get an umbrella to stay dry and I needed warmer clothing. Suddenly, I realized that my throat was a bit sore. This was usually an indication that a cold or worse was on its way. I cursed the timing of this and on the way to the station. I stopped at a small corner store and asked for some sore throat medicine.

"Would you like some Tickly Cough?" The man behind the counter asked.

A British lady near me heard my accent and looked at me. I tried to look respectable, but felt very out of place.

"I'm sorry, I've never heard of that." I said. "Is it

good for a sore throat?"

"The best." He said. I paid the man and left for the station.

Tickly Cough? What if I had diarrhea? Would they sell me *Shitty Shitty Bum Bum*?

I bought a round trip ticket from a very rude Chinese man behind the glass at the small outdoor station at Salford's. Hearing his English accent startled me a bit, kind of like if my dog suddenly meowed. And why was he so crabby? I was the only person at the station, which was really nothing more than an uncovered, raised concrete platform. It was not like I was holding up the line, or cue, as they called it.

The morning rush had already passed, so I had the platform to myself. I looked around and down the long train tracks that led off into infinity. Suddenly, I felt very lonely. It was miserably cold and wet. I was 8,000 miles from California, alone and heading to one of the most famous cities in the world. I was in such a hurry to leave the hotel that I'd forgotten to eat or to bring any water, so hopefully the trip would be short. I tried to catch some of the rain on my tongue as I listened for the train.

CHAPTER TWENTY-ONE
There And Back Again

The ride on the train from Salfords to Victoria Station was fairly uneventful. There was not much to see out the window. It seemed that trackside buildings and homes in England were just as shabby as they were at home. As we sped by, I did notice that the graffiti was just as prevalent as back home. However, the spelling appeared to be much better. I wasn't surprised. The English language *was* created here. There was one graffiti conversation I saw that read something like this:

"Frank's a wanker!"
"Frank is a mate. I demand that you retract your statement!"
"Apologies, mate. I did not know Frank was your mate."
"Right then. All is settled and I have satisfaction."
"Cheerio!"
This place WAS different.

John met me at Victoria Station, which was an absolute blur of activity. Like most things in England, the station itself was not massive, but the energy and action was electric. There were people everywhere hurrying from place to place, vendors with their carts selling everything from snacks and tea to perfume and chocolate. The walls were lined with more vendors,

284

small shops and restaurants. Just as I began getting interested in some of the compulsion shopping items, I saw John walking up to me at full speed.

"Have a good kip?" John asked and he motioned to an exit that led to a busy street.

"Kip?" I asked. "Oh yeah, *sleep*. Not bad. I was pretty tired."

"Knackered." He said. "You were *knackered*, mate. You're in London now. Might as well speak *English*.

John immediately took me on a whirlwind walking tour of London. We speed-walked down thousand-year-old streets as he spoke quickly and smoked incessantly. About an hour into the trek, I realized I had not only brought the wrong clothing, I had also brought the wrong shoes. I was wearing leather dress shoes and my feet were killing me. John smartly had worn trainers, but he was not on his way to a job interview. He was always about five paces ahead of me explaining the history of the next thousand-year-old church, while I was still trying to get a snapshot of the last thousand-year-old church.

Americans had to get used to the "time inflation" of London and most of Europe. When they said something was "old", they meant from the days of the Romans. A five-hundred-year-old church was just getting broken in by English standards. The odd part for me was that the five-hundred-year-old church sat right next to a modern glass and metal monster building. I saw this odd architecture and juxtaposition everywhere in London. It was very hard to get used to seeing a gothic cathedral next to a building shaped like a man blowing a pink bubble gum balloon. Modern architecture was in full-bloom in London.

"A lot of the older buildings were bombed to their

foundations during World War Two, mate." John explained. "We ended up rebuilding what was lost and preserving what was left."

"You ended up with some very strange juxtaposition, my friend." I said.

"Is that English?" He asked.

"Yes, I'm fairly sure."

He nodded and probably made a mental note to research the word later, instead of just ask me what it meant.

We trekked onward.

John's walking pace was about equal to that of a medium jog. This American had not been fed yet, was miserably jet-lagged, and had blisters forming on each toe. My head was swimming with thoughts of my impending interview in an hour or so, while taking in all of the sights. I tried to enjoy the experience, but I was freezing and my feet were really starting to hurt.

"John, are we going to see all of London in one day?" I asked.

"Well, not *all* of it, no. London is quite large and very dense, you see." He said. Apparently, sarcasm sometimes does not translate even to English-speaking people.

"What I mean is, can we slow down a bit? I'd like to take some of this place in." I pleaded.

"Well, we just don't have much time, mate. I've got to get you over to the office for your interview at 11 AM and there is so much to see before then."

"Right. Well, I'd rather not arrive a sweaty mess. And I'd better get some different shoes if we're going to run a marathon." I joked.

"Marathon?" He asked. "Oh no, there's no time for sport. That's the last day when we go to Twickers for the rugby match."

"Dude, you're killing me. How about some new shoes then?"

"Right." He said as he thought for a moment. "I know just the place."

John took me to a nearby sporting goods store where I bought some eighty pound shoes that were so comfortable I almost shed a tear. The dollar was doing poorly against the pound, about 2 to 1, so the shoes cost me $160.00 US. They were worth every penny.

"OK, mate now that you are properly fitted." John said grinning at my new trainers. They were indeed the most comfortable shoes I'd ever worn. Probably invented right here in England, John would say. So I just kept quiet about the shoes.

"Did you get hold of Beth?" He asked as we left the store.

"Sort of. There was no phone in my room and my cell won't link up to any network here. I think I was able to pinch some free Wi-Fi and I emailed her. I'm not sure if she got it, though." I said. "Hey, did you know that Attila the Hun choked to death from a nose bleed?"

"Yes, in 453. The same night he married the barbarian princess Ildico." John said matter-of-factly, as if everyone knew this fact. "What makes you bring that up?"

"I'm not sure." I said. "I think I dreamt it. But I did leave the TV on last night."

"Well, good thing you at least spoke with Beth. I promised her I'd bring you back in one piece. Now she won't worry." John sighed.

"Again, I'm not sure the email even went through. But she'll worry anyway." I said. And John nodded and smiled. He had been married.

John led me further into London, explaining every building, structure and bridge along the way. John was

287

like a walking encyclopedia, if encyclopedias could run and smoke at the same time.

Finally, John said we would head to his corporate office where I was to have my interview.

Running so much in the cold weather inside my heavy jacket made me pour sweat the moment we got inside the warm office building. We approached what appeared to be a large pile of broken glass, about ten stories tall, with little metal sticks that pointed at odd angles, when John suddenly stopped and pointed.

"There she is." He said, beaming.

"That's your building?" I asked.

"Beauty." He said.

But he was an engineer. To me it looked like a failing grade in a freshmen year industrial arts class. It also looked like a crate of glass Coke bottles broken up with some welding rods sticking out here and there.

We quickly headed inside and John told me to wait.

I whipped my jacket off to avoid soaking my shirt, but it was too late. I began to get nervous, which did not help my situation.

This area of the office appeared to be a computer clean room. There was probably not a speck of dust on the whole floor. It was sparsely furnished with huge ceilings and glass walls everywhere. The place did not appear occupied. Then someone walked by, heels clicking loudly on the concrete floor, looking like the cover of Paris Vogue.

"Good morning." She said.

Then she kept walking, but she did throw one more look my way. Sure, she had to stare a bit at the sweaty stranger. I was so sweaty that I probably looked like I'd just walked through a car wash. How was I going to dry myself off and get through this interview, which would just make me sweat more?

John came back and then he led me to a small waiting area, which was actually a small stool and a counter with a coffee machine and some napkins. He then left me again and I did everything I could to calm myself, changed my focus to the task at hand, and dried off my shirt and skin.

I wiped myself with some brown paper towels I found next to the coffee machine as I dreaded what would come next: the interview. Job interviews were like a first date. You were on your best behavior and you still knew you're most likely not getting laid. And even as nice as that might be, you tried to pretend that you were not that kind of person. Having sex on the first date pretty much doomed the relationship to be short-term, but you didn't want to appear to be the clingy, serious "marriage-minded" guy that most women ran from even though that's what they really wanted. You had to act a bit aloof, but interested, interesting but not dangerous, caring but not weak... ahh, the first date. What a lot of crap. Most people were so screwed up in the head that they had no clue what they wanted. They kept chasing the best balance they could fathom eternity with, just enough crazy to be fun, but not enough to cut the crotches out of all your dress slacks.

I sat down on what may have been either a silver trash can, a dentist's spit sink, or a modern artists' version of a chair. I could not recline or fold my legs, and the stool was so narrow it was in danger of giving me a prostate exam. I never got the whole Euro-minimalist thing. I sat there balancing myself on this circus prop, trying to mentally force the sweat to disappear from my forehead and look cool.

Busy people walked by in a hurry like people do in the movies about huge corporations. But this was not movie. This was a huge multi-national corporation. I felt a little sorry for myself as I sat there alone, so many thousands of miles from home, soaked to the skin in clothes that I was sure were not as nice as the two-legged fashion magazines that kept walking by.

London, like Paris, was full of people that were very concerned about how they looked. I was just a California beach kid that bounced on a Caribbean beach before landing here. I checked my appearance in the reflection of a stainless steel piece of artwork and I began to check my attitude. I needed to man up here and do what I came to do.

What did I really have to lose?

My resume honestly listed my skills and experience, but I knew nothing about being a Quantity Surveyor (QS) like John. I remembered: a QS was like an accountant/engineer for large commercial construction projects. We didn't really use them in the USA. The largest construction project I ever worked on would not hold most of these people's shoe collection but they did not need to know that. The only reason they would even consider me was because I had already lived in the Bahamas and John had told the owners that he would be able to train me. My background in construction and commercial fire sprinklers would certainly help. According to John, they were very light in the fire sprinkler system area, so I had a chance. I would focus on that aspect of my skill-set, but I was certainly feeling pretty small.

Where the heck was John?

Thankfully, I sat in that break room, storage area, or whatever it was with ample time to dry off for quite a while until John and another man finally came to greet me. The other man was older, but seemed energetic and friendly. He invited me back to a very small interview room. Inside there was a small, round table and four chairs. I squeezed myself around one chair and then wondered how I would actually sit at the table. The chairs touched the wall and the table. Was this some kind of engineering test? Or was it a joke?

"Go ahead, mate. Have a seat." The man said. "Coffee?" And normally I'd say no, but I needed time to work the chair puzzle out.

"Thank you." I said.

"Sugar?"

"Sounds great."

"Milk?" He asked and did not look the least bit like he was testing or teasing me.

"That would be lovely." I said and immediately kicked myself in the mental crotch for saying "lovely". Well, it was England. They did say things like that there.

"Be right back." He said and he was gone for about ten minutes.

While he was gone, I figured out a way to sit at the table by removing two of the chairs and lodging myself into a corner. Opening the door would be a trick for him, but at this point I did not care. How the heck did they not use some of that cavernous space just outside this office for the interview area?

We spoke for about thirty minutes. The room being so small that our knees kept rubbing the inside of each other's thighs the whole time. This was odd. But, he acted normally so I did too. I remembered the rumor that the Eskimo man insists that you sleep with his wife if you're a guest in his igloo. I was the stranger in this man's stack of ice blocks, and there was no way I'd say no if he handed me a nightshirt and his wife's hand. I wanted this job.

The whole process was not at all what I had dreaded. It was actually very comfortable and positive.

291

He did not seem overly impressed by my knowledge of his company and its history, but he did like my resume and reiterated what John had said about the Bahamas lacking tradesmen with fire sprinkler skills. He hired me on the spot, and said that the details of the job offer and compensation package would follow soon via email.

As I walked back out of the interview room where the man led me back to John, I was in a daze. Maybe it was the new shoes or maybe it was because my feet were no longer touching the floor, but I felt like I was floating. I had just gotten the job. I figured that he had already decided to hire me from my resume and John's recommendation. I figured that he just wanted to meet me and make sure I was the kind of person they wanted. Most interviews are mere formalities anyway.

We headed down in the elevator in silence. Once we were back on the street, I almost shouted.

"John! I got the damn job!" I yelled to the sky.

"Well, I always thought you would, mate." He said calmly.

"Don't be so cool, bro. I was nervous as hell! But he really liked me and hired me right there in the office."

"Well, he's one of the owners so he can do that." John said. "Congratulations, my friend and *colleague*. I knew he'd hire you. Were you really that worried?"

"Are you kidding? Never mind. *Fancy a drink*? I'm buying." I said.

"I never thought you'd ask." He said grinning. "Come on, I know a pub."

I was pretty sure he knew a few pubs.

John took me to a restaurant that was actually below the street level. Apparently, it's original purpose was a butchery and there were meat hooks hanging on the walls to remind patrons of its' legacy, or what the barman would do to you if you stiffed him on the bill.

We sat down, had ordered a quick beer and one of the tiniest bacon sandwiches I had ever seen. I did not touch either. I was almost in a daze. But I did find a moment to complain.

"How the heck did you English get bread that is even thinner than the bacon itself?" I questioned the whole room apparently because they all looked at me for a moment.

John just smiled. Another reason England ruled the world and the rest of us just lived there, his face said as he smirked and raised his eyebrows nodding at me.

"Dude, seriously. I could eat thirty of these!" I exclaimed.

John saw someone he knew and introduced me, but I was in my own world. I did not care about London, the rugby game, skinny bacon sandwiches or anything else right now. All I wanted to do was call Beth and tell her the good news. John chatted to a friend he used to work with, introduced me to her and her friends, and they all talked. I was fading into my own mind and the jet-lag was making me willing to pay $1,000 for a pillow on a soft bed with nothing to do for two days.

* * * * *

I finally figured out how to get my laptop to attach to the hotel Wi-Fi cleanly and Beth and I were able to instant message each other and have an actual conversation. This was before Skype was so popular, so we just spent over an hour instant-messaging each other. It was kind of romantic waiting for her next reply to pop up as a small electronic chime rang out on the laptop. It reminded me of how much I missed her. She was thrilled to hear my news and said she wanted me to

293

come home soon. I was only going to be gone four days, but it was somehow reassuring that I was missed by my family.

* * * * *

Two days later, John and I were headed to a suburb of London called, "Twickenham" to watch England play Ireland in the Six Nations rugby tournament. In typical English form, the historic and even ancient town of Twickenham had quaint pubs, small cobbled roads, and homes the exuded old English charm right next to a behemoth stadium that held over 90,000 people and looked like a space ship from Mars. It would take a while to get used to this place.

National pride was heavy at that event, but there was no trouble. Perhaps John was right about this being a gentleman's game. The Irish fans and the English fans all proudly wore their flags and jerseys right next to each other, and I saw nothing that resembled animosity. Perhaps they just hid it well.

The fans absolutely flooded the subway and the small road that led from the train station to the stadium was a wall of slow-stepping flesh. As we walked the narrow roads of the village shoulder to shoulder, the crowd made me a bit claustrophobic. From the tube station to the stadium was a long, slow walk. As we approached the modern stadium, it grew in size and the closer we got the more it looked completely out of place, apparently having traveled through space from an advanced race of people. They must have run out of dilithium crystals and had to park here until the space version of AAA arrived. I had a lot of fun teasing John about this, but in the end I was left wondering, where the heck were they supposed to put the modern buildings? They did not want to get rid of their historical landmarks and they'd been around so long. Kind of like living in one house your whole life, marrying, raising kids and retiring in that same house. Moving would be a bitch! The things we accumulated. Well, the English had been here for a long time and ran out of closet space sometime in the 1940's.

John and I enjoyed the rugby game, drank a pint to England's victory, and met some of his friends for dinner after the game. Oddly enough, we went to a Indian curry restaurant.

"You know mate, the English invented curry." John explained.

"I kind of figured that." I smiled.

* * * * *

It was another long, cramped train ride back to London. The train was full of drunk rugby fans and true to the stereotype, there was a large group of young Irish fans that were absolutely blotto. We teased them a bit and had fun with them. At home, someone would have been shot by now, so I felt pretty out of place, in a good way.

We got out of the tube in London and then switched trains to Salford's where our inn was located, but it was worth it. John kept shouting, "Swing Lowwwwww...."

And the English fans would all join in and sing along, "Sweet Chariottttt... coming for to carry me hommmmmme."

No matter how many times he started the song, they all finished it together. We had nothing like that. But we're a young nation. Give us time to steal a slave song from some foreign nation to use as our game day sing-a-long and we'll get there.

This was our last night in England together, so John and I parted ways at the closed hotel bar once more before retiring. It was getting to be very late and we'd been hard at it for hours, but we were coming to the end of a great trip. We both understood.

"I won't see you tomorrow, mate. My plane leaves very early and yours leaves very late in the day. We'll have to catch up in the Bahamas." He said.

"I have about a 12 hour layover in New Jersey and I think I get there late at night, so I'll just sleep on the floor in the airport. You'll beat me by almost a whole day." I griped.

"Well, it's been a great four days. You got to see London, the countryside, where I grew up, a great rugby match, and you got a job. Not bad, eh?"

"*Race-Walking Through London with John* should be marketed. A great way to work out any moisture you have in your body and right into your clothes just before a very important interview... Spend a thousand pounds to lose ten pounds" I pontificated.

"*Drink London Pride, break wind through all of Blighty whilst still holding on to your Natural American Swagger!*" John laughed.

"Not a bad book title, except that it's longer than most books! But seriously, thanks, John. For everything. I owe you." I said.

He just grinned. He knew he had done well.

We shook hands. We walked together back to our rooms and said good night.

"See you in the Bahamas." He waved.

"Yep, see you there, pal.

I decided to put off packing until the morning as I had hours before my flight. England had been a very full trip, full of sights and new experiences, but little sleep. I decided to get some. My ears were ringing and my body was buzzing from all I'd just done and seen. Did I really just fly to London and get a job back in the Bahamas? As excited as I was, I needed to crash for a few hours. I instant-messaged Beth on my laptop for a while and fell asleep mid-sentence.

* * * * *

I flew back across the pond on Virgin Atlantic, comfortable and giddy. It was really not much more than an expensive nap. I landed in New Jersey at around midnight and had almost twelve hours to kill. There was nothing open, and no one at the gate so I found a place to sleep under a bank of payphones that lined a wall. I was able to put my belongings behind me for safety and after a short while I dozed a bit. I felt like the Omega Man. The airport was completely empty. I only allowed myself to doze as I was worried I'd miss my flight. But like most things I worried about, it didn't happen and I got home safely.

* * * * *

Back in the Bahamas, Beth and Jake picked me up at the airport.

"Successful trip, hmmmm?" She laughed as she hugged me.

"Oh yeah." I grinned.

Jake jumped all over me like he usually did. I held my little family and breathed the warm, wet air.

"I missed you two. It's good to be home."

John met us at the condo and we all shared photos, stories and beers. I told John I had taken over 600 photos and he almost choked.

"Six hundred?" He laughed. "Why so many?"

297

"Well, we were running through London so fast that I figured it would be the only way I could remember what I'd seen."

"Well, we did have a lot to see and only four days. I must say, mate you saw more of London than most locals do in a bloody lifetime."

"Yes I did. Thanks to you."

"Hey-ho, no worries." He said grinning.

* * * * *

The waiting game was on.

I followed up my visit to England with an email to John's boss, thanking him for meeting with me and expressing my gratitude for the opportunity to work for his company. It was the professional thing to do, but what I was really prodding him for was some sort of official agreement or contract outlining my duties and my compensation package. I'd been hired by one of the owners and I figured he'd pass me on to someone from human resources for the details and paperwork. I really knew nothing about my position other than it was mine.

After a week of not hearing back from the London office, I approached John and Mongo. We were sitting on John's balcony overlooking the ocean through the palm fronds.

"That's one of the things I truly detest about our company." Mongo said.

"What's that, their complete inability to follow up with new hires?" John asked.

"Well yes, that and the fact that they've just hired Jim and now left him in complete limbo. They should have given him a new hire packet on the spot, something to study... something." Mongo griped with detest.

"I got nothing." I said, trying not to sound negative. "But he did hire me. I'm sure of that."

"Oh, I have already gotten confirmation on that, mate. Don't worry. You've got the job. I just wish they'd get you moving forward so I can begin training you." John assured me. "This is really weird."

And here we go with the statement that I seem to hear more than I should. I'd be rich if I had a buck for every time someone says to me any of the following:

"This is very odd."

"Hmmm, this never happens."

"Well, that's really weird."

I had heard sayings like that so much that I've concluded that it's a conspiracy against me. Perhaps my imaginary anti-paranoia meds were not strong enough. With my luck, my doctor was probably in on the conspiracy. Damn him.

I fought it with all of my will, but I began to feel the darkness of doubt creep into my otherwise sunny outlook as the days of waiting turned into weeks with still no confirmation from London. I tried to keep a smile on my face, but Beth was able to see that I was worried.

Jake's school year was almost over and if we were to extend another year here, I'd need to know that I could support my family. Business at home had slowed down so much that had let my last employee go and had stopped accepting orders. It cost too much to keep the doors open with so little business. I needed to make a decision soon. We were either going to stay in the Bahamas with a job at Club Caribe, or we would have to head back to California where I'd begin rebuilding my business.

Beth made no bones about it. She wanted to remain in the Bahamas, but she was not realistic. Arguing with her about it was like bringing someone out of a dream. It was not something I liked having to do. I just avoided the topic and planned on making that decision with her only when we absolutely had to do so.

After picking Jake up at school, we were walking up the garden area to our patio when I heard John's voice from his balcony on the second floor.

"Hey mate. Come up when you get a minute, alright?" He yelled.

I waved at him and nodded. While I took Jake into the house I thought to myself, this is it. It's either good news or bad, but now I'll know.

Jake sat with Beth as I walked up the stairs. Beth knew that I was going to hear something that would alter our future and she was visibly worried. I smiled at her as I left and she tried to do the same.

"Hey mate, come on out to the patio." John said. He had left his front door open, so I let myself in. Mongo was there with him on the balcony.

"Kind of early for you guys to be home, isn't it?" I asked. They had about ten beer bottles around them on the table and were clearly tipsy. I did not need to hear their words, the message was clear. My chest sank.

"We've all been let go." John groaned. "They called us into a big meeting and we were told to go home. The project is on hold indefinitely."

"Something about the credit crunch, the economy, the... whatever." Mongo growled angrily. "We're not sacked but this project is done for now."

"I guess that's why they did not send me anything from London. They must have known this was in the wind." I said as I sat down. "I just wonder why he hired me in the first place. Do you have another beer?" I asked.

"Help yourself, mate." John motioned towards a small cooler. "It's business as usual right up to the twelfth hour with these blokes. I'm sure it was full-steam ahead until the decision was made. I'm terribly sorry."

"Why are you sorry?" I asked. "I'll drink this and then go tell Beth. She's going to be pretty upset. Jake will be thrilled. He wants to go home. I guess I have good and bad news to deliver."

"I wish there was something we could do. Perhaps you could work elsewhere on another international project in the interim? John began to think out loud. "I believe they're sending me to Amsterdam."

"I'm headed back to London." Mongo groaned. "I'm sure they have something for you in Dubai, Jim. Tons of projects there."

"Yeah, maybe." I said and tried to sound hopeful.

Working somewhere else sounded like an option but did I really want to uproot my family and go to work in Dubai? At that moment, it seemed like a better idea than going back to California. I'd have to talk to Beth and wait to see if there was even a job available for me.

I went down and told Beth, but she said that she had been expecting the news. She said it just seemed too good to be true. That statement made me feel like I'd really let her down. She had tears in her eyes as she walked out to the sea wall. I knew she was preparing herself to leave and decided to just let her be alone for now.

I could have guessed it, but the London office finally made it very clear that they only wanted me for the Bahamas project, not Dubai or anything else. The economy was limiting their options abroad. I was not that interested in bouncing around the globe with my family anyway. I wanted to place roots and raise my son either on the island or at home.

Beth began to accept the fact that we would be leaving and she asked me for a date. We had to sell some things, see about renting out our place, and pack up what we'd take home. After talking to the airlines and Beth with a calendar in our hands, we decided on June 30th, 2008. We'd be home in time for Independence Day. It seemed like an appropriate holiday to share with our friends at home upon our return to the good old USA.

CHAPTER TWENTY-TWO
Rich Man Poor Man

Beth and Jake were asleep and once again, I could not shut my mind down long enough to sleep so I got up to think. I poured a tall glass of wine. Tall? OK, it was in a beer stein with a handle as thick as an umbrella. I planned on being here for a while. But the wine was a mere prop. I did not drink a drop.

I sat by the pool, at our back patio; the one that overlooked the beautiful sea during the day. It was such a perfect view in daylight. It really was not such a great view during the night as the sea was so black and calm. It was actually a bit creepy staring out into the eternal darkness.

I lit a cigarette and fired up my laptop. I knew I'd trash whatever I wrote this night, so I felt free to say what I really meant. That was the plan, anyway.

I began questioning my decisions. Why was I here in this foreign place? I had traded my life for this and ultimately...I hated it. Didn't I? I could finally admit it to myself. It's too damn hot, the people here don't get us, and we thought they were playful but odd at best. We'll never truly relate to them. It's terribly expensive. And... I can't get a job. Add to that that I'd spent almost $700K of our money on this so far and the world economy world was about to collapse.

Could my timing have been any worse?

Shit.

What have I done?

I did not move here. I escaped the US. Perhaps that's what I wanted all along. Did I hate my home that much? Or, was I just feeling like a failure there?

I decided to figure this out this night. Bottle or two, whatever it took. I'd pour it all out on the ground. The wine may have been a poet's prop, but my plan was that I'd be honest with myself, write down my thoughts and then burn this crap in the morning. Again, that was the plan.

We were successful at home. We were a team. Everything we did seemed to work out. But we were cautious and methodical. This move was planned, but escaping to a cheaper place would have been smarter. And then...of course, I had to choose this place. This place where our money would disappear faster than a drunken groom's new mother-in-law cried after he threw up on his new bride.

For some reason I smiled.

I loved those videos on TV where the drunken groom passed out in front of all the guests. I felt that way at my first wedding. I just wish I would have passed out or threw up before I committed to that woman. I was not drunk. She wasn't bad. We just were better off a short affair, instead of the stupid forever shit I'd proposed one night. She took me seriously and I did not have the balls to just leave. Before I knew it, her parents were spending money on our wedding like the country club automatons they were. I did not see a way out... it just felt like it was too late, the die was cast. I was stuck.

Two years later we were divorced. What a mess.

Perhaps, I should had passed out or thrown up all over Beth before we really went through with this move. It was a very stupid thing we had done. Leave

Cali for the Bahamas... what was I thinking? And why did she agree with me? Was I so convincing?

Yes, I was.

I was absolutely in love with the idea and the place. It drew me like a moth to a porch light. Part of me stayed there in the Bahamas and would not leave: a simpler life that was bound by the ocean and the sand. An island always appealed to me, more than a city. But I had to admit that my sister wasn't right. Everyone wanted to live there when they were on vacation. Then you go home and get back to real life. I went there on the vacation just like everyone else. I just never went back home.

What I needed was a permanent vacation, but our money was not enough for that dream.

What was I running from?

I guess I was just so damn disappointed in my life. I wanted to be a rock star, or a confused poet with a short life, and here I had become a husband and father, a college grad, a business man with responsibility and mortgage in tow. My old, torn jeans did not fit me now, and my black leather biker jacket with all the spikes and paint on it was hanging in the hall closet next to our vacuum cleaner.

I once wrote a poem that described the world as a place that I once wanted to just burn down and piss on, but then I had realized it was people and property that meant something. I wrote that after my son was born. He grounded me, or tethered me. I'm not sure which.

The Kool-Aid was blue and brown. I bought it from the Clampdown. I bought it at the Clampdown company store and I was chugging it by the gallon. Get along. Get along.

What was I escaping? What was I running from so hard?

I had a beautiful wife and a healthy son! I had a successful business that allowed me to pretty much do what I wanted. I had a nice home, a Jaguar and a BMW in the garage. Weren't these goals for most people? They were for me and then I got them.

Brilliant!

I was running from success and happiness, so I chose a successful and happy place to do so. A vacation destination! That made zero sense. I wish I could say I had seen this happen in other people's lives, but I could not and now it was happening in mine. I'd never seen anyone so disappointed when they got all they wanted and then seen them run away from it all.

But we had all seen people we thought had it all, suddenly spiral out of control and lose everything. Was that me now? Maybe I should have been a rock star, or a confused poet. They burned so brightly and then fizzled out quickly (at 27 or so), usually a bloated, irrelevant and sad piece of their earlier incredible light.

At 19, I asked an Army friend if he knew what it was like to peak at 18 and he laughed at me. His name was Rich. He introduced me to a band called The Smiths that is my favorite to this day. *My wife calls it "red wine and razor blade" music" but I still love it.

Rich and I talked a LOT. We talked about important things in our lives. It turned out that my friend Rich was gay and to his dismay, I was not. He was a couple years older and had lived an interesting, rough life. His stories were fascinating in the early morning hours of a long weekend. Rich was one of those apparently incredibly clever people who had the whole world figured out when you met him, but a year later when he was still spouting the same crap, you realized that he was just another outcast that would probably be the angry older guy behind the counter at the sandwich store in another five years.

We had a lot of fun in the Army and we partied hard a bit down south in Austin, Texas. We learned each other's life stories one night when our ride ditched us, and we hitch-hiked the 70 or so miles north back to Fort Hood in the dead of night. I-35 was a desolate and lonely place at 3 AM. It could have even been dangerous, but Rich was one of those gay guys you just did not screw with. He'd cut you to ribbons. I carried a switch blade and a butterfly knife everywhere I went, and I was good with both. But, I still felt safer with him by my side on that long, dark walk.

We finally caught a ride from a pretty blonde girl who drove a huge Lincoln. All of her windows were down as it was still hot and sticky in the Texas summer night. She did not say but a few words when we got in. She could take us to our base. She drove with her left foot on the dashboard, somehow, smoked incessantly and listened to what sounded like Nick Cave and The Bad Seeds. She and Rich talked the whole way. I was amazed at how quickly he made friends. Before we got out, they exchanged numbers.

Rich died five years later. I was in bed with a girlfriend in Sausalito, California when an ex-girlfriend from Texas called me at two in the morning to tell me he had died. My sleeping girl woke up and cursed the old girl, and I felt caught in that similar circle of jealous shit again. My friend was dead. Couldn't these two just park their insecurities and hatred for a minute?

I hated both of them.

I could not even mourn him properly. I had to pay attention to the barking voice next to me and get the girl on the phone to stop calling, crying and asking me to join her at Rich's funeral. I stamped out the whole pain

307

process and wrote the event off as a sad, careless affair. He should have died years earlier. He was a reckless man and we used to be reckless together. But I went home, and then to college after the army. Rich had carried on.

Yet, here I was alive and he was dead. I'd grow older and fatter, while his body went back to the world, his memory fading in all of our minds. His name was Rich, but his life was poor. And that was one of the reasons I loved him. He was a gutter punk that glowed in the darkness along a desolate highway. He looked best under the midnight glare of a 7-11 sign's fluorescent glow. He came from nothing and nowhere in Newport News, Virginia. I just remembered that he smoked Newports. I wonder if that was on purpose. No clue, but he died and very few gave a shit, no matter how wonderful I thought he was.

And I cried for him. I missed him. In a short while, he had taught me a lot about life and even more about myself. He told me how wonderful and special I was. He'd laugh if he were alive to see me now. Pitiful prick lamenting that I'd peaked at 18. He laughed at that one, but he was also angry because I was wasting something he saw as unique. I was given so much. To be bitching about it to him was a crime.

He might laugh at me now, or maybe we would share a glass of wine. A tall one in a beer stein glass this tall with a handle as thick as an umbrella would do the trick. And together perhaps we'd figure out why I had been running from something I didn't understand. It was probably the same thing I ran from ever since I knew him in the army in 1985. Why could I not be happy even when surrounded by wonder and joy?

Here in the Bahamas in 2007, none of this made any sense and that was why I chose to burn what I have written here about him and that time in my life instead of publishing it here. Whoops, now it's published.

So much for my plan.

I had gotten nowhere this night in my quest to learn what my problem was here. But I remembered a line from a movie I had seen: *everywhere you go, there you are.*

I had brought sand to the beach. There was no changing that. I had not finished my negative trajectory. Like most of us, I had my fun and then I wised up, finished my degree and went to work. My rock star life path could have ended up similarly to Rich's. But one thing was for sure, I had turned out to be the last person I had expected I would, but that person was a good one. A lucky one. A blessed one. I was still alive, so I'd better get back to living. Somehow, I'd have to shut out the negative thoughts that plagued my mind and learn to bask in the wonderful place in which I dwelled.

I looked at the cigarette I had lit and the wine I had poured. The cigarette had burned a three inch ash and was out. The wine stein was still full. I walked to the sea wall, did the gangster thing, and poured my wine out onto the sand in front of our place, hoping Rich got a drop or two, wherever he was.

CHAPTER TWENTY-THREE
Heading Down Fast

After the big Club Caribe letdown, poor Beth had to go back to California for one last business trip before we moved home. We still had months before we had to move.

Before she left, we had decided that Jake would finish the first grade in the Bahamas. There was no way we'd make him switch schools mid-year as I'd had to do so many times as a child. We'd have to focus on selling our Bali-Hai, the Honda, and a lot of personal things we could not take with us, but did not want to leave behind.

Jake was feeling a bit torn. He wanted to go home, but there were some things he liked about our adopted home. He knew his parents were upset even though we tried to hide it from him. After we dropped his mother off at the airport, he went into his room and moped. I did the same thing and worried that I was somehow making him feel responsible for our move. I did not want him to carry any guilt. The truth was, he was a big part of our decision, but the economic downturn was forcing us to leave. We could have sold a condo we owned in Belize. We could have sold our home back in California, liquidated everything, and truly separated from the USA. And we did have some money left in savings. It was just too much of a gamble for us to go "all in" as so many others we knew had done. My last name is Reno, but I'm no gambler.

I sat on the couch flipping channels and felt sorry for myself for a while, but the day outside was so beautiful that I decided we needed to go and enjoy ourselves. It was like pulling teeth but I finally got Jake to suit up for a day at Atlantis. It was tough to get him out of the house if he was not in the mood.

We arrived at Atlantis, a place we usually escaped to when we wanted a quick dose of a more Americanized Bahamas. Atlantis was like Disneyland, a huge resort and we sometimes called it our country club. Everything at Atlantis was over the top. But it was clean, safe and of course... very expensive. It was a place to get away from the sometimes gritty reality of the Bahamas. All the years I had spent pining for a life in the Caribbean never took into account the crime, the restrictive government, and never once did I think about the high cost of living there. Like most, I just pictured a carefree life where I rented Jet-Skis to tourists and made a fortune in bare feet.

We needed to feel like tourists again for a day. We were happy when we were tourists. And while we spent many happy days as residents, most of my thoughts had been spent insuring we could afford to stay. I wondered if my life there had been tainted by that little monster that crept around in my mind: worry. As a kid, my life was very unstable. Nothing was guaranteed and even major things like where we lived, what school I attended, and who my parents were changed frequently. I made a mental note to get some serious psychiatric help when we got home. Either that or look into just having my memories of my first seventeen years on the planet erased.

* * * * *

I remembered that movie "Total Recall" where Arnold Schwarzenegger had an adventure trip implanted into his brain. I dreamt of doing the same thing.

"So you don't want to be a millionaire playboy?" The Recall tech asked me she filled out my entry form.

"Nope." I said.

"You don't want our NFL quarterback Super Bowl win package?" She asked.

"No."

"You know, in that package you not only win the game but you get to date Halle Barry."

"Not for me."

"OK. So let me get this right. You want to be Beaver Cleaver and live in a sterile, black and white Hollywood version of the American Family." She asked.

"That's it. But only as long as you can insure that my own childhood will be erased and replaced with the Beav." I said.

"Oh, that's the easy part." She said. "The hard part will be linking your present with that kind of past. It will surely change some things and we can't control just what."

"It's worth it." I said.

* * * * *

At Atlantis, we paid for our "local" (discounted) day pass tickets at the front desk. In order to use the facilities and beaches at Atlantis, you needed a wristband proving that you'd paid for the privilege. You either had to stay in the hotel or buy a day pass. Since I was not truly local and did not have a work permit, the only way I could do this was by showing my California

312

driver's license and a copy of our local phone bill showing my name and a local address.

Once we had been approved for entrance, we headed straight for the lazy river. We were in line for the floating plastic donuts and Jake, as usual, was dragging his feet, whining a little about how he did not want to do this... but I ignored him and we went anyway. The water in the lazy river was very warm. It felt like a big flowing bathtub and Jake liked that. We had been given a big double tube with two holes (built for honeymooners I guess) and we began our float.

After about ten minutes, we were diverted at a fork in the lazy river for what looked like a tunnel and Jake got anxious again. I kept him as calm as I could. Jake was a tough kid, but he was never the kind to try new things without trepidation. I was the same way when I was young and I cursed myself for passing this wimpy trait onto my child. Perhaps he'd outgrow it like I did.

The tunnel turned out to be some rapids that bounced us around a bit. He took that pretty well. Then we were blasted by some cold water vapor at the end that jolted both of us. I got Jake to talk about it as we floated, and he began to think we were actually having fun. His distrust of the whole experience faded and he loosened up. After some more talking and rapids, he began to really enjoy himself. Toward the end of the ride he was really having a blast. As usual, he just needed to adapt.

We took a second loop on the lazy river (which is a long ride in itself), but this time we were diverted in a different direction a juncture called "The Tower". I didn't mention anything to Jake, but this looked like it was going to be more advanced. He was 48" tall (the minimum they would allow) so I figured it was ok. After a long, slow and winding ride through the waterway we

313

skidded onto a rubber conveyor belt that carried us upwards at about a thirty degree angle. Jake was really getting nervous again. There were really scary machine-like creaking noises emanating from somewhere above us as we ascended. I was sure this was part of the experience but Jake was getting nervous. He started asking me questions about the screams we kept hearing in the distance and I told him that I'd never been on this ride before so I really did not know.

At the top of the conveyor belt, we floated around through some more winding turns but now we were very close to the other riders in what appeared to be a floating holding area. Everyone was cueing up for what looked like a big fall.... the ride operator was stopping everyone, apparently to give them one last chance to get off the ride. We were at the top of an artist's rendition of a huge Atlantean pyramid about four or five stories high, and now it had become very dark. The cavern had mist everywhere and incredibly loud, bass-laden, eerie music playing. It sounded like there were machines fighting each other somewhere in slow motion. The sounds were not really music at all, more like a spooky soundtrack. Jake was really getting nervous, but I was determined that we would finish this ride. We had started it, he was old enough and he was big enough. We were in for the duration.

"Just hang on to Daddy, OK?" I said.

"Is it a roller coaster, Daddy?" He asked. Roller coasters were a big no-no in Jake's sheltered world. He hated them.

"No, Son. It's just a hill with some water." I explained.

He hated roller coasters just like I did when I was his age. Another wimpy trait I'd passed on. I was wondering if we should get off the ride now. But how would we feel about ourselves if we chickened out now? Right next to us, there were little girls Jake's age that had obviously been going on this ride all day. I did not want the Reno boys to be the only ones doing the walk of shame down the ten flights of stairs, carrying this gigantic, orange, stupid double-tube.

We got to the operator of the ride and our tube stopped and angled upwards just slightly as he put on the brake. There was some platform beneath us that had raised us partially out of the water that continued to slowly flow past us now. At this slight angle and in our reclined position on the tube, we could not see what lay ahead.

The operator asked Jake to get out so he could measure him. He happily leapt out of the tube to safety only to be tall enough to have to get back in with Daddy. He was not happy now and began to protest. I told him there was no other way down, so he sadly got back in.

When the ride operator pushed the big red BUTTON the tube angled downwards and we saw a huge plunge ahead of us. Jake stiffened up and I wrapped my legs around him tightly as we quickly descended with water splashing all over the place. We hit a jump and seemed to catch air right before we hit the next section of descent, gaining speed as we headed upwards and into a very dark tunnel. As we shot through the blackness at top speed, I kept telling Jake that I have him and that he'll be ok. He was not saying a thing. We thrashed through the tube blindly, sliding up the walls as the tube turns left and right.

Finally, there was light at the end of the tunnel (not often that I get to use that phrase literally instead of figuratively), and we splashed down into the lazy river again. After a moment, all was calm and the fifteen seconds of watery violence was behind us.

I asked Jake how he was doing and he shouted at me:

"THAT RIDE SCARED ME TO DEATH!!!"

He was pretty shaken, and to be honest I was surprised that the ride was as advanced as it was. I had no idea what to expect and felt a bit guilty for taking him on the ride at all. But the images of the little girls his age riding the thing over and over again never left my head. His mother would have never taken him on a ride like that. It was up to me to get him bumped and bruised on the way to manhood. I hated this part of my role as a father but it had to be done or he'd be raised up like a veal.

Jake had some tears, but we talked it over and he agreed that since he survived the ride that crying was not the thing to do. He was proud that he lived through it, but made me promise that we would not do the tower or the lazy river again that day.

We shook on it.

CHAPTER TWENTY-FOUR
Home

The last few months on the island were a combination of happy parties and sad good-byes. As expected, John was relocated to Amsterdam by his company and we had a sad send off for him at a local beach restaurant. The restaurant was right on the beach, just a bit west of our place. The Aussies were there with their kids and we watched as the three boys played with Jake at the edge of the ocean just yards from us.

"It's not over." He spoke lowly as he sipped his gin and tonic.

"We'll always be friends." I said. "Is that what you mean?"

"I know, mate. But what I mean is... this... this whole thing here in the Bahamas... it's not over." He shook his head.

I really did not understand what he meant by that, but just nodded and gave him a hug when I dropped him off at the Nassau airport the next day. He had left me with his little SUV as I was to handle the transfer and sale to the Texans, a last minute deal.

We had more time to sell our stuff than John had, but we had a lot more stuff. We sold most of the personal stuff we'd accumulated that we did not want to leave or bring home. The Weber barbeque, the electronic keyboard that Jake reluctantly was learning to play, the kayak... all of it had to go. We put the boat and Honda up for sale. Mr. Texas' boss took the Honda, but the boat had to be left with a broker as she did not sell while we were there.

All of this was really just drudgery and details that felt like blood dripping from a dying man's body. Each thing represented a trip somewhere, a journey for a project, or something for Jake. Every single thing had a memory, a reason for being with us.

Like the little plastic cooler we had used so much on the beach and the boat. We would fill it with Kalik and ice, prop it up on the sand against the sea, and take photos that we'd email back home, as our friends and family all cursed us.

"I'm sitting at my desk right now listening to my asshole boss and you're looking at this?" They would email back.

That little blue and white cooler had traveled with us to Jake's soccer games, beach parties, carnivals and boat trips to nearby islands. It had served as a cooler, a seat, a cutting board and now as a doorstop, propping open the door as we moved things around. I hated looking at it now, knowing it was going to stay here and have more beach adventures without me.

There was my little toolbox in which I had painstakingly collected a small arsenal of household tools. With everything being so incredibly expensive in the Bahamas, I usually tried to fix anything that broke or wore out. Our master bathtub had rusted a hole through the top edge where the leaking faucet had dripped right through. I fused the hole in the tub with some industrial glue and some white shower tile I'd bought, and not only sealed the hole but fastened some very decorative looking shaped tiles.

I hung our flat screen TV's to the walls to save dresser-top space. I'd installed night locks onto our

318

huge sliding glass doors when the robbery happened. I'd dealt with our leaking washer countless times, always managing to fix it enough to prevent me from buying a new one. When you live on an island, you had to be more independent than when you were on the mainland where "things" were more available and inexpensive.

Beth's telescope would have to stay, but we'd leave it out like furniture and hope that the new tenants enjoyed it as much as we did. We looked at stars through the jiggly lens at night, looking up constellations on my laptop. We used it to spy at the party people on Sandals Island... never really much to see there. It was not like "Hedonism" or other clothing-optional resorts. My favorite thing was watching the boats go by. Sailboats barely large enough to make it to Florida, motorboats carrying dirty Bahamian fishermen, huge zillion-dollar yachts, and the large water-tanker "Titas" that brought fresh water from Andros.

Lots of things like this would have to stay and it hurt a lot to sit there and decide. The Titanic was going down. Women and children first... but the china, the artwork, the piano, heck the whole band, must stay. We had the same nine suitcases and two carry-ons each that we brought with us here. The Reno Family had arrived first class and we'd depart the same way. We would have a comfy seat, but what we really needed was the extra baggage they allowed in first class.

* * * * *

The day we were actually leaving was particularly difficult. Beth and I had stayed up very late the night before. I anticipated a four-alarm hangover, something

I hated traveling on, but it was our last night and there was a lot to talk about.

There were many rounds of *"Well, we gave it our best try."* And there was even some *"There was no way we could have known without trying."* And even *"It's the best thing for Jake"* showed its head.

But the overall mood was one of serenity. We had done something no one else we knew would even try. And we lost nothing. We had kept our home in Walnut Creek and we were not going to sell the condo in the Bahamas. I still had my company and Beth still had her job. We'd spent a lot of money during this venture and would have some debt when we got back, but we agreed that it had been worth it.

* * * * *

"I would not change a thing." Beth said. "Except that I want to stay!" She laughed.

"I know, I know." I lamented. "But we were not willing to cash out of California completely so it was that much more difficult to grow here. Had we sold the house in Walnut Creek..."

"There was no way I could do that." Beth said.

And she restated the impossible circumstance she had given me. She wanted both homes, up and running full time, at all times. That was very expensive. Add to that the lack of work for me and the economic collapse in 2008, it was a perfect storm.

"If just one thing had been different. If I'd gotten the job at Club Caribe. If we'd sold the Walnut Creek house. If the economy had done great instead of terrible. If, if, if. Screw it." I cursed.

"Don't be bitter." She said. "Don't leave here and let things be ruined."

"I won't. But if I had it to do over again, I would not have come to this island. Schools, doctors be damned. I'd have taken us to Eleuthera. At least there you can sleep with the window open... well if the mozzies don't eat you alive!" I laughed.

There was no perfect answer. But I knew that Nassau and the island of New Providence were history for me. I had a LOT of memories here, but I could revisit them all in two days and then be off to the Family Islands (anything but New Providence and Grand Bahama... the little ones), the places that the locals called "The Real Bahamas."

"Next time?" Beth said.

"Heck yeah. Another chapter in our story." I said.

* * * * *

Jake had a hamster that Beth had planned on smuggling home, but we talked her out of it as it at the last minute as it could be a crime to bring rodents into the USA. It turned out that it was.

We were actually packing our mountain of luggage to the waiting row of cars just outside our building that would take us to the airport when the decision to leave the hamster was finalized. Beth and Mrs. Texas sat with Jake as he cried. I was too full of my own remorse to deal with that situation, so I just kept lugging our bags outside with Mr. Texas.

* * * * *

I was still thinking of the night before when Beth and I had sat up very late on our back patio sharing some drinks and talking about our experience.

"I'd do it again." I said.

"I would too." She said. We watched over the sea wall at the dark water and listened to the small waves. The moon glowed and hung low over the ocean.

"I'm sorry." I whispered.

"Sorry? For what? For bringing us here? It was my dream too." She exclaimed.

"I've always thought I dragged you into this. I know you grew to love it but it was a leap of faith to come here, wasn't it?" I asked her desperately.

"It was trust." She cried. "I trusted you. We trusted you. We always have and we always will!"

"Mr. Texas told me once that when they came here, they went all in. They sold everything and left nothing behind. We didn't do that. Maybe that's why we failed." I explained and apologized sincerely.

"Who said we failed?" She yelled at me. "We got to live a *dream*, something most people never even try. And we still own this place. We'll be back. *It's not over.*"

* * * * *

I knew I'd play these conversations and thoughts over and over again in my mind over the rest of my life. Heck, I'm doing it right now. The day we flew home was a nightmare. The power had shut down again, so the airlines were forced to write tickets and boarding passes by hand. The manual luggage screening process quadrupled the amount of time it took to check in and adding to the misery: no power meant no air conditioning. I was hungover, depressed, and there was no cold beer in sight to help ease the pain.

The Nassau airport felt like a greenhouse and everyone inside it was getting short with each other. I was sweating and feeling a bit ill from the night before.

I hated situations like these. Crowds were not for me and added to it was my personal situation, leaving our adopted home, but then as I thought of it, none of these issues bothered me now. Suddenly, a huge weight had been lifted from my shoulders. As I stood there in the middle of the Nassau airport with ten thousand other hungover, sun-burned tourists, I felt a huge sense of peace. I realized it was because now there were no more decisions to make. No more worries. The end of the dream was finally here.

I wondered to myself if this was what I had secretly wanted all along. I felt like I did when I was in the Army. The sergeant told us what to do. We got up at 5 AM, exercised at 6, ate at 7, and went to work and the rest was pretty much the same every day. We wore the same uniform every day and performed the same tasks. Why I was thinking of this, I did not know. Was it freedom from decisions? Or was it just security? I remembered feeling very secure in the Army. I knew where I'd work, sleep and eat every day. These were things I did not grow up with (thoughts for another book someday, maybe). Getting away from the constant worry was a huge relief.

We shuffled through the airport, line after line after line, dripping sweat and leaking oil, but eventually we boarded the plane and watched the islands disappear under the clouds as we flew home.

* * * * *

Almost exactly as planned, we had gotten home on July 1st, 2008. It felt great being back in our home. As it had so many times before after being in a third world nation for months, our home now felt like a palace. Our little town of Walnut Creek was so clean it felt like Main

Street USA in Disneyland. The power never went out. The AC worked very well and inexpensively. There were no robberies. We had left three cars behind and they all ran well, gas was cheap, and the roads felt incredibly smooth and safe.

One phenomenon I noticed was that after driving on open roads and so close to the ocean so much: the roads at home felt like driving down long, green hallways. It felt like being in a corridor for some reason. Although it was July and the hillside grass was now yellow, the ubiquitous trees and shrubbery at home lined the street on both sides. It felt like I was driving in long channels and that feeling stayed for a while. I likened it to "land sickness", or the feeling one gets after a long ride on a boat. When you step back onto land you expect the land to sway with your adopted inner rhythm. But it does not. The land stood still while I still rocked side to side. I expected this would not last long, but I was wrong. To this day, I still sway a lot on the land. I still have not regained my comfortable footing. And I will probably never be totally comfortable here again.

* * * * *

Jake and I were sitting in our pool on the 4th of July. Our friends were up on the deck with Beth listening to music and enjoying some barbeque and beer. I looked up at the sky and smiled. The sun that warmed us here was the same sun that warmed us on the island. My good friend Bill came down from the deck and lowered himself into the pool with a huge "Ahhhhhhh." He reached out and rubbed Jake's head the way men do, roughing up the kids hair.

"Jake." I said.

324

"Yes, Daddy."

"Are you glad to be home?"

"Oh yes. I get to play football starting next month. And it's fun to get to see grandma and my cousins too." He said.

"What about me?" Bill splashed him a bit.

"You too, Uncle." Jake chuckled.

Bill smiled.

"Did you miss it here?" I asked.

"Yeah. I guess I did, Daddy." Jake looked upwards at the sky as he said this. Perhaps he was remembering the same thing about the sky I was thinking, how it linked us to the whole planet.

"Did you hate it in the Bahamas?" I looked at him and he looked back at me.

"No, I did not hate it. But I hated trying to sleep when it was so warm at night. I miss my hamster. And it was fun playing at the beach with you and Mama. Lots of different stuff, I guess." He smiled and played with the pool water.

"Yes, it was. May I ask you a question?"

"Sure, Daddy."

"What is your favorite place in the world."

"Walnut Creek, Daddy." He said quickly and without hesitation.

"Right here?" I smiled at him.

"Yes, Daddy. What is your favorite place in the world." He asked and looked back into my eyes.

"Yeah, bro. What is your favorite place in the world?" Bill grinned as if he knew.

"You first. What's your favorite place?" I asked him.

"Walnut Creek." Bill said and gave Jake a high-five. "I like it here, too." He grinned at Jake.

I loved seeing them both teaming up on me. Bill was his godfather.

"So, what about you, Jimi." Bill asked. "Where is your favorite place?"

"In the whole world?"

"Daddy, quit fooling around. What's your favorite?" Jake asked as he splashed me.

I put my arm on Jake's shoulders and reached out my hand to Bill. He shook it but I held his hand for a moment longer.

Home." I said. "I like it best at home."

THE END

AUTHOR BIO:

Jim Reno was born in Palo Alto, California, the son of a surfer and a beauty queen. His parents raised him in Santa Cruz, California. They taught him to dream and raised him to think independently.

He discovered at age ten that he loved to tell stories to his brother, sister and cousins. He soon learned that writing them down helped him remember the detail, dialogue and settings. He quickly found that writing was a powerful way to get the attention of others. It was also an easy way to extract anything he felt inside, good or bad. And sometimes...others liked what he wrote. Evoking an emotion from another person merely with his words on paper was intoxicating. He was hooked.

Jim has written his entire life. He has written a lot of poetry and short stories. He has written one really bad screenplay. This is his first full-length book and he sincerely hopes that his family will still enjoy his tales and his unique style of story-telling.

He hopes that this book will expand his literary family. It's his dream that there is a library or book store in Heaven so that his Mother may still read along with him, listening and laughing for hours as he read to her. She was his angel on Earth. Now she is his angel in Heaven.